JACE DEKKA...

still called **"Commander"** by the many slaves he once liberated, he is an enhanced super-being, possessing a genius intellect, the strength of several men—and the superheated libido of many more. His work against enemies from his past continues without rest even as he struggles with his personal demons. But he knows he cannot save the Solar System alone, so he has created an elite cadre of eight queer young men that he calls

THE UNSUITABLE BOYS...

TRACE Battle

A former sperm-slave and elite rentboy, his body riven with sexual enhancements, he fought alongside Jace during the secret "Dirty War," and has the uncanny ability to almost instantly learn new languages.

BRADEN Vaieux

Jace's adopted son, he is a touch-telepath who can experience other people's thoughts and interior monologues in the form of strange and symbolic stories—during intense sex with them.

ZANE Brace

An aetherspace engineer by training, he discovered as a youth an impossible ability: he can, with the power of his mind—and while in a state of fiery gay lust—teleport himself and others to any point in the Solar System.

ANDO Natahn

A hacker of extraordinary genius, he can commune with artificial intelligence in both cyberspace and aetherspace—and his body is an arsenal of erotic modifications.

TIMOTHY Arush

Once a child prodigy who trained himself as a biologist and a physician, he was rescued from a sinister enterprise by Jace Dekka and is now the team's doctor. Reclusive by nature, he harbors a frightening sexual secret.

PATRICK Confessori

A brilliant tactician and game theorist—and an intense and amorous lover of men—the youngest of the Unsuitable Boys employs his formidable talents to keep them all safe.

ETHAN Komorford

This neuroatypical youth can see beneath the substrate of reality and show people astounding visions of what's real and what is yet to come with his drawings and paintings. Occasionally his intense curiosity (and intense sexual arousal) leads him into danger.

COLIN Vorta

He "hears" an underlying music in the aether and can sometimes make it audible to others through his mysterious songs. A Venusian "maph," he has the ability to bear children…and a nearly insatiable appetite for the bodies of his teammates.

COMMANDER JACE AND THE UNSUITABLE BOYS EPISODE #5

THE INTERSEX BOYS OF VENUS

M-Brane Press

Saint Louis

Cover illustration: "*Fucking Around with Henry Scott Tuke's 'After the Bath' in GIMP*"
Interior scene-break image derived from original material.

Book design by Christopher Fletcher.

Printed in the United States of America.

www.mbranespress.com

ISBN: 978-1-945945-00-7

THE INTERSEX BOYS
OF VENUS

It begins...

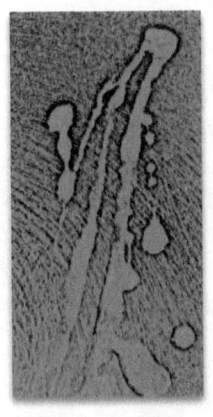

Colin "heard" in his body a lush, pulsing, throbbing new song in that singular way that only he can hear, and while it had lyrics that he could neither sing nor write down after they evanesced inside his hot consciousness, he could still sing loudly its crying melody and tell his friends about the sultry and gaudy impressions that it had left upon him, and how it told to him a story of a vast treachery yet to be uncovered, of two naked and sweat-slicked boys on steaming tree-shrouded Venus, of a father or a prince in an ancient compound of ivy-shrouded towers where a series of books perhaps, or letters perhaps, or voices perhaps would show him the key to an answer for which he does not even know the question. Colin, smooth and shiny like new porcelain, damp like a lover on a hothouse world, pulled back with both hands his shaggy black hair and gripped it, as if squeezing the song from its strands and Ethan watched him, listened to him, thrilled to him.

Ethan drew a vast and stormy and light-streaked picture with chalk and charcoal and pastels and ink on many pieces of thick rag paper that he stitched together into one huge sheet — one enormous picture with many smaller ones nested within it, like a free-form graphic novel page. His montage of images included lithe athletic boys on simmering sun-soaked Venus, glossy and lusty youths with stiff and dripping cocks, and someone else, too — a shadow — moving among towers of stone and ivy, and many, many books and keys and a twisted thing that looked like a twirling helix, spinning like a violet and a blue tornado. Ethan crawled naked and sweat-shiny over its surface, the palms of his hands and the tips of his fingers and now his kneecaps stained with pigment, adding more and more little bits of color, deeper and deeper inky details, and Colin sang to him until he was done and until he needed to drift sideways into a dreamless, cavernous, silent and starry sleep.

1.

The clairvoyant boys present Commander Jace and Ando with a new mystery; Timothy designs a virulent sex-package intended to infect and influence Braden and Patrick.

From Jace Dekka's journal:

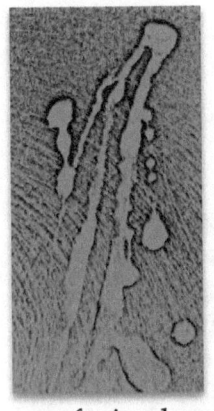

The irritating trill of the phone alarm woke me from dark and carnal and confusing hangover dreams and I remembered why I needed to get out of bed yet again. Of course, I had asked Ando for his thoughts this morning, as I often do when these two boys— eerie and musical Colin and luridly visual Ethan—seem to be having a clairvoyant episode and when they seem to be having the very *same* one in their own ways. Solid Ando—he of the steel-grey gaze and the logician's mind, scalpel-sharp Ando—doesn't let himself get too easily swayed by his or anyone else's emotions when faced with a preternatural puzzle. He sees with a cool clarity a symbolic logic in these iterations of the precognitive boys' intuitions, and he can often tell me not necessarily what they "mean" but what sort of action we should take to *learn* their meaning. It does not disturb his scientific at all at all that there is no credible rationale that explains Colin and Ethan's strange episodes. It's sufficiently obvious to him that they *are* real whether we understand them or not, and so we proceed from that standpoint.

I tapped a confirmation message to him, asking him to meet me in my office in a few minutes, forced myself upright from the bed and walked into the big adjoining slate-floored shower room. The skylight and windows inside it were open and I enjoyed, despite the hangover, this morning's breeze, its coolness on my bare skin. I enjoyed much less my appearance in the mirrors: I looked pale, a lot the reddishness in my hair looked to be going to ash and my eyes — normally green — seemed as grey as the slate on the floor. I dismissed these observations — I'd see the doctor about them later — as I washed off the residue of last night's sweat and spunk and spit, the smell of my long three-way with Colin and Ethan, accreted on my skin as I'd tried to understand what they were showing me. But I'd become too drunk and stoned to do anything but fuck them.

Under the hot water jets, I considered my upcoming journey to the Academie Bishonen and the cute faggot students I'd likely entertain there. This got me stiff, so I decided to beat off: it would make me feel better anyway. I remembered Ethan's soft lips last night on my nutsack, my tongue deep inside Colin's warm and weeping cunt, and I dropped a big and satisfying spatter of thick clotty cocksnot on the tile at my feet. I figured that this would have the side-benefit of relieving some involuntary morning-horniness long enough for me to concentrate on a problem. I toweled off and put on a pair of mesh shorts just as Ando arrived.

I drew him into my work area. I opened the blinds and threw open the patio doors. I prepared a big screwdriver, offered one to Ando, but he passed. We looked at Ethan's artwork, the enormous drawing spread in its many tape-stitched panels over the entire surface of my giant bamboo table. Or rather, Ando looked for a while I watched him and sipped my cocktail. I'd seen this picture already, so much so that I doubted I could see anything new in it without help.

"This just seems almost too obvious," said Ando, pointing to a smear of pastels hatched through with tiny details of ink that suggested to me a run of ivy-clad stone buildings, crumbling under the weight of centuries. "And an image like this is suggested in Colin's song as well." But *I* still didn't see what *he* was seeing in it, so I waited a beat for him to start to explain it: "You are going to the Academie Bishonen this week for that conference. These are the kinds of buildings that they have on an ancient school campus like that."

"But," I said, "the Academie really doesn't look much like this at all. It's not this stony and craggy, not so much overgrowth and ruin."

"It's not to be taken so literally as that." Ando combed back his thick hair with a sweep of his long fingers, nails glossed with black polish, and he frowned. He rubbed the thin line of dark beard on his jaw and wiped his eyes with his palms as if fighting drowsiness. I offered a drink again, and again he declined. He peered again at a piece of the image. "The ivy and the stony buildings are a common representation of a place like that, and Colin and Ethan have probably never been there and have no idea what it really looks like. It's just their idea of what a place like that *should* look like. But I think it still must have to do with your trip this week, and I think it means that you *must* go to find out what the rest of the clues mean."

"But what about this?" I wondered, pointing to large swath of imagery in Ethan's huge drawing that Ando and I had agreed suggested Venus and some treehouse-style cabanas in a forest of monstrous cloud-scraping trees, homes to billions of birds. These things seemed to be echoed in Colin's strange song, its opaque lyrics that suggested "love" and "essence" and "an answer" on Venus. Colin's song also suggested two lust-filled boys on Venus, and Ethan's pictures *showed* them again and again, naked and stiff, exaggerated *hentai* cocks leaking long drooly falls of preek.

"I'd say a couple people here are due for a vacation," Ando said. "On Venus."

"That *feels* right somehow, but who is supposed to go? Do you have any idea?"

Ando pointed to a frame of Ethan's drawing, a tiny one that at first glance seemed to contain no legible imagery at all. He opened the magnifier on his phone and showed me this: tiny and minutely-detailed ink drawings of what were clearly young men. These weren't stylized and indistinct like the larger boys elsewhere in the image. These were meticulously rendered: one had blond hair with kinks and curls, and the other had moppy black hair, and even that weird little fold in his upper ear. They carried bags, one of them plainly Braden's olive green purse, the other a black pack strapped over Patrick's naked shoulders. "Am I taking *this* too literally as well?" I asked.

Ando looked at me for a few moments, red-stained lips pursed. "My instinct is no, you're not. I am inclined to trust this." He waved open a desktop screen and called up Braden's schedule. Over the next two weeks, it held very little other than some questions marks around the words *"¿Jace gone — maybe a vacation somewhere for me too?"* So he was thinking about going somewhere anyway. Ando next opened Patrick's calendar, and it too was largely empty over the same period.

I scanned over some more of the smaller images with the magnifier and stopped on one, showed it to Ando. "It looks to me like some of you may need to come along with me to the Academie." In the frame, we saw perfectly-rendered little comic book images of more boys. They were plainly Ando, Trace and Zane, easily recognizable if a bit stylized and exaggerated in their features.

"Wow," Ando said. "Well okay, then. I guess I'll pack my bag."

"Bring all this info from Ethan and Colin as well. Maybe don't discuss it too much with Zane and Trace. It seems like we might alter the flow of events too much if everyone gets too self-conscious that we are on some kind of mission."

Ando agreed: "In fact, let's not even tell them at all why we are going with you. Just tell them that they need come along. It won't be a lie, just more of an omission. And *we* don't really know yet anyway."

I wondered about Braden and Patrick and what it would take to induce them to vacation together on Venus just now. "I can easily convince Braden to ask Patrick to go with him on a private fuck-cation with his favorite bro— and he was probably already planning something like it anyway—and Patrick will readily agree to some nice alone-time with Braden, and he won't care much at all where they go so long as they get to go together. But what if Braden is thinking of something more like a week of narcowhirl and fucking and rentboys at the beach house at Maya Plaxa or something like that somewhere else on Earth? I wonder how I make them go to Venus in particular without too much suspicious prodding."

But Ando was tapping at his screen, bringing up travel info. "Simply buy them the tickets. On this big cruise ship, which is headed for Venus." A little image of it rolled in space, its glittery spires and sails trailing ribbons of rainbow. "It's Braden's twenty-second birthday next week anyway. Tell him it's an early gift. Just tell him the rest of us are busy with other things, and to take Patrick along." He purchased two tickets, assigned them to Braden and Patrick, and pointed out the date and time. "They leave early tomorrow morning, and they will get there super-fast—this ship will catch an aether hyperstream in upper Earth orbit and they will land at Athenus Vaginus in two days."

"But one problem," Ando continued, "is that you shouldn't tell them much about any of this, in the same way that you shouldn't bias Zane and Trace with too much information. I feel that if they just go then they will somehow end up doing what they're supposed to do as suggested in the picture and the song. But we don't know what any of it means yet. Should we try to make a biological command packet out of it?"

I agreed that this was probably the best plan, a little extra insurance that they would find out about their mission themselves without me biasing the results. Likely they would be annoyed when they discovered the existence of the so-called "packet" in their blood, but they'd probably forgive me for it.

"I guess," Ando said, "we ought to take this information to Tim[1] right now and have him help us make the packet. It will take his AI a little while to figure it out."

I noticed he was gazing downward at my crotch, the tentpole in my shorts probably brought on by considering the actual mechanics of the packet, the thing that I would need to do to give it to Braden. "But can you concentrate on it? Have you even gotten off yet this morning?" he wondered.

"In Ethan's mouth and in Colin's pussy really early this morning before they went back to their own

---

[1] A mostly self-trained physician, Timothy Arush received a medical degree in Kruze Republic when he was only fourteen years old. He later dedicated himself to what he called "biopunk aetherology." A few years before the events of this tale, Jace Dekka disrupted a plot that the young doctor was involved in with the Tong Tiphon and the Draku Rouge, and Dekka convinced him to join the Unsuitable Boys. Of Dekka's coterie of exceptional young men, Tim Arush remains to this day the one least well-understood by historians. Unlike Dekka and Braden Vaieux, Arush kept very sparse personal journals and was quite secretive about his own thoughts and beliefs.

quarters," I said. "And then I beat myself off in the shower a little while ago, thinking about Ethan and Colin and how I'll probably fuck a bunch of the students at the Academie. That was just before you got here, but I could go again whenever. You wanna dock with me?"

We stood and stripped. I was wearing only the mesh shorts that I'd donned after the shower, but Ando had a t-shirt, black denim shorts and a shiny silver jockstrap to get rid of. He did so and I could smell the sweat of his crotch, of his thick black pubic thatch, and I stiffened and dripped instantly. Once naked, Ando stepped close and we stood cock-to-cock — he's nearly as tall as me. He pulled that extra-long extra-wet dick-sleeve of his over his mushroom head and then over mine, covering it completely in its slippery and sticky dampness. I felt my preek flooding over both our cockheads, further lubing the inside of his foreskin. Carefully and slowly, to keep us docked together, he stroked both our rods with both his hands. "Let's time it," he said, he gasped, "so we blow at the same time." We did what he said, kissing and drooling into each other's mouths as he stroked us, keeping in time with each other until I told him I was ready. "I'm close," he whispered into my mouth. "Just a couple more seconds." And when he said *now*, we both let loose and immediately Ando's hands were filled with a surf of our white goo busting out from under his skin, lathering both our dongs, dripping from his fingers and falling onto our feet. He wiped his hands off on his chest, wetting and matting down the light layer of gossamer fuzz over his pecs. He wiped some of down into his pubes and smeared some of it with both palms against the scruff of my chin. And we put our clothes back on and went to visit Tim in his lab.

A summary of the workings of the Venus Command Packet (from Tim Arush's notes):

While its construction is quite complex and based in some science that we don't fully understand, once constructed and deployed, its operation couldn't be simpler. It is basically an artificial virus that, once injected into the testes of the carrier, hitches a ride on the carrier's sperm. He spreads it to the intended recipient like a highly contagious STD through amorous intercourse — preferably anal-penetrative sex with the ejaculation of his semen inside the recipient's body.

The carrier generally has about three days to achieve this transmission before the virus times out and ceases to be carried by his sperm. In the case of the Venus Packet, in addition to its intended carrier, Jace, I made Ando and myself carriers as well to increase the likelihood of someone fluid-penetrating Braden with it in case, for some reason, Jace fails to succeed in this assignment. The recipient will later, generally within a day or two, gain an unconscious but pressing sense that he has received this packet

17

and that he must act on it. In the case of the one I designed for Jace to give to Braden, it has a aethero-chemical sequence that will make him feel rather strongly that he needs to share the contents of the packet with Patrick in particular. This sharing is designed to happen through sex between them, preferably anal-penetrative sex with Braden as the insertive partner, but he will be likely shedding so much of the package data through all his bodily fluids at this point that it can probably be transmitted to Patrick through almost any kind of physical intimacy between them at all if Patrick has at least some soft-tissue contact with Braden's fluids, whether it be his spit or his semen or even his sweat. It would probably work the other way as well — with Patrick as the carrier — but Braden is a particularly good choice of vector for such a method as this because of his innate aethero-telepathic ability.

Once it has entered Patrick's bloodstream, the affected pair will start to have a transaetheric psychic episode in which they come to understand together that they were sent to Venus for a purpose and that they should follow a series of clues that will feel to them like simple gut instinct even though they will be aware that this data is acting upon them. These clues encoded in the package derive from what little information Ando, Jace and I could glean from Colin's song and Ethan's picture. But *how* this actually works and how the clues end up coded into the package, we really have no idea. My lab AI, which has an aether-core logic center, does the actual encoding, and after using this method a few times in the past, I have come to trust it as being reasonably reliable, but for reasons that I don't understand. What we do know, however, it is that it is a good way to give someone a mission without prejudicing its results with foreknowledge gained through Ethan and Colin's clairvoyance. Ando considers this to be of paramount importance, and he speculates (rather outlandishly, in my opinion) that if we are not as careful as possible when handling the kind of insights that we get from those weird boys, then we could accidentally damage the course of our own futures or possibly — in an extreme case — create a temporal paradox that could imperil the entire universe.

2.

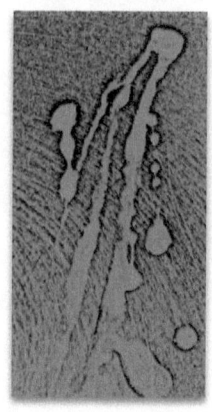

Braden and Patrick board a lavish aethership; en route to Venus, they indulge in each other's bodies, and later, during lunch, witness an amazing phenomenon; Braden falls into a raging amorous fever and exposes Patrick to a stunning secret.

From Braden's journal:

Jace booked us in first-class on a shuttle that rocketed us off Earth slantwise into space and upward to our rendezvous with the vast aethership that would sail us off to Venus. Though we did our usual bickering *en route* to the spaceport (the Sea Road is faster than the Hill Road! You'll want a jacket! No, I won't!), I was so glad that Patrick was my companion — and my *only* companion — for this unexpected vacation. I guess because I hadn't been all alone with him for a while — and away from the other guys and our daily routines — I noticed for the first time in a while just how fucking pretty Patrick is, how bright his blue-green eyes are, how pink and pouty his thick and soft lips are, how exotic his waved and twisted blond hair is. How fucking *hot* he is! It's almost as if I had never quite noticed it before even though he's been around the Home for almost two years and I have boned his sweet mouth and his tight clenching ass scores and scores of times.

Shortly after take-off, I considered trying to take Patrick into the restroom with me for a quick airborne fuck on our way to the rendezvous with the Venus cruise ship, but this journey was to be a very short one—just from the planet's surface to a dock in low orbit—and he was sipping and smiling over a green and bubbly cocktail and happily telling me about cruise ships and aether-streams and Venus.

He paused and said, "You're *looking* at me while I talk to you, but I don't think you're *listening*." And he laughed and I wanted to bite his lips and lick his teeth.

I wanted to tell him that I can't focus upon whatever it is that he's saying *because my body loves his body so much that I want to open his fly and spear myself raw on his pretty cock right fucking now,* but I didn't say that, but I think he knew somehow that I was feeling like that, but he probably attributed it to my normal horniness, and he leaned into me and gave me a quick but sweetly wet kiss and continues with his lively chatter about Venus. Even *that* turned me on, the sound of his voice and the way his mouth moves when he speaks, the flash of his teeth and the wetness of his tongue. I was not wearing any underwear and my cock was tenting my linen pants and dripping out a soaking preek stain into them. I ignored this and tried very hard to listen to Patrick.

We dock with the ornate and gigantic cruise ship, a vast aether-sailing ornament in space. Its name is the

Queen of the Aether—cheesy name, yes, but the ship itself is astounding to see as we draw near it. It's not easy to even perceive its structure and design concept as one approaches it in a shuttle as it seems to be compiled of a vast number of gilded slabs and opalescent pods and silvery spires and domes and filaments that seem barely connected one to the other, but the whole thing is lit wildly with swinging spotlights and strobing bursts, and what look like rainbow streamers of silk billow and pulse for kilometers behind it as it rolls through space, a thing so gorgeous—though perhaps gaudy—that it seems as if it is there to compete with Earth itself as a spectacle in space.

It occurs to me that Patrick and I—at least by virtue of our association with Jace and our membership in the Home—are probably among the wealthiest people on the planet and yet I had never been on a "luxury" cruise ship before, and I wonder aloud if Patrick ever has. He looks at me, pauses, kind of frowns a little bit and he says, "No. I never even dreamed of it." I am not sure at first if this is just an off-hand remark or if he is saying something sincerely about his past dreams. But he adds: "We weren't rich like this when I was a kid. I never thought I'd go anywhere."

I have nothing to say to this and I want to pull him close and press my mouth into his but the pilot is announcing that we are about to dock with *Queen of the Aether* and to raise our tray tables and remain seatbelted until the light goes off.

The docking was a quick affair and, since Patrick and I were in first-class and very near the front of the shuttle, we were off quickly with our bags, and we stepped into a vast promenade that reminded me a bit of the gate area at the spaceport—with all its shops and cafes—but this was much more ornate and livid with activity:

Hawkers entreated people to enter bars and coffee shops.

Kiosk vendors sold souvenirs and tickets to on-board attractions.

Circus performers enacted athletic and magical tricks, including a quartet of naked avian Martians who cavorted in a towering laser-lit fountain.

An aether-light show whirled in an overhead sky-light, complete with tropical birds spinning about, playing with knotted twirling tops.

Narcowhirl dealers wandered with cigarette trays hanging around their necks.

Electronica noise throbbed loud and hard from a dark smoky doorway and a few rentboys in harnesses and metal codpieces danced outside it and motioned come-hither at likely clients. Patrick stopped briefly to flirt with one of them—a very black boy with shock-white whorls of tattoo ink encircling his nipples and winding down his belly into his navel and back down into his crotch.

"You want?" Patrick said—to me, I realized after a beat, gesturing with a bent thumb at the rentboy. "My treat!" He laughed.

I only want you, baby, I wanted to say, but I didn't say that because it would have sounded stupid even to me. Instead I said, "Maybe later. Let's find our room!" And I pulled Patrick away from the cute black queer and led us further down the promenade, not really sure that we were even going in the right direction.

But somehow, someone found us. "Master Patrick and Master Braden," said someone. We both turned and saw the dude who was evidently speaking to us. A ship bellboy, he said: "If you are ready to see your stateroom, I am available to take you there." The way he said it made me want to get there *now*. The way Patrick looked and me and the way he smiled at me made me *need* to get there.

That bellboy, a pretty red-skinned Martian kid with short black hair and purple eyeliner and huge green eyes and big black osmium studs in his earlobes, led us to our stateroom through a series of lifts and moving paths that somehow pulled us through the structure of the ship (Patrick closed his eyes a few times during this, alarmed by the height and openness of it all). When we got to the suite, the bellboy briefly toured us through its rooms, showing us the functions of the bathroom and the location of the wet bar and the access panels to the ship's computerized amenities.

Patrick offered the boy an extra-large tip in exchange for a blowjob for *me* — a rather unexpected gift. "The dude's practically in rut for some reason," Patrick said to the boy, glancing sideways at me and winking. *He had sensed it.* He knew that I was in a strange kind of state even before I had fully realized it myself. "He needs it bad, and your mouth looks like one he'd like."

The offer was accepted and the bellboy went to his knees in front of me, and he opened my pants fly with his slender reddish fingers — I always fix upon a dude's fingers because I know that he used them sometime very recently to grab his own cock. Patrick told the bellboy to remove his fancy black-and-gilt uniform jacket "so he doesn't accidentally get his cocksnot all over it." The boy removed the jacket and an undershirt as well, stripping bare his toned and hairless torso, showing me his wide stiff nipples, the deep dent of his navel, the thick snarl of his black armpit hair. As the bellboy blew me very professionally, sliding his tongue up and down my shaft, jerking it with gobs of his spit, squeezing my nuts, Patrick jerked himself off, his tool sticking out through his fly, fucking his fist. We came at about the same time, me in the Martian kid's mouth and Patrick on his neck and chest — and it was really seeing Patrick jack off that made me cum more than the pretty Martian fag slobbering on my dick.

The dude wiped Patrick's gob-splatters of spunk off his neck and chest with his undershirt, which he then put back on, evidently not caring that it was now cum-damp, thanked us for the bonus (which was probably more money than he usually made in a month), put his uniform jacket back on and left us to settle into our quarters.

Jace had, of course, booked for us first-class accommodations aboard this ship. The huge bed chamber was spanned from one end to the other and from floor to ceiling by a window that let us see into space and to see the varicolored whorls and streamers of the aether flashing with light from the sun. Patrick stepped toward that window very slowly. I knew that he was probably feeling some vertigo — he is a little bit afraid of heights — and he was trying to get used to this view into the void as quickly as possible. He stood directly in front the glass and then lowered his head, very slowly as if daring himself to look down. And he jumped back a little bit and I caught him and hugged him from behind. "I won't let you fall, baby," I said into his ear and kissed the back of his head and licked his hair and tasted its grease.

Patrick was, like I said earlier, very beautiful that morning. Granted I always feel a lot of intense hot attraction to him, but he somehow seemed especially appealing and undeniable right then. He was dressed stupid-handsomely in a dark grey suit with a four-button vest, clenching knee-length pants, a lavender short-sleeved shirt and a yellow bowtie. But I wanted him naked, and I asked him if he would do me before we go to lunch. "I know I just got head from the bell-boy like five minutes ago, but I am fully loaded again already!"

"If I can put my dirty pole in your pussy," Patrick said and kissed me and started removing his clothes.

We both decided we needed to take a dump before fucking, so we repaired to the almost gaudily ornate bathroom with its gilded fixtures and dark wooden floor, some of it covered in a thick shaggy Persian-style area rug. Patrick went first, squatting on the gleaming commode bowl. He spread his legs wide and pushed out shit and squirted some piss from his erect tool. I stood between his knees and aimed my dick downward and pissed into the bowl in between his thighs and soaked and his cock and ballsack and stubbly shaved groin. He finished his dump and we switched places. As I unloaded, I licked and sucked at his piss-damp junk and he cooed like a bird.

I washed my ass and his in the bidet, and noted just how generally dirty Patrick was and how good he smelled under his arms. I never tell him this and usually berate him for his bathing habits — even though I devour like a prized delicacy his particular flavor of boy-funk. But his ears clearly needed a good swabbing, which I did with my tongue, my hands caging his head, and he giggled through this procedure because it tickles him.

After his ears were eaten out sufficiently, I got on my knees in front of him to inspect his dong. I pulled his long foreskin back and — as I suspected — the head and that first chunk of the shaft behind it were clotted with cock-cheese. He clearly hadn't washed the thing in a couple days. I did it for him with my tongue and he moaned and leaked streamers of preek. I took him to the big bed and he took my ass first, from behind, me on my hands and knees. After he spunked out inside me, I rolled him onto his back and pushed his knees to his chest and jammed my stick into his hole. I slammed him fast about ten dozen times and made him sweat and cry and say my name a lot of times because he knows I like hearing my name — like hearing him scream it: *Braden! Braden! Braden!* — when I am fucking a guy's ass and I pulled out and put my jizz on his face. During this, I felt flooded over with heat over how fucking hot Patrick is, how perfect it is to fuck him, how much I love him, how badly I wanted him in that moment. This isn't, at least on paper, all that unusual in the sense that I *do* love him (as much as I fight and bicker with him in regular life when we are not on vacation) and that I do love boy-on-boy fucking with him (he is probably my most frequent partner after Jace), but this particular moment of fucking his pretty faggot ass was exceptionally cum-tastically perfect and I was made almost breathless by my pleasure in it — almost *dead* by it — and the intensity of my lust with his body. *More on this later.*

We went together to the shower and washed each other's bodies and dried them and dressed them. Patrick resumed his suit vest but omitted the tie and the shirt; I chose dark close-hugging jeans and a black sleeveless button-down shirt. I molded my mess of hair with beach wax and painted my lips pink and we went to lunch.

Lunch was in a giant restaurant on a deck elevated above the main body of the ship and with a wrap-around panoramic view of the open aetherspace around us and a huge skylight above us, darkened to obscure the sun. We could see the blinking and sparking flashes and streaks of the aether stream and the thicker clouds of visible ray-lit aether perhaps millions of miles further away that glowed and flared like aurorae. I asked Patrick if he was okay with this, and he said that he was adjusting just fine, and that if we were to be on this ship then he just needed to get used to it—this ship's apparent design-determination to aggravate his acrophobia—but he did ask if we could have a table further away from the window.

This high-flown restaurant's host, a middle-aged man of about seventy or eighty years clad in white suit that included a kelp-lavender vest and an osmium chain-link necktie, took us to a little square concrete table with high-backed leather arm chairs near the center of the vast dining room and asked us on the way there if we "two boys" were "traveling alone" or if "your parents are with you." We laughed politely at this, lied that we were married, but it briefly annoyed me that this might be a place where we would need to show our ages to get served alcoholic beverages, as I fully intended to have a ton of cocktails and wine with this lunch. Of course we *were* old enough to drink legally (me, twenty-two and Patrick nineteen) unless this was ship was run by ultra-puritan zealots. And, of course, Jace had equipped with us with our usual fake documentation to hide our real identities, but every time we had to show those docs it was another opportunity for us to get hacked and I didn't really want to have to constantly show ID just to drink.

But Patrick, who seems to know everything about law and order throughout the Solar System, said that there was nothing to worry about since this was a Venusian-flagged ship (clade of Vepaja-Amtor) and that these people "by pan-clade law" impose firm age restrictions upon neither drinking nor sex and that "they litigate individual or social problems with each on a case-by-case basis."

After we were seated, I noticed a red-blond and alabaster-skinned boy at a nearby table who looked to be about fourteen or fifteen or maybe even sixteen, lunching with adults who looked like they were probably his parents—though he resembled them not in the least—pouring himself a big water-glassful of white wine (Paul Pernot Chardonnay, 3116) from a glistening huge jeroboam-size bottle. This reassured me.[2] Patrick saw the resemblance to the laundry boy

---

[2] This wine-guzzling kid looked almost exactly like a somewhat younger version of Cade, the college kid that Jace hired a couple months ago to do laundry and make beds at the home after I complained that it was ridiculous that we were doing our own laundry constantly. Though Jace prefers that we not have sex with our occasional employees—and he tries to hire women or straight

dudes in most cases to prevent this—this Cade kid is a total fag and he was easy to seduce. The day before I left on this vacation with Patrick, I went to the laundry room and fucked the shit out of Cade (kind of literally—right after I pulled out of his tight ass, he took an uncontrolled dump right on the floor—this embarrassed him but I thought it was kind of cute and I cleaned up after him and fucked him again). I pulled a piss-and-cum-stained jock from Zane's laundry bag and stuffed it in Cade's mouth and he sucked on it while I drilled him that second time. Then he was very cute in the face when I rode his pole and made him put his spunk inside me.

Later in bed I jacked off to my memory of fucking Cade and embellished it with this fantasy sequel: I imagined that Cade was married to a much older man, like someone in his forties, and that when Cade returned home from his laundry shift that day, his husband (who I named Kyler) restrained him with straps and a harness and put his feet in stirrups and elevated and spread his legs. He pushed a footlong dildo into the kid's ass and swabbed juice out of it which he touched to a test strip. This test strip was then fed into a hand-held device called "*Fag IDentifier*," a thing that could detect DNA and match it to a genetic record in the database of all queer males in the Solar System. The thing would beep and display on its screen this message: "**Positive ID: BRADEN VAIEUX**." And it was also possible to pull up on the screen naked pics of me, sex videos of me, and a complete sexual history of me including my masturbation fantasies and porn preferences. Kyler was disgusted with Cade and said, "I knew you'd fuck around behind my back working at that house, but I can't believe that of all the dudes in that place you actually hooked up with Braden Vaieux, that dirty little fag-twink!" Kyler then headed to the Home to confront me. In fact, he intended to beat the shit out of me for fucking his young husband. But I quickly seduced him and ended up sucking him off and letting him fuck my ass. We agreed that going forward we would share Cade's pussy and that Kyler could have mine whenever he wanted.

at the Home without me even mentioning it. "Mini-Cade," he whispered with a grin, gesturing toward the kid.

"Have you fucked him yet?" I wondered.

"*That* kid?" Patrick looked confused. He looked at the wine boy.

"No, dumbass! *Cade!*"

He laughed. "Oh yeah, yeah, yeah, of *course* I have! Who hasn't? He's a huge slut. Like you!"

"Jace really tried to discourage me from doing Cade for some reason," I said. "Not that I care."

The server arrived, yet another red-skinned Martian dude like the cute cocksucker bellboy, but this one was wearing a simple black t-shirt and black-on-black pinstripe pants. He also wore white-framed Ray-Ban eyeglasses and held an order tablet at his side. We ordered elderflower-gin coolers and a bottle of the same wine that the kid at the other table was slurping and an appetizer of mixed sashimi.

After the waiter dashed away to get these things for us, Patrick said, "You do know, right, that Jace kept Cade overnight one night last week? In his bed."

"Interesting! And, no, I did *not* know that. Where was I?"

"You were home but you spent the night in bed with Zane and Ethan, I think."

I remembered. "Oh yeah," I said. "That makes sense."

"Jace actually called the dude's *mom*—Cade still lives with her, which is weird anyway if you ask me—boy his age!" said Patrick, "and he asked her if she was cool with Cade staying overnight! Apparently, she said she was fine with him staying at the Home all hours of the day or night as long as he was earning some money!" Patrick detailed how Jace did, in fact, pay some extra money to Cade for going to bed with him, including his normal hourly pay that he gets for doing laundry plus a bonus for each time that either Jace or Cade came during the encounter. "So you can imagine," said Patrick, "that the kid had a nice incentive to keep the semen streaming."

I sighed. "See, this is what's wrong with Jace and his entire household economic system." The waiter arrived with our drinks. I thanked him and gave him our main course orders. I continued: "There was no need at all to *pay* the dude! He totally would have fucked Jace all day with no compensation. I'm telling you, the dude is insatiably horny. Now he isn't going to want to do the laundry anymore because it's so much more profitable to just get Jace's rocks off. Either that, or we're going to end up with the highest-salaried laundry boy-slash-rentboy on the planet."

"He'll probably decide against going to college," Patrick said, swirling his drink around with its straw, "because there is no more lucrative profession one can get than doing laundry for Jace Dekka."

I heard the wine kid say something in some kind of Germanic language — maybe German itself — while gesturing toward us, and I watched when his mom or perhaps older sister shushed him while looking quite embarrassed. I didn't understand what they were saying, but Patrick did. "He thinks we're cute," he whispered.

"Settle down," I said. "Don't even think about it. He's way too young!"

The appetizer arrived, and as the waiter set it down we felt *something* run through the ship or perhaps through *us*. The waiter said, "You may feel some momentary discomfort. The ship is going to pass through an aethereal cyclone in a few moments, but you will hardly notice it. Just a little trembling through the ship. Please ignore it and continue to enjoy your lunch."

Even from our distance from the wrap-around windows, we could see the ship's great sails — more like rigid wings actually, but they were called sails — extend outward like vast scoops, painted floridly like the wings of birds of prey. I knew that these would somehow ease the ship through the cyclone, and along with gyro stabilizers, make it possible for us to pass through this phenomenon without noticing much turbulence.

"It's fantastic!" I said, watching the wings deploy and the sparking arcs of energy lance around them as they contacted the storm swirls. But then I looked at Patrick and he was staring down at his drink, his hands balled into fists. "Oh, baby," I said, taking one of his hands in both of mine. "I'm sorry. I know you don't like this kind of thing." I always feel protective toward Patrick, but I felt strangely more so than ever right then, as I if needed to not just take his hand but fully hug him into me and hold him.

"It's okay," he said. "I'll be okay in a second." Then, very deliberately, he looked up and gazed around the room, seeing what was happening out-side. "See? It's fine. I know we are totally safe. But it just kind of freaks me out because *I know what is actually happening* to the ship and it's so weird that we actually can't feel it." He knows more about this than me and he told me what was actually happening to the ship: *"It is tumbling end over end and being whipped around, like a chew-toy in the mouth of a dog, at a significant fraction of light speed. And we can't even tell."* That was, I must say, pretty fucking freaky to contemplate.

A few minutes later, the storm was evidently past us and the vast wings began to retract. The waiter arrived with our main courses and poured more wine into our glasses. I received a tart filled with chorizo, dates, eggs and chard. Patrick got a thick Kobe burger on a glossy brioche bun topped with a slab of foie gras and a smear of piccalilli, and on the side a little nest of golden parsnip fries speckled with black salt.

As we ate our meals — which were delicious *as Patrick's spit and sweat*—and drank the wine, I found it increasingly difficult to concentrate on anything but an intense fuck-lust for Patrick. My cock was steely stiff in my tight jeans and I laid my napkin over my lap to conceal the spreading wet stain of preek pulsing from my cum-slit, soaking the denim over my inner thigh. I found that I was barely eating my own lunch because I was so captivated by watching Patrick eat his, his wet mouth chewing tender meat.

Of course I always like fuck-time with Patrick, and have had plenty of it with him since his very first day in the Home when Jace summoned me to his apartment where he suggested that our new colleague and brother bugger the hell out of my ass. But this time was different: I wanted it with him in a way I don't think I ever have before. No, I *needed* it. It was not just that my body was craving sex in general, but rather it was a very specific deep-down need for Patrick in particular as if our very recent fuck in the stateroom had never happened and he had been keeping me waiting for him forever.

"Are you okay?" he wondered, pausing mid-bite, half of his burger hovering in front of his chin. "You look kind of flushed."

"I'm okay," I said. "You just look really, uh, *nice* today."

"To where I am making you blush and sweat? *Really*, dude! You are a mess!" He laughed and resumed munching on his lunch.

We ate without much more conversation until the food was gone. Patrick pondered a dessert, and I could tell that he really wanted a scoop of chocolate malted gelato with candied cherries on it—*and I dreamed of feeding it to him with my hands, his teeth nibbling and tongue licking my sticky fingers*—but he ruled that he was too filled up from the burger and would rather instead just drink some more wine. Our plates were cleared by the waiter but we kept the rest of the wine bottle and told him that we'd remain for a bit and finish it. By this point, I think the preek stain in my jeans had nearly reached my left knee as I continued to press fabric against the leakage that throbbed out of my dong onto the skin of my thigh.

It turned out that smoking was permitted in this dining room—a fact brought to our attention by the wine-slurping mini-Cade when he lit up during his dessert, a giant ice cream sundae with cookies jammed into it—so Patrick hailed a busboy who sold us an open pack of Venusian cigarettes that he was carrying in his apron. Patrick lit two of them at once and handed me one. I imagined being in bed with him, *Patrick pinioned on his back underneath me, transfixed on my just-spent cock, me sweating and maybe even crying over him, thoroughly fucked out inside his pretty body and lighting up one of these smokes and sharing it with him, feeding him drags of it, with my rod still in his chute.* I came in my pants, without even touching my bone. This wasn't just more pre-jac: I fully shot a big load. And I felt like there was another one immediately chambered up right behind it, meant for Patrick.

Patrick chattered on about Venusian tobacco and drugs and customs and features of the planet while I pretended to listen with interest and slugged down more wine and felt like I was being set on fire from inside my body with my need for him. And then this happened:

You hear your phone ring but you can't understand how to answer it because you're in a dream and whichever way you swipe or tap at its screen it does not open and you cannot read the incoming call message because it's in an alien script, full of crooks and whorls unlike any language you have seen before, but the ring is insistent: it must be answered at all costs. Patrick — your boy-shaped fuck — clasps your hands in his, cradling the phone with you and he says that the call is for both of you, that he will help you answer it.

"I think we need to take you back to the room for a little while," Patrick said. He stubbed out his spent cigarette. Mine had gone out, only half-smoked. I was sweating, the wetness chilling on my forehead and soaking me under my arms. He had never said anything that I had agreed with more: *yes, he needs take me back to the room. Now!*

The walk back to our suite woke me up a bit, pulled me back into reality slightly, at least enough to understand what was actually going on inside my body. Patrick was going to be pissed off, but I needed to give him the information that I could no longer deny.

We entered the room and closed the door and I said, "I need to tell you that I think Jace gave me a biological command packet before we left. I just...um, *found* it. Felt it, I mean. Like, I am really *fucking feeling* it."

His face fell and he clamped his hands to his head and gritted his teeth, bit on his lower lip. "Jesus Christfucker! Are you fucking *kidding* me? That's why you're feeling like this?" He stalked around the room in a circle for a minute and added, "I should have known that there was no way he was sending us to Venus just for rest and recreation. And I even *asked* the motherfucker! Directly! Why does he do this? And don't say *'lucid situational insight'* because it's complete assfucking bullshit!"

"Well, you know that's what he'd say." This "lucid situational insight" was a major premise of Jace's decision making—at least when he was making decisions for the rest of us. The idea was that one could get better in-the-moment insight into a problem and thus better problem-solving ability if one didn't really even know what the problem was in advance and had to process it as it emerged.

"My job," Patrick continued, "in our dumb organization is supposedly to be some kind tactician, but Jace never tells me *shit* about what's going on! Instead he gives it *you!* Why? Obviously because he likes you best—everyone *knows* that—but it makes no fucking sense! If he wanted us to succeed in whatever mission is in this stupid fucking command packet, it would have been better if he'd just told us—and especially *me!* —what the *fuck* the godsdamned mission *is!*"

I told him to knock it the fuck off, and that I was about to belt him across the face if he continued ranting in such an extreme fashion. I told him that he knows damned well that sometimes our missions don't become clear to anyone, even to the Commander, until we are ass-deep in the situation. "And you can scream and yell and cry like a little bitch all you want," I said, "but we still have a command packet to deal with. It's a fact. And it's also a fact, as you well know, that we need to *fuck* to unlock it. It's giving me a fucking fever, dude! It's going to fuckin' *kill* me unless you help! I need to fuck *now* and fuck *you* now to unlock it! So, do you want top or bottom? I couldn't care less. I just need you!"

He scowled at me and said, "I'll take bottom. It will set the mood for how totally fucked I am going to be before this mission is over!"

Despite the fever of my lust and love for him, I got totally annoyed with Patrick during the required fuck. He insisted on staying in that mood with that scowl-face even during the whole time my bone was sliding up his chute, him on his back, me mounted on top of him, piston-pumping his hole. I seriously started to worry that I was never even going to nut off despite how badly my body told me I needed to do it. I usually have almost total mastery over when I fuck out my juice, but he had pissed me off so much that it seemed like I couldn't even hate-fuck his punk ass hard enough to force out a spunk-load, and it got even worse when he actually *asked* me, after maybe five or eight minutes of thrusting, if I was ever, ever, *ever* going to cum. I told him to *shut the fuck up, shut your boy-bitchy mouth*, and he smirked and asked me if I hate him. "Yeah," I said, "I fucking hate you, you little faggot!"

"Good! he said. "*Spit*," he told me. "I'm trying to help you, dude. Spit in my fucking mouth!" I hawked up a big snotty glob of throat-spit and drooled it into his open face-hole. And then I came. It just happened, without any control at all. I shot off inside him, pulsed inside him for a minute, and then pulled out and realized that I wasn't done. I had a full-on double orgasm going on, and I spewed out some more dick-juice on his smelly junk. Which I sucked, of course, eating my own cum along with his preek, and he unloaded himself in my mouth in less than a minute.

The virus infected him instantly *and I heard it inside him* as I let my mental shield fall all the way and he let my mind touch his and we had together a peculiar moment of contemplation wherein we vaguely apprehended the meaning of command packet, like a thing seen through stained glass, and we learned something about the situation we were in, or at least where to go to learn something about it. Basically, we answered that ringing phone. Patrick asked me how I felt. "How do *you* feel?" I said. *Good. Really fucking good!* he said and he leaned into me, his mouth into mine.

3.

Trace and the boys find unexpected delight in their travels with Jace.

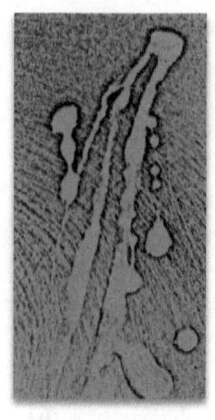

From Trace's journal...

Life with the commander can sometimes be trying and exhausting, with
all his manias and depressions, all the
crazy projects he continually sets us
upon, but despite all these deficits of
personality and management style, he knows how to
take good care of his men. Ando, Zane and I were not
exactly elated at first when he informed us that he
wanted us to accompany him to the *Conference on
Erotic Atavism in the Novels of A-R Kanayda* at the Academie Bishonen, a conference for which he giving the
keynote address and conducting one discussion session. It made no sense on the surface of it why anyone
needed to go with him to this boring and absurdly es-
oteric academic affair, nor why it needed to be the
three of us in particular. Ando seemed to not care one
way or another about tagging along, but Zane was
pretty disappointed when he asked to bring Ethan
along as well and Jace told him that Ethan needed to
remain at the Home with Colin and Tim for some kind
of unspecified project. Evidently they'd had some
kind of joint fugue the other day.

But when we arrived, we were presented with the
awesome details of our housing. Jace was given his
own quarters in an on-campus house for visiting VIP

guests, but he had arranged for the three of us a suite of rooms in a building called Edom Hall, which was also the primary gay boys' dormitory. He had, in other words, housed us in the same building as several hundred young queer male students. I doubted, given their living arrangement—a testosterone-hazed, semen-reeking nest of queer-boy horniness—that there'd be even a single one of these kids who still needed to be rescued from the oppressing chains of his virginity by me and my bros (this was after all the very school where Braden took a formal master class in sex when he was a student here), but I was certain we'd still find a bunch of young/dumb/full-of-cum dudes with whom we could entertain ourselves during our stay on campus, hundreds of horny lads, accustomed to daily sodomy. I intended to fuck my way through as many of them as possible while we were there and leave dozens of samples of my boyjuice in and on them.

We settled into our quarters, ordered the delivery of a bunch of booze—which arrived quickly—and had a couple cocktails while looking into what we might do for dinner. I scanned a homepage for Edom Hall and found something quite entertaining. "Check this out," I said to Zane and Ando. "This school offers helpful meat-beating advice to its horny young population." I read aloud to them the following:

From the Student Handbook ch. 17 on male students' sexualities and sexual health...

This school believes that physical and mental well-being are a human right, and we also believe that sexual health and sexual satisfaction are inseparable from physical and mental well-being. To this end, our health department offers an array of information, advice, tools and tips specifically tailored toward each physical sex, gender identity, gender presentation and sexual orientation, whether you are male, female, or of some other non-binary gender identity or physical sex; and whether you are straight, gay, bisexual, polyamorous, asexual, or any other shade of human sexuality.

This section is focused specifically on the specials needs of physically male cis-human students and may be equally applicable to such males of any sexual orientation.

Most male students of this school are within an age range from mid-teens to early twenties, an age range in which their bodies are experiencing peak sexual urges, needs and capacities. It is entirely normal for young men in this age cohort to be continually seeking sexual gratification, even sometimes to the distraction from and detriment to other important priorities.

With few exceptions, young men in your age cohort have a real and inescapable need to release semen from their bodies with great frequency, generally daily when all other health indicators are good. This is a very normal and healthful thing, and we encourage the young men on our campus to achieve this release with as much frequency as needed and desired both through masturbation and, when available, through sexual activity with willing partners. We attach no stigma of any kind to these behaviors as we know it is in the inherent nature of being a young man and entirely outside his control."

"Seriously!" Zane said. "They find it necessary to explain all this in a, uh, *hand*-book?" Ando laughed at this.

I continued to read:

"Some common advice that we give:

Studies indicate that a young male sleeps better if he ejaculates prior to settling down for sleep. It seems equally beneficial to him whether his ejaculation is the result of an orgasm during sexual activity with a partner or the result of self-stimulation. In any case, orgasming prior to sleep is recommended for most young men. Similarly, we find that male students have better concentration and productivity for their morning activities if they have another release of semen shortly after awakening. If a sex partner is not available in the morning to cause him to ejaculate, a young man ought to consider masturbating to orgasm in his bed upon awakening or during his morning bathing activities. If the consumption of pornographic images or literature is helpful to this end, the school library hosts a vast catalogue of such erotica on its server and in physical form at the library itself. Again, no stigma is ever attached to this at the school. Some of you may have come from cultures with different norms and where you may have been shamed or ridiculed or even punished for normal behavior such as masturbation, but here it is considered a standard part of most young men's daily lives and is encouraged as fundamental to their good health."

"This place is a really a *school?*" Zane looked at Trace in wonder. "Why couldn't *I* have gone to one like this!"

After we had settled into our quarters, we made some dinner plans and discovered an online campus social network where guys could go to arrange on-campus sex hook-ups. This also revealed the existence of a shower room, which happened to be on the very floor of the building in which we were staying, and which appeared to exist just for cruising. Since the individual suites of rooms all contained their own bathrooms, it was clearly unnecessary for any of these boys to bathe together for the sole purpose of washing their bodies, so it rather made sense for such a shared dorm shower room to just be a place for exhibitionism, public masturbation and gay sex.

Also, there were dozens of public cams in it. We opened one of them and saw one guy under the spray of an overhead shower nozzle, soaping his hard-on. Near him, two other guys under the spraying water cavorted, one on his knees with other's cock in his mouth.

Ando stood next my left shoulder, naked, not having dressed for dinner yet. He stroked his big hooded tool while watching these shower boys. "I won't be able to wait until later, dude," he said. "I need to let some of this out of my nuts right now." When he was ready, he asked me to open up. I turned my head toward his bone, mouth opened wide, and let him unload on my tongue. I swallowed his hot cocksnot, switched away from the shower cams and found a page full of postings by dudes who were making themselves available for sex now or later that night. It reminded me a bit of the customer service page for rentboys at the hotel where Jace bought me from my previous owner, with pic and stats and profiles and little icons indicating if they were available now, or later or if they were currently hooked up and therefore not available at the moment. That last status was indicated by an animated emoji resembling a grinning yellow anime cartoon boy being buggered by another.

I figured we'd get back to this later, after dinner.

4.

Back on the aethership, still not quite to Venus, the horny lads find entertainment in a lavish queer bathhouse and later educate an inexperienced young man in the ways of homosexual intercourse...

From Braden's journal...

We were still most of a day away from Venus, and while we felt a little bit of unease as to what awaited us there, we decided there was nothing to be done about it, and we still felt a lot of the initial euphoria from the unlocking of the command packet. Things would happen as they would happen no matter what we did now, and I felt a lot more stable in my mind and body now that this unlocking had finally happened with Patrick's perfect cock-help.

While browsing for some evening entertainment for us, Patrick discovered that there was a queer male cruising area on the ship, an actual old-timey bathhouse on the bottom-most deck. It seemed like an unlikely amenity for a cruise ship, but it was a very *large* such ship, carrying nearly eighty thousand people. He paid the premium fee for us to visit it and, after a light supper and a couple drinks and a few lines of narcowhirl and few tabs of Erec-T, we made our way down there. Even if it ended up being no fun, we reasoned that it couldn't be worse than some of the ship's other evening entertainments on offer such as a musical concert by some has-been popstar, a show of "Light and Magic Amazement!" and a "Fun Family Dance Party!" It's weird how when one is on "vacation" one feels pressured to do deliberate and contrived activities that one would not normally even consider on a regular day. We both laughed about this and agreed that if we were home on this particular evening we'd probably be doing nothing in special and be very happy with that situation. But there we were, on a cruise ship — on vacation! — and an activity was called for. So, to the bathhouse we descended.

The entrance was a sort of airlock and, once through it, we could smell the aromas of a swimming pool, feel the humidity of hot tubs and saunas and a faint underlying pervasion of male sweat. We stripped off our clothes (save for our rubber sandals), secured them in a locker, collected towels from the desk attendant who helpfully offered free condoms and lube should we need it. We passed on the rubbers[3] but took a tube of lube. Patrick wrapped up the

---

[3] We don't see a single instance anywhere in the *Unsuitable Boys* accounts of any of the main characters using condoms during gay male sex acts. Elsewhere in this story, Patrick refers to having worn one once to prevent himself from impregnating a maph, but he is never seen doing so during his sex scenes with males. In the episode *The Hypnotic Lawn Boy* (episode #14), Aaron Ansible offers to put a condom on his penis before anally penetrating Jace Dekka, but Jace dismisses the idea. A footnote explains: "While it is true that there is still occasionally an outbreak of a sexually transmitted disease to which males who have anal sex with other males are susceptible, it had already by Jace Dekka's time been centuries since any were serious enough to encourage widespread

tube in the towel that he had no intention of wrapping around his waist in the fashion of many of the men in this place. Before we proceeded inward, Patrick remembered something and went back to the desk where he collected a code to a private room should we find someone that might want to fuck in seclusion.

The place had a strange maze-like layout that made it feel much larger than seemed possible. We peered into a swimming pool area and then another one and then passed a couple saunas, rounded a corner and found a big bubbling hot tub with naked male Roman-style statues in it as well as several naked living males. We entered a door that promised a "Garden of Ephebos." We passed into a short length of corridor that had moving images of gay sex illuminating the walls, mostly middle-aged men fucking young twinks. This corridor opened into a room that looked at first glance to be literally a patio garden with huge potted plants, a floor material that looked like cobble paving stones but which was made of some kind of softer stuff, fountains, huge hanging baskets of flowers, vines trailing about, the whole thing lit in a yellow-green glow. At first it seemed that no one was in

---

condom use among gay men. Then, as now, condom use among gay males is principally a niche fetish thing during sex or sometimes during discreet masturbation in public places as they make it possible for a guy to cum in his pants without making a stain. No sign exists in Dekka's copious sexual records, however, that he ever had any particular use for condoms and it is doubtful that if he had ever cum in his pants that he would have cared in the least about letting anyone see a visible wet spot."

here, but we could hear the noises of guys copulating coming from somewhere.

We passed to either side of two tall stone vases which sat in between rows of what looked like wine grape vines and eventually the garden path opened into a large clearing with benches and lounge chairs set about, most occupied with a couple dozen men, and most of these men were having some kind of sex. But a few were unoccupied and a couple of them took note of Patrick and I appearing in their midst naked and stiff-cocked. I was startled to realize that one of them was that kid from lunch, the wine-guzzling "mini-Cade." He was lounging naked on a purple pleather Old Martiana-style couch with the older male that had been at lunch with him.

This older dude—a good-looking well-toned, brown-skinned, black-haired man of perhaps thirty-five or forty years—was unique among the people here in being semi-dressed. He wore a white skin-tight tank-top and white boy-briefs with black fly-seams. He cradled the young white boy's red/yellow-haired head against his belly. At lunch, I had assumed this older dude to be mini-Cade's father, but now see-ing them so close together like this it seemed quite weird if that were true, and unlikely biologically at least given how different they appeared in their eth-nicity, the boy's skin almost shock-white against the man's deep brown. The kid sat up and pointed when he saw us: "It's *those* boys!" he said. The older dude waved us closer.

We approached their couch and the man said, "This little faggot was checking you guys out in the restaurant this afternoon." He spoke with a Britannic accent that sounded a lot like Patrick's. "He's obviously thrilled to happen upon you now in your bare state."

I was not at all sure that we wanted to have anything to do with these people, but was also kind of like what the fuck, we can at least be polite for a moment. We made introductions and learned that the kid's real name was Axel and (to my relief) he was actually a fair bit older than he appeared — at lunch I had guess him to be sixteen at oldest, but he turned out to be fair amount older than that.

"I am, since just a few months ago, in an obligatory clan-marriage of convenience to his mother," said the older man, whose name was Blake, "due to shared business interests. Which is not ideal, but the acquisition of this slutty white boy faggot makes it somewhat worthwhile." We learned from Blake that his marriage to Axel's rich mother (who was evidently passed out on booze and pills in their suite at that moment) made young Axel a piece of property owned, under the rules of their clade, by Blake until the boy reached the age of twenty-three. "I don't fuck him a lot myself," said Blake, "but I enjoy giving other men the consent to do so."

I wondered how Axel himself felt about this relationship, but his calm presence there and the sudden mouth-lock that he applied to Blake seemed to suggest that he was fully on board. Axel broke the kiss with his owner/step-dad and stood up to face me. He stroked fingers over my chest and did the same to Patrick. "You guys are fucking *hot*," he said in his German accent. "It's ridiculous — really! I have never seen such beautiful boys. Are you married to each other?"

Patrick laughed. "Fuck no!" he said. "But if we were, we'd still share each other."

A blond-headed Asian dude wearing a harness and a metallic purple jockstrap appeared next to me holding a tray of drinks, frothy and frosty double-imperial pints of beer. I had not dreamed that it was possible to get drink service in this place. Blake explained that he had paid for premium service, drinks included, for this particular couch and for a private room. Patrick mentioned that he and I had also secured a private room, but Blake said, "You probably just got one of those closets with a little fuck-cot in it. I arranged for something much better."

We each, all four of us, accepted an enormous glass of beer from the waiter. It was a refreshing if rather light pilsner. I took a sip and asked Blake what was available here that was "much better" than the room that Patrick and I had reserved. He told us that he had held for the next couple hours something called "the Trough," and that Axel "really likes to be pissed on." I understood then why we were being fed, of all possible drinks, giant beers.

We put Axel and Patrick together into the Trough, which, as one might expect, resembled a trough-style urinal but it was made of some kind of rubbery fabric, perhaps the same stuff that the fake cobblestones in the garden were made from. Patrick kissed the boy for a minute with a lot of spit steaming over their chins. I told Patrick to suck on Axel's stiff skinny little cock, "but don't let him cum," I added. "Slap his hands away from his prick if he tries to cum." Patrick sucked on the boy's meat for a minute and Axel cooed with pleasure and then I tapped on Patrick's head and made him come up to receive some more beer. He drained the glass in one long chug then went back down on Axel.

"They are pretty together, aren't they?" Blake said, and he pulled me into him and kissed me roughly, scratching me with his hard ragged chin stubble, but I liked it. He gripped my penis and tugged on it and me kissed me for another minute. I felt his rod through his briefs and wished they were off of him but it seemed like a hassle to try to undress him. I was more interested in Axel and Patrick and their cute lovemaking in the trough. And so was Blake.

"Hey, Mister Patrick," Blake said. Patrick raised his head from Axel's crotch and looked up at us. "Do you think," Blake continued, "that you could piss right now if you wanted to?"

Patrick affirmed that indeed he could, and Blake said, "Then do it right now. All over Axel."

Patrick knelt, straddling Axel's knees, and released his bladder. Hot Patrick-piss sprayed the youth, first soaking his thatch of pubic hair and then filling his navel and spattering all over his belly and his chest. He aimed his hose into the dude's armpits and then onto his face, hitting his chin and open mouth. Axel groaned with delight and rapidly stroked his piss-wet cock as Patrick finished emptying his chamber. Patrick batted Axel's hand. "You're not allowed to cum yet!" he said, and then he descended back upon Axel, licking his ballsack, his belly, his nipples, his face, cuddling with him in the remains of his own piss.

Blake told me to go ahead. "Patrick, look up here, and open your mouth!" I said. "You, too, Axel!" They followed orders and I let loose my stream. I aimed at their open mouths, first Patrick's, then Axel's, and back and forth between them filling their mouths, splattering their faces, soaking their hair. Patrick tended to swallow it while Axel let the piss fill his mouth and spill out on his chin.

Then Blake let loose. He pulled his cock out through the fly of his shorts — a big thick veiny meatlog — and sprayed the boys in the trough. As he did so, Axel opened his own stream and fired it into Patrick's face and upon his chest. Once all this piss-fire dribbled out, Blake said this to me: "Go ahead and tell *your* boy to fuck *my* boy. I wanna see your boy *nail* that fuckin' kid."

I hadn't, of course, been regarding Patrick then or ever as "my boy" in the way that Blake seemed to mean it, but the idea of Patrick fucking Axel in front of us was in itself hot and the way that Blake was making this decision for the lads in a way that excluded them from the process was kind of sick in a way that made my cock throb and drip. Of course, the two piss-drenched dudes heard this exchange and looked up at us smiling and waiting for their orders, so I said, "Patrick, I want you to fuck Axel's ass."

As they got into position—Axel on hands on knees, Patrick kneeling behind him—Blake said to me, "And while they go at it, I want to bang *your* white-boy hole."

I can't recall having ever before been called a "white boy" not even by the blackest dudes who have ever fucked me. While I am certainly lighter in tone than Blake, I am certainly not "white" in the way Patrick and Axel are, with my mostly-brown background. But if it was a turn-on for this dude to regard me as a "white boy," then I was happy to play.

I assumed a position bent forward, hands resting on the edge of the trough, feet spread apart. This stance was great both for Blake's access to my cocksocket but also my view of Axel and Patrick as *my* boy boned *his* boy. Axel and I groaned and gasped as we were fucked, him by Patrick and me by Axel's dad. Blake's dick was rather thick and it made quite an impact inside me as he poled in and out with great speed and force. In this position, I was leaning directly over Patrick's head. I told him to look up and open up and I dropped a big spit-load onto his tongue. He bent lower and took my cock, which was hanging over the edge of the trough, into his mouth and sucked wetly while he continued to drill lithe and pretty little Axel.

Blake announced that he was going to breed my white-boy ass, and Patrick informed Axel that the same was about to happen to him, and in another minute it was done, Patrick and Blake cumming nearly simultaneously, filling my hole and the boy's with jizz. They released from our asses, Patrick sitting up and slumping back against the end of the trough, Blake leaning on its edge next to me.

Blake asked me if I wanted to trade places with Patrick and have a turn on Axel's cunt. I hadn't cum yet during this encounter — and neither had Axel — so I agreed immediately and hurried Patrick up and out of the way so I could do it to the young dude. I wasn't fully comfortable, however, with the way that Blake was making all of Axel's decisions for him, so I did lean into the boy's face and ask him if it was okay if I fucked him. "You fucking kidding?" Axel said, grinning. "Get on me *now*, you little faggot!"

I still found it a bit hard to believe what they had told me as Axel's actual age. But on closer inspection it seemed more plausible that he was, in fact, Patrick's age, though I decided that I didn't need to care too much since he was evidently some kind of youth-slave, owned as property by his step-dad, who could grant or deny sexual consent on his behalf until he turned twenty-three. So I slid my rod into the cum-mess that Patrick had left inside Axel and pumped a few dozen times into his socket. Axel jerked himself furiously the whole time. He told me to tell him when I was ready to bust and he'd do it with me. And so we did, me inside his gut and him all over his smooth belly. And then Patrick and Blake pissed on us. My dick was still inside Axel as the other guys hosed us and I told him that I could probably piss again and asked him I could do it inside him. "Fuck yeah, brother," he said. "Do it." I pushed in as deeply as I could and let loose, draining my bladder into his gut. Sometimes when I attempt this, the piss just kind of squirts right back out around my cock, but sometimes it actually goes in and stays there for a minute, as it did with Axel this time. After I pulled out and sat back, Axel rose into a squat and shat out my piss-load — and some actual shit as well — to Blake's approval, Blake who kept saying "good boy. Very good boy. Both of you."

It somehow seemed that our liaison with Blake and Axel was concluded at that point, and so Patrick and I left the Trough room and found a shower room — we both probably needed to rinse off pretty badly. We were, at first, the only two dudes in the shower room, but two more guys joined us shortly. They were both extremely tall and quite stocky Latinos, their brown skin riven with black wiry tattoos. They grinned at us, removed towels from their waists and let us see their stiff pricks, their bushy pubes, their low-hanging ballsacks. "You guys having fun?" one of them said.

"We have been having fun," Patrick said.

"I suppose we could have some more," I said.

The other dude — the one who hadn't already addressed us — said, "You little faeries wanna suck our big dirty man-cocks?" He stepped closer to me, ran thick nail-bitten fingers over my cheeks, and added, "You have a real pretty face."

"I want the blond one," said his partner, stepping up to Patrick.

"Story of my life," I said to the dude who was leering down at me. I gestured at Patrick. "When *I* am with *him*, they always want the blond one."

The dude laughed. "Not me," he said. "I like queer little darkies."

Without any more conversation, Patrick and I accepted the proposition and lowered ourselves to our knees in front of the big dudes, Patrick and I shoulder to shoulder and the men hip to hip. We each started sucking and slurping on our guy, and then after a minute or two, without deciding consciously, Patrick and I did this: we switched hands. I grabbed the base of Patrick's guy's cock and started stroking while Patrick sucked and he pulled on my guy's pole why I sucked on it. In this way, they were getting the benefits of a joint blowjob from both of us at once, and it did not take much longer for both of them to launch their loads. My guy put his in my throat while Patrick's dude pulled out and pumped his out onto Patrick's face.

This seemed to end the encounter as the two dudes drew away from us, got under the shower sprays and laughed and joked with each other in their own language, sort of ignoring the fact that Patrick and I were still present. So we rinsed again, left the shower room, dried off, retrieved our clothes from the lockers and headed back toward our room.

But on the way back, Patrick was attracted by the site of a cocktail lounge that hung aloft from a loggia above a promenade and suggested we stop there for a drink. We seated ourselves at the bar and each ordered a gin and tonic and a cigarette and sipped and smoked quietly for a few minutes. Patrick showed me something on his phone. It was evidently a queer sex hook-up app. A grid of selfies of shirtless dudes filled the screen, most with "on-line now" indicators glowing green. He tapped on one—a pic of a chubby cherub-faced fag with moppy red hair who, despite his smile, looked positively uncomfortable standing (at least mostly) naked in front of a bathroom mirror with his phone. "Check this out," Patrick said, and pointed to the screen. *"Distance: 4.613 meters"* it said. "Look behind you," Patrick said. "Act casual about it."

I swiveled my seat slowly and saw him, this kind of fat and kind of cute red-head kid sitting alone in a booth, sucking on a glass of white wine and holding a smoldering black cigarette in one hand. He looked down at his phone which was lying on the table in front of him. I completed my slow swivel and Patrick showed me this dude's profile info. He had just finished high school and was on a vacation with his dad and step-mom and sister. He was a closet homo from a conservative clade, and he was *"hoping to get my v-card punched"* on this voyage aboard *Queen of the Aether*.

"I think," said Patrick, leaning close into me, "that if you wanted to pop that boy's cherry, all you'd have to do is offer the service."

Patrick was correct. The red-headed boy, though quite nervous when we approached him, readily agreed to accompany us to our quarters. His name was Hansel, which I thought was hilarious given that he was a little chubber who'd probably be a delicious dinner after being roasted like a pork butt in a wicked witch's oven, his melting fat-cap basting the sinewy boy-meat cladding his bones. But I did not, of course, relate this observation to the lad since he was so obviously self-conscious and nervous over the imminent prospect of his long-awaited first time with another man that I would never have compounded his anxiety by letting him know that I was fantasizing about barbecuing his rich and marbled meat.

Patrick, never one to take anything slowly, stripped himself naked as soon as we got into the room. Hansel looked at him wide-eyed, perhaps alarmed, perhaps fascinated since he'd supposedly never been in a sexual scenario with anyone before.

He'd probably never even seen another gay dude naked in person, much less one naked and with an upright and preek-drippy erection standing within a few feet of him.

Hansel gaped as if he wanted to say "oh...wow" but instead he said — face flushed — "Could we have a drink first? Do you have anything to drink here?"

Of course, I said, and led Hansel to the wet bar where I poured him a big shot of aquavit. He downed it in one fast gulp, then stood there cringing for a couple moments. "Another?" I offered. "Fuck yeah," he said and took down the second pour, but more slowly.

Patrick stepped up the bar and pulled open a drawer. "Let's get this cute little fuck stoned." He pulled out some weed and some narcowhirl and some rolling papers. "I saw you smoking a cig in the bar," he said to Hansel. "Do you smoke anything else?"

Hansel blushed and admitted that he smoked weed sometimes.

Patrick went to work in his way, expertly crafting a fat joint of part weed and part tobacco and laced with narcowhirl dust and a couple powdery crushed tab of Erec-T. "This," he said, holding up his creation for Hansel's inspection, "is going to both whack your ass and get you horny as fuck." He leaned forward and surprised Hansel with a quick kiss on his mouth. "And then you're going to want either me or Braden to terminate your virginity at long last."

We smoked the joint, passing it among us, for about five minutes and it had its intended effect almost immediately. All three of us were stoned as fuck, high as kites, but also so freaking rock-cocked that we could do nothing else but get right to business. I stripped off my clothes and Patrick and I together set to work stripping Hansel's body. Under his clothing he was about as chubby and jiggly as I expected but his fat-layer belied a very firm undergirding of muscle. What I had expected to be soft and almost girly boy-boobs were quite firm pecs. He gasped when I tongued and nibbled his pink nipples and licked the faint fuzz of chest hair in the center of his breast and cried out in surprise when Patrick dropped his knees and took the boy's long thick prick in his mouth. "Step One," I said into Hansel's left ear with a lick of spit, "toward the end of your virginity: you have your cock in another man's mouth right now."

Patrick stopped the blowjob probably just shy of making moaning Hansel squirt and pulled him toward the bed. "You need to get officially deflowered, dude," he said. "Let's get that over with now and then we can expand your education at a more leisurely pace afterward."

Hansel accepted Patrick's directions to get on his hands and knees on the mattress. He whimpered and moaned a little bit when I spread his big asscheeks and pushed my mouth into his crack and tongued his sweaty cunt. "Oh, fuck!" he said. "That's amazing! Oh my god! What are you even doing!"

"Foreplay, baby. Braden loves eating a faery's ass before he fucks it."

"I can't believe this is really happening!" said Hansel.

"That you are finally getting laid?" said Patrick while I continued to tongue the red-head's funky ass-pucker.

"Yeah, and that I am doing it with *two* hot dudes at once!"

I told Patrick we should do him from both ends. I volunteered to take his mouth and told Patrick to do the deed in Hansel's ass and it was on Patrick's pole just a moment later that Hansel's anal virginity ended. Patrick warned Hansel that it will definitely hurt at first but he needed to be brave and take it and soon enough it would feel just fine and that it might even make him cum.

And the dude did take it very bravely at the moment of penetration. While Patrick drilled Hansel's hole, I sat in front of the boy with my legs spread and pulled his mouth down onto my cock which he slurped and slobbered upon hungrily, with the innate understanding that every male has of how to suck a dude's dong even if he has never done it before. "I'm not going to pull out when I cum," I told him, "and I don't want you to pull away when I do it. I'll hold your head down on it if I need to. Do you understand?" He sort of nodded and grunted assent as he soaked my stick and slid up and down on it with a tight fist. "You need to experience what it's like when a man cums in your mouth and you need to at least try to swallow it this time, too. Later on, you'll figure out what you like and what you don't like but you need to do everything at least once first."

Patrick started making his usual pre-cumming noises and grunts and cries. "You're going to breed him, right?"

"Fuck yeah, I am! Right now!"

I let myself release at the same time, and in that one moment Hansel was flooded inside his mouth and inside his tight rectum with two dudes' streaming semen.

We all three collapsed to our backs on the bed, Hansel the fresh new non-virgin in the middle, and we breathed for a couple minutes. "We're not going to be able to cover every possible sex act that fags can do together," I said, "but there's one more major one that you need to try before we're done with the key initiation."

Hansel had not cum yet, and his bone was livid purple and rock-stiff and leaking preek. I raised myself over him, straddled his hips, grabbed his tool with one hand and aimed it at my cunt. "Oh fuck!" he cried. "Really?" Yeah, really kiddo, I said, and I slowly seated myself onto his dick and wriggled ever downward upon it, admitting it inside. I didn't lube my ass nor his cock beyond his leaking pre-jac, but I was still slick inside from Blake's breeding earlier and entry was easy. I told him to thrust up against me, push in as far as he could. Patrick grinned at Hansel and said, "You're fucking that hot faggot in his boy-cunt, baby. For real. You like it?"

Hansel's answer was a whole lot of gasping and moaning and yelling and it didn't last too long and he couldn't hold it in anymore and he let loose inside me. We relaxed and smoked some more, had another drink, and then continued young Hansel's sex education for a couple more hours.[4]

---

[4] From Braden's journal: "Rather surprisingly, Patrick and I received a message from Hansel today — that chubby ginger boy that we fucked on the cruise ship to Venus last year. He said that he had defected to a new clade and was in school to learn aetheric engineering. His parents were pissed, he said, because they had finally found him an arranged corporate marriage to join, this being a common solution in his former clade to the 'problem' of homosexual boys. They'd be forced into group marriages and procreation with females for reasons of social acceptability and would be relegated to having to seek gay sex on the down-low, often with the other men in the marriage, and always in danger of jeopardizing their livelihood if caught. So he said fuck all that and joined a gay-sex-positive clade and said he was very happy. He thanked us for his initiation on the cruise ship."

5.

Jace meets an old acquaintance and is entertained by a closeted queer boy.

From Jace Dekka's journal…

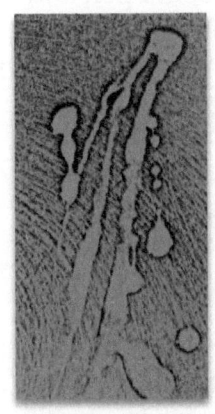

The bedroom suite that they gave me for my stay at the Academie Bishonen was surprisingly huge, airy and well-appointed. Occupying the entire fourth floor of the large house, it was a vast expanse of shiny wood flooring, walls of beige plaster, a vast coffered ceiling laminated with elaborate tin work, several crystalline chandeliers depending from the center of large medallions of stamped gold. a dozen beds of various sizes and a sitting area of large over-stuffed leather furniture furnished the huge room. I assumed it was either normally, or had once been, a dormitory given the number of beds and the bath-room with its huge open shower stall large enough for a dozen or more dudes to shower together, a bank of sinks and mirrors sufficient for a bunch of boys to shave or do their hair or make-up at once. I didn't think that I was to actually have any roommates while here, but I was pleased that I had plenty of room should I want to entertain some guests while here.

I spent a moment organizing my belongings in a deep wood-paneled and sky-lit walk-in closet and stripped out of my travel clothes, thinking about showering before getting ready for the seminar. While I was in there, I heard the door to the room open and a few footsteps and then a familiar voice: "Jace Dekka! Are you in here?"

I stepped out of the closet, still naked, and saw Matteo Ngau, the longtime director of the Academie's sex education department. "I wasn't necessarily expecting to see your cock this morning, Dekka, but I can't say I am disappointed." He stepped toward me, we embraced, kissed briefly. While I've never found Matteo to be hugely arousing (he is a bit older than my usual range for erotic objects), the brief contact with him did stiffen my pole a bit, and he even gave it a quick squeeze. He stepped back, assessed me with a head-to-toe gaze and said, "You never, ever age, Dekka! It's amazing!" I couldn't say the same about Matteo Ngau, of course. We were nearly the same age chronologically, but he looked a bit closer to his actual fifty years, while I hadn't noticeably aged in appearance since my early twenties. But he remained a handsome man nonetheless, made as he was of planes of muscle and shimmery hair and nearly-glossy brown skin.

"How is my favorite former student doing? Your boy Braden?"

"He is quite well," I said. "I might have brought him along on this trip but he is busy on another project for me this week."

Matteo asked if my relationship with Braden was still that of father and adopted son. I told him that no, it was not, and that we did in fact start a sexual relationship as soon as he moved to the Home, that I quickly thereafter fell in love with him, that he is my most frequent sex partner, and that I would likely marry him one day if he wanted the same, but we were not going to discuss it until he passed the age of twenty-five, which I consider to be the bare minimum age for a boy to really be sufficiently a "man" enough to make a commitment like that.

"You did a fine job with him, Matteo," I said, suspecting that he was hoping for such a report. "He really learned a lot here. He is the most astonishing lover, an absolute pro in every position, technique, game, fetish, everything. And he is quite popular with all the other dudes in the Home as well, to the point where I sometimes don't get quite enough of him myself. But I am happy, as always, to share all of my lovers."

"Does he still look the same?" Matteo wondered. "I was always in love with those cute little bent ears and that thick mop of hair on his pretty head."

I opened my phone and showed him a recent picture of Braden, of Braden squinting at the camera, his mouth open and filled with a blob of white ice cream. "He cuts it in different ways sometimes, but much the same, yes. I did give him a couple of sex organ enhancements even beyond what he received here—we have a doctor in the Home who is an artist with such things. We increased his testicular volume even further, doubled (again) his Cowper's glands. I had Tim—our doctor—also reinforce his asshole and rectum. He has cocks in his ass so often—often several times a day for weeks at a time—that I didn't want

69

him to eventually get too stretched. He was also partially circumcised when he came to us — his father personally did that for him when Braden was a child; I actually watched him do it — a strange thing to recall now after all these years — but he decided he wanted to have his whole foreskin back after becoming captivated with that of one of the other guys in the Home. So we did that for him as well."

Matteo nodded and grinned. "He must be quite the young rakehell!"

"He's gorgeous and loving," I said. "And perfect. I hate even being away from him for a day, but we had important work for him to do off-planet."

"I know you have a session later this morning," Matteo said, "and I should be getting back to work anyway, so I won't detain you further if you'd like to relax for a bit and get dressed. Would you, however, like to put that cock in a pretty dude's mouth? I can send Kiel up here to entertain you. He's the guy at the desk downstairs, the one who gave you your room key."

I nodded. "Yeah sure. He's cute. He can suck me if he wants. Send him up." I found this to be an unnecessary consideration on Matteo's part, but whatever.

"I'll have him join you right away." Matteo smiled, evidently quite pleased to be offering me this deluxe room service. "Be aware, though, that he probably won't want to do anything more than suck you off. He is actually mostly straight — married to a woman and with four kids even. But he has an intense fetish for orally servicing gay men. But he doesn't fuck ass in either position, and he won't cum at all unless you ask him to jack off. He will let you suck his cock if you want, and you can kiss him if you want, but he won't stay very hard for long — if he even gets hard at all in the first place — and he claims that he is capable of orgasm only by way of masturbation, even while having straight sex. He once told me that in order to knock up his wife he had to jack off until he was on the brink of cumming and then stick his dick inside her right at the point of no return. So if you'd like a more diverse and capable partner who wants to do more than just suck your rod, I can probably find someone else for you easily enough."

"No," I said, "a blowjob from Kiel will be fine for now. I don't have a lot of time this morning anyway. And I suspect I will find some more fun later in the day."

Since Kiel would supposedly be there directly, I decided to stay naked. I change my mind from time to as to whether it's a bigger turn-on for me to just be naked already when a new guy sees me for the first time or to be dressed and then strip for him. But this time it was just simpler to not get dressed. I prepared a vodka tonic at the wet bar, gulped it down quickly, made another and sipped it while smoking a cigarette.

Shortly after, a knock sounded against the door and I told him to come him in.

Kiel was a white dude and he looked a bit flushed in the face, as if he were either hot or a little bit embarrassed. His hair was dark brown and molded into a short crest atop his head, his eyes were either hazel or green and he had fat pouty lips that looked like they'd feel nice around my pole. He seemed rather too young to be married and with four children as Lyndon had said, but I suppose it's possible that he was from some kind of religious clade that had placed him into an arranged marriage at a very young age so that he could start to fulfill his breeding duties as early as possible without the aura of sexual immorality surrounding his fervent and fertile fucking.

I asked if he smoked and he accepted my offer to share a narcowhirl joint, and he seemed almost a tiny bit relieved that we had something to spend time with, to break ice over, before getting right into the business of putting my dong in his mouth. He sucked hard on cig and concentrated his gaze on a spot on the floor.

As we smoked, I asked him about his love of cocksucking and he admitted that he was aroused by a kind of *humiliation* that he felt when he had a man's penis in his mouth. He kept glancing at mine, which stood fully stiff during our conversation. I told him he should probably get started on getting me off. Would you also get naked, I asked, so I can see your pretty body? He obliged, removing first his shoes and socks, then unbuttoning and discarding a black button-down short-sleeve shirt under which he wore a black ribbed tank top. He peeled this off and I saw he had little whirls of dark hair around his pink nipples but none in his armpits, which was a little disappointing but I didn't figure I'd be putting my mouth in them anyway. He undid his belt, opened his fly and dropped his pants, stepping out of them carefully. He wore sheer white trunk-style underwear through which I could see the darkness of his pubic hair, the general shape and size of his pole and his nuts.

As he stripped himself completely naked, I actually added some things to my body: shoes, a cricket cap, sunglasses. And I had him put back on a necklace and bracelet and an anklet—all black rubber with magnet clasps—that he'd removed with his clothing. I considered having him add back his shoes because I usually like seeing an otherwise naked dude with shoes on, but they weren't very cute shoes, while his bare feet were very cute, a bit too big for his body, and—though I didn't touch them—they looked to have soft heels and soles and neatly trimmed nails. I asked him if he liked to be on his knees when he had a dude's dick in his mouth. He nodded, said that he very much did like that. I asked him where, when I cum, would he want my load? In your mouth, or should I pull out and shoot it somewhere else? "On my face please," he said, voice a husky and bashful whisper. I liked that choice. Though it often feels amazing to let a blowjob go all the way until I actually cum inside the dude's mouth and he swallows all of it, I still really like to see my spunk on a guy's skin, and better still on his face, in his eyes, and in his hair.

Since this sex session with Kiel, based on what Lyndon had said about him, would consist solely of him sucking me off, I was tempted to spend a long while getting blown, really stretch out as much as possible how long I took to cum, but time was getting short, so I figured I'd limit this pleasure to maybe eight or ten minutes. He was a good cocksucker, with decent hand-and-mouth technique, and he made quarts of spit. It literally dripped from my crotch and wet the floor at my feet. He didn't forget about my nuts, taking them both in his mouth one at a time while jacking on my pole. I noticed how slender and pretty his fingers were, wet with spit, polishing my knob. He even wedged his head fully between my legs and lathered my taint with spit, quite nearly touching my asshole with his tongue, making me wonder (hope) that he was going to eat my cunt, but he stopped short of that and went back to my cock with his spit-glossy lips and tongue.

After another minute or so of this, I realized that he was doing such nice work on me that I was very close to cumming even though I might have wanted to hold back a bit, and that I really didn't have a whole lot of control left to exert over it. Part of it was just physical pressure: I hadn't shot off in hours. I hadn't beaten off at all that morning, and my last release was unloading my first-thing-the-morning cum-wad inside the cabin boy on the airship during the last leg of the trip here, but that had been hours ago. (After that unload, my dick didn't droop at all, and I kind of wanted to go at him a second time, but I needed to get ready for arrival, so I just washed my junk, took a dump, washed my ass, and the cabin boy just jerked himself off quickly, jammed a tampon in his hole because he wanted to keep some of my juice inside all day, pulled his pants back on and left).

But, even as pressurized as I was anyway, Kiel really was very good at sucking dick, and I did want to just allow myself to let loose and pack his throat full with a big load of cocksnot, but I honored his request to not jizz inside his mouth. I withdrew my stick from between his fat spitty lips, grabbed it with both hands, tugged a few times on it, his spit soaking my fingers, and I launched my load in a few spatters on his forehead, eyes, nose, lips and chin. And then I realized I was going to have a second uncontrollable back-to-back full-on climax, and took that opportunity to squirt white goo on his smooth alabaster chest as well. A stream of it drizzled from between his nipples and down the center of his belly and settled into the short black hair above his prick, which I noted was now quite fully erect. "You need to cum, too, baby," I said. "If you want me to try to help you do it, just ask. But otherwise, you need to jerk yourself off now, right here in front of me."

Kiel looked down at the floor and told me that it embarrassed him to be seen with a hard-on, shamed him to be seen so plainly aroused in front of another man. But I understood that this was the key part of his fetish: this shame was in itself the actual turn-on for him. He was a straight married boy who had just been on his knees, a cocksucker for a big-dicked queer, and now he was being seen by that same faggot showing his raging shameful sinful preek-dripping boner. I needed to respect this fantasy and help him play it out. "Do it," I said. I bent low and spat heavily on his cock, and he cried out, a long moan. "Do it, you little faggot," I said again. "Make yourself cum like a fuckin' homo. Right in front of me."

He beat his rod stiffly, like he wanted to hurt, and moaned, gasped and literally cried, real tears soaking his cheeks as he pushed himself to release. I know a lot of people think it's ridiculous and insufferably embarrassing when a guy cries during sex, but I tend to love it, and I find it to be very endearing and arousing when the boy is as pretty and vulnerable and earnest as Kiel was.[5] When he did finally achieve his kind of relief, his batter shot out in several sharp and full bursts, a lot of it hitting my shins and landing on my shoes.

He remained on his knees for a minute or two, still crying, but soon he regained his composure, looked up at me and actually *thanked* me. "Come here," I said, reaching down and helping him stand back up. "I need to leave for my appointment pretty soon, and you probably need to return to work as well, but we're kind of a mess. Especially you." He still had cum and spit all over his face and chest and prick. "Let's get in the shower and wash up before we get dressed." I could feel him recoil from this a bit from

---

[5] "Braden is really good at that," Jace states in one entry from his *Fuck Record*. "He will sometimes play the part to the max, fully sobbing while fucking me and getting his rocks off in my hole, tears falling from his face, bubbly snot-streamers dripping from his nose into my mouth. It's ridiculous that he can just turn that on and off like that. He is a fuck-superstar."

this suggestion. "Don't worry. I am not asking you for any more sex," I said. "But let's just clean up. We would enjoy it."

I led him into the subway-tiled bathroom, into the huge open shower chamber, turned on a few of spray nozzles. I kicked off my shoes and drew him with me into the water. I told him that I like bathing cute dudes, and that I'd get him all freshened back up for his return to work. He let me paw away the spunk from his skin and rinse his hair. He smelled so sweetly, however, that I decided to not use any soap on him so as not to ruin fully his natural man-smell. He surprised me by letting me kiss him as water poured on our heads. "Lyndon told me that you're married," I said. "Is your wife cool with this thing you do with guys like me?" He surprised me again by sprouting a fresh erection when I rubbed running water over his nuts.

"She has no fucking idea," he said. I have never told her. "She wouldn't get it. That I like sucking gay cock. She'd think I was a faggot. But," he said, "I do it almost every day. There's lots of queer dudes on campus. I guess I'll get caught eventually."

We stepped out of the shower and I dried him off with a thick white towel, taking care to get under his arms, deeply into his crack, in and behind his ears, into his crotch. I made him raise his feet one at a time and I dried his toes. I towel-dried his hair and re-styled it with glossy and sticky pomade. He allowed me to help him back into his clothing and he even let me kiss him again, which stiffened my stick again though not his again. While helping him dress, I asked him if he'd let me keep his underwear, those sheer trunks. "I'll give them back tomorrow if you want, but I'd love to keep them for tonight if you can get by going commando for the rest of the day."

He said nothing, but allowed a shy smile, set the trunks on the bathroom counter and pulled his pants back on over his bare ass and nutsack. I imagined this: me in bed at the end of night, naked on my back on top of the sheets, fucking my left fist with Kiel's dirty underwear stuffed in my mouth, his sweet and stale crotch-sweat stench in my nose, jetting hot bedtime sperm all over myself. "Keep it," he said, "forever if you want." [6]

---

[6] Several years later, Kiel Bartosa came out as queer and moved to Chako Paul City to work in its porn industry. He narrowly escaped being a victim of the so-called "Scando-Noir" serial killer who preyed on male sex workers and porn industry workers and is thought to have slain over a hundred queer men and boys mostly by strangulation before his spree of terror suddenly ended for reasons unknown. Bartosa, as the only known survivor of the Scando-Noir's depredations, provided a good physical description of the killer, but this bit of evidence never helped crack the case, which remains cold to this day. A fictionalized Kiel Bartosa is a major character in the crime thriller film *Don't Wake Up*, loosely based on events in Chako Paul during the time of the Scando-Noir killings.

6.

Meanwhile on the planet Venus, Braden and Patrick find the person who can unlock the mystery of their mission. But will he?

From Braden's journal…

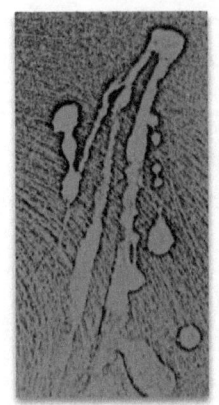

We fell toward the Venusian aetherport in a shuttle much like the one that had brought us up to *Queen of the Aether* from Earth at the start of this voyage. I held Patrick tightly against me and literally covered his eyes with my hand so that he did not have to see the perspective of what seemed to be our free-fall toward the forest-canopied planet but he broke away and said, "I'm okay, baby! I really want to see this." He paused. "Well, *want* is maybe overstating it, but I *should* see it. New experience!"

I waited for him to change his mind—or possibly faint or puke—but he held up well, nose pressed against the glass as we fell into Venus. It had been a few years since I'd last been to this planet, but Patrick hadn't been there since he was a toddler and had no real memory of it.[7] Even though he was in no real danger, I thought he was kind of brave in a sweet and endearing way how he insisted upon swallowing his fear of heights and tamping down with sheer force of

---

[7] Patrick's parents had attempted to get into the wine-making business on Venus, but their enterprise failed quickly and they returned to Earth.

will his vertigo so that he could see our arrival on this planet, so that he could experience it with me and not miss out on any aspect of something that we were doing together.

The shuttle completed its fall and settled onto a pad that seemed woven of vines or tree branches and which was, in fact, held aloft between a couple of towering trees. I still worried about Patrick and his acrophobia and how this entire journey so far had seemed built to aggravate it, but he was calm as we stepped off the shuttle and proceeded to the customs checkpoint. Our fake ID papers let us through without comment and soon we were descending to the ground level on a lift made of wood planks and plasteel poles.

Along a cobbled street, red clay stones with black mortar, a line of taxis — old-style electric motor cars clad in shiny chrome trim and tail fins and big headlights, and blazing with wild enameled paint colors which shimmered in the bright but diffuse sunlight that filtered through the leaves and limbs of trees that rose hundreds of meters above us — waited for fares. Cabbie leaned on their cars and smoked black cigarettes, sweaty and bright-eyed shirtless kids sold what looked like big puffy empanadas and bottles of pink juice to passing tourists. We walked, without really thinking about it, toward a purple car, and its driver noticed us and starting waving us toward him.

But we did not know where we were supposed to go.

But, somehow, we *did*.

Patrick stopped our forward motion with an arm across my chest and looked at me, eyes wide. He said, "I think we are supposed to take that purple car. Do you feel it, too?"

I admitted that I did. We agreed that we'd do it. A moment later, we were seated in the back of the car, sinking into its leathery tufted seats. Neither Patrick nor I can remember it specifically, but we are both still quite sure that we never spoke with the driver as to where to take us.

The driver, a stocky brown-skinned dude with mirror-shiny sunglasses and a big grin, helped us load our bags into the boot of the car, opened doors for us and got us situated. It was warm in the car, but it either did not have air-conditioning or the driver was declining to use it, but we traveled with the windows down. This ended up being the best thing: the breeze felt like cool feathers on my face and Patrick and I were delighted with the fruity forest aroma of Venus. "Do you smell it?" said Patrick. "It's like orange peel and kiwi and lemon grass." The driver lit a black-papered cigarette and offered them to us as well, passing the open pack and his lighter back to us. The flavor of the smoke tasted like the forest smelled. I'd been hoping there'd have been a little weed or narcowhirl in it, but no such luck.

We rode for maybe ten or fifteen minutes along a smooth jungle road, leaving behind the aetherport, rolling forward into what felt like ever-deepening forest, trees reach ever higher over us. We met not much other traffic, just another car occasionally heading the opposite direction, probably more cabs full of bags and passengers for the cruise ship and its next port of call. A flight of dozens of huge varicolored birds passed low over us, flapping vast translucent wings, heading the opposite way, and Patrick leaned out his window to better see them and laughed. "Those are so cool!" he said, and I wanted to lean into him and kiss him.

Then I realized that *we had been riding for maybe ten or fifteen minutes already* and had not exchanged a single word with the driver about where we intended to go. It's not like we were booked in a hotel somewhere already that this taxi driver somehow already knew about.

Patrick and I looked at each other at the same time, and he said that he felt like something very strange was happening. But I asked him this: "Does it worry you? Are you at all worried about it right now, at this moment, as it's happening. Be honest."

He shook his head. "No. Not at all. Not even a little bit. But *that's* weird in itself."

"I'm not either. I say we roll with it. See where we end up."

We didn't know *where* we were, but once we got there it felt like the place, like we'd gained some certainty over the sense that we were going to uncover some piece of an unseen plot, and that it was going to involve somehow the inhabitants of Cabana Vepaja-Aknathus, the small arboreal village where we found ourselves housed after the ride in the purple taxi.

We rose from the sidewalk by the taxi stand into the trees by way of a lift like the one that had lowered us from the aethership dock to the ground upon our arrival on the planet. As we rose higher, I watched Patrick pointedly *not* look down or at anything at all for too long a spell. "This part is actually okay," he said. "I know that when we get up there into the village, it won't *look* as much like we are in free-fall."

He turned out to be correct in that hope. Once we were up there, it felt more like we were on solid ground again, a cobbled street under our feet, even cars again—though all much smaller and less gaudy than the ones at ground level. We walked into what appeared to be a town square with huge trunks of trees piercing its cobblestone pavement here and there and rising hundreds of meters above us, their distant canopies dappling the intense glow of the sun, so much larger and hotter in the sky here than on Earth. Locals smiled and waved at us as we passed, occasionally issuing a bright ¡hola! There were a fair number of tourists as well, easily identifiable because they looked a lot like Patrick and me: way overdressed, sweaty, laden with bags and back-packs.

"Over here!" Patrick said, and he took my hand and drew us toward a palapa-style structure housing what looked to be a bar or a restaurant under its thatched roof. At first I figured I was simply once again fortunate to have at our command Patrick's un-erring ability to spot a bar — and I was really thirsty! — but then I heard or maybe *felt* this: *Go in there! You're too thirsty.*

"You feel it, don't you?" he said, pulling me along. We entered the palapa and took seats at a cocktail table topped with brightly painted clay tiles, dropping our bags on the thatch floor at our feet.

Without bothering to ask us for an order, the bartender — a muscly brown-skinned and black-haired twink, shirtless with barbells through his big nipples-set in front of each of us some kind of drink in a tall and weirdly carved cup, like it was made of wood (but it was actually made of porcelain) and intended (I think) to resemble a collection of Cthulhist icons. It had a tall steel skewer transfixing assorted fruit rising from it and a pink umbrella with silver glitter speckling it, and a very tall transparent straw.

The drink was thickly fruity, full of pink pulp and little specks of black seeds, and had what tasted like a lot of rum in it. I started noticing the other people seated at the bar and at a scattering of tables around the palapa's perimeter. We seemed to be the only tourists in there, and based on what I could see of the locals, I wondered if this town was just some weird place populated somehow entirely by brown teenage twinks. This would make more sense later when we figured out that they were all maphs, and mostly actually in their twenties and thirties and forties. And every fucking one of them. We learned this fact shortly after someone joined us at our table

Kyler FEY

"Mister Vaieux, I presume!" he said to me, and "Mister Confessori, I presume!" he said, grinning at Patrick.

It wasn't clear as to how he knew ours names nor why he was looking for us, but it felt like a reasonable development. He introduced himself as Austin Bajer, and he said that he was the "tanjong" of the community, sort of their prince or chief. He seemed at first glance to be too young for the job because he looked to be about sixteen, shaggy red-brown hair, dark eyes, skin the color of a caramelized chess pie. But he was actually forty-five (that Venusian air for you), and that greater age came across when he spoke. "You gentlemen," he said, "have been expected for some time. I hope you'll trust me when I tell you that you must — I insist! — dine with me this evening."

He invited us to his cabana — a sort of deluxe tree house in which he lived alone. Though pleasantly appointed and comfortable, it seemed like a very modest dwelling for a tanjong, but I didn't know much about Venusian aristocracy. We got there by way of a quick jaunt in a cab and then a ride in a lift. He cooked us an abundant and delicious dinner of local meats and vegetables, fed us chilled orange wine and regaled us with gossip about the village.

85

Later, we fucked. Austin told us that he liked the way we smelled, that our Earth sweat and the oil in our hair and the smell of our armpits were different than that of Venusian boys — both the maphs and the *cis*-boys. He was fascinated by our uncircumcised penises: maph cocks don't have foreskin to begin with and most *cis*-boys on Venus get cut upon their "coming of age."[8] His foreplay with us included a lot of playing with our dick-sleeves, smelling and tasting what were to him alien cocks. Patrick had the first spunk-out of the session, startling Austin with the volume of jizz that he launched onto the Venusian man's face. "Even *this* tastes different," he noted, swabbing Patrick's white juice from his chin and cheeks into his mouth with his fingers.

I was pretty fascinated with Austin's body as well. Sex with a maph wasn't new to me — Colin is one and

---

[8] A custom rooted in "Enphasma" a Venusian spiritual tradition compounded from Cthulhist mythology, veneration of the "Old Trees" of Venus and sympathetic magic. Boys who practice the faith will, when "ready for awakening to the Old Trees" — typically around the onset of puberty — spend a period of weeks in the forest meditating and living off the land by foraging for food. They typically do this alone but are periodically looked in upon by a spiritual guide who eventually performs the ritual circumcision and returns the youth to his community where he is regarded as having entered the "second age" of his spiritual and ethical life. A modern variant of this custom practiced by some wealthy urban-dwellers skips the period of meditation in nature, substituting it for a week at a summer camp followed by a big "coming out" party that resembles a Terran wedding reception or bar mitzvah party. This abbreviation of the custom is often regarded by people outside that social stratum as being inauthentic and missing the point.

I get in bed with him a lot—but the Venusian tastes and smells of Austin's body were probably as unusual to me as mine were to him. It was as if the fruit and spice of the sky-scraping trees and massive flowers and humid air were baked into his skin, into the flavor of the cum that he pulsed into my mouth from his vaj when I licked his internal clit. I wanted more of him and felt like I could have gone on for hours eating out his cunt and his asshole, fucking him in both of those holes, making his long slender dong squirt in my mouth, kissing his mouth and sipping of his spit, but he decided we needed we to take a break. "You'll get plenty more later, baby," he said and licked his own juice off my lips.

Patrick and I were hungry again so Austin made us a snack of smoked fish and flatbreads and a creamy labnah-like cheese. We drank a lot more and smoked a fruity local variant of narcowhirl, and Austin Bajer suddenly clarified the viral command packet. He simply told us why we were there.

"You are familiar, obviously," he said, "with the ornate depredations of Tiphon."

We said nothing at first. Honestly, I was so stoned at that point that I wasn't sure if I was even hearing that correctly. Did he really mean Tiphon, the same Tiphon that we're always hassling with at our Home for Unsuitable Boys? That very same villain that Jace has been at war with pretty much since his birth? How does this twinky maph know anything about that shit? And who even says in normal conversation—most particularly while freshly fucked and drunk and stoned—such an outlandish phrase such as "the ornate depredations of Tiphon?" Are we in a bad movie? Are we caricatures on the pages of a dumb pulp novel?

Patrick may have been slightly more sober than I, so he answered: "Yeah, we know all about that dumb shit. I assume that's why we are here. It turns out that we were 'ordered' here by our boss, though that info didn't come across my desk until a couple days ago, and this fucking cocksucker *[jabs thumb toward me]* didn't unveil it even though he knew godsdamned well that this was the case. So, what up, bro?"

I must assume that Austin Bajer had no difficulty at all with parsing Patrick's profane dialect and simulating it, because he answered thusly:

"This is the shit that's gonna knock your faggot socks off, if you were wearing socks. Do either of you even own socks?" Neither of us answered this outré question. "On Venus, we don't wear socks much unless it's to a formal event requiring decent shoes, and then only if such shoes are too fucking uncomfortable to wear without them, because sometimes you need them to increase how long it takes to get blisters on your feet from wearing shitty shoes. But that's not important right now. But *this* shit *is:* Tiphon is preparing to shoot some kind of beam at Venus that, once shot, will cause the pregnancy of every woman and maph[9]

---

[9] This persistent use of the term "maph" to denote the "manyn" — a mostly-Venusian subset of humans whose bodies bear genitalia resembling those of both typical males and females and who can bear children — is currently considered problematic by many gender scientists and social activists. It is obviously derived from

who is fertile for such a thing at the moment this beam blankets the planet. I know that sounds ridiculous, but we here on Venus—victims of history, all of us! — tend to take world-wreaking psychopaths at face value. That's why you're here. In my opinion."

Patrick rose from the couch. I almost thought for a brief panicked moment that he was going to go ahead and put his clothes on and back slowly out of the place with some polite thanks for dinner and for getting us wasted and possibly even abandoning me there to sleep it off with Austin Bajer because I wasn't likely going to be getting up from the couch right then even I had wanted to. But instead he went to the kitchen island and poured himself more wine, and he said, very soberly, "It *is* ridiculous. Perhaps the most ridiculous shit I ever heard in my life. *But* we *also* take the Tong Tiphon at face value. Is this it then? Are we now to just to go home and get to work on stopping this?"

"hermaphrodite," a long-discredited term that centuries prior to these events was applied as a slur upon people with non-binary physicalities. Its use in context among manyn is considered comparable to the way *cis*-male queers will often use terms like "faggot" and "faery" to refer to themselves and each other but which they would consider inappropriate for use by heterosexuals. In the case of the Venusian manyn, most of them present as gay males and they are almost universally sexually oriented toward other manyn and *cis*-males, upon whom they rely for sperm to reproduce. An often-overlooked fact in Braden Vaieux's biography is that his birth-mother was a maph and that he is a very rare *cis*-male offspring from such a union.

Austin Bajer rose from his couch, naked, his long skinny cock fully stiffened. "Yes, but there's something else we need from you boys first," he said.

7.

Jace attends his seminar and is later entertained by sixty randy young fags.

From Jace's journal…

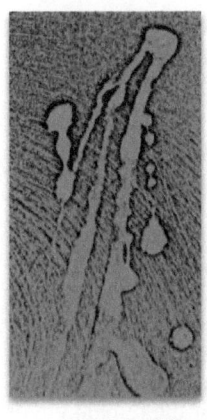

They'd made posters and flyers, featuring a stylized and somewhat cartoonish depiction of me, that characterized me thus:

"*Jace Dekka: Freedom Fighter, Public Intellectual, Homosex Radical, Social Gadfly, Father of Millions, and Possible Super-Being, joins us to present the Keynote Address of our Conference on Erotic Atavism in the Novels of A-R Kanayda.*"

This was entirely over the top, but I liked the phrase "Homosex Radical"[10] even though I really had

---

[10] Given that this was an academic conference, it could refer to any number of "radical" statements that Dekka had made in various writings on sexual matters, including some that earned a fair amount of displeasure from less "radical" commentators. One item in particular was his article from several years before this conference titled "*Son-Swapping: Boy-Man Marriage Among the ZenAmish Polygamous Cult of Terraphis.*" Negative reaction to this piece was based on a superficial reading of his thesis as actually being supportive of the now-extinct ZenAmish clade's acceptance of a marriage practice wherein married men with adolescent gay sons would sometime arrange the marriage of those sons to other men in their cohort. Under this bizarre arrangement, it was possible for such a man to enjoy carnal intimacy with such a boy without incurring the stain of adultery (because they were married to

no idea what exactly the author of the poster meant by it beyond the fact the I'm a hugely promiscuous

---

at least one other woman, and plural marriage was permitted) and without the stain of "fornication" since sex outside of marriage was prohibited, and without the stain of the other major sin of male homosexual behavior since that, too, was prohibited altogether unless it was in an arrangement like this between an otherwise hetero-married man and his arranged-for male bride, and naturally without the risk of any unwanted new children since obviously neither the man nor his young male bride could get pregnant through their intercourse, and the younger man was forbidden altogether from intercourse with any of the female wives (not that this injunction was always successfully enforced). A full reading of Dekka's text leaves no doubt that he did *not* approve of this as any kind of reasonable social arrangement that other societies ought to emulate, and that he found it to be one of the many aberrant forms of marriage and religious practice that had evolved in the centuries since humanity had broken free of the bonds of Earth and splintered into hundreds of thousands of clades. But he did observe at some length how the "swapped sons" tended to fare much better than other members of their families in the long run because of how their husbands treated them in relation to their female wives and their own children. They tended to be better-educated and more materially "spoiled" than anyone else in the society, and thus tended to rise to the top of the patriarchal and heterosexist hierarchy. This stands in contrast to the usual academic view that these boys were simply rape victims and sex-slaves. The swapped sons also tended to repeat this odd practice in the next generation after achieving their emancipation into adulthood at age twenty-three, siring their own sons and then later trading the boys into marriages with other fathers. It is evidently this acknowledgment that some social advantage to this practice accrued to many of the swapped sons, and that they did not necessarily live lives of unalloyed victimhood, that caused for Dekka a stream of social media hate for a short while, but it appears that he ignored it entirely.

faggot who also lives with a bunch of young queer dudes that I fuck routinely.

My keynote address was politely received by the students and faculty attending the conference, and many of them had very perceptive questions to ask during the question-and-answer period, nearly all of them staying on the academic topic and avoiding the topic of me as a personality. The speech itself, after a brief overview of Kanayda's erotic literary atavism, focused on the evolution of Puck, the main character in the gory fagsploitation novel *This is My Rust, My Love*. This book focuses on the coming of age (and then wild disintegration) of an orphaned youth who is inducted into a gang of serial-killing rentboys in a strange bombed-out city in a country that's never named and which seems to be the entire world (I am not going to reproduce it here, but the text of the speech, if anyone is interested in reading it, can be found in *Phaeton's Cum-Lit Rag-Mag* #413).

After the speech, I sat in in on a seminar session which ended up focusing for most of its duration on what the professor contended is a "dialogue" between some of Kanayda's work and my own book *If You Were My Boyfriend, My Fucker*.[11] I enjoyed (though

---

[11] This book by Dekka, sometimes described as a metafictional novel or a long prose-poem, is derived from his relationship with Echo Rajer, the med-tech who midwifed Dekka's clone-birth and became his lover for several years before being tragically killed in an attack by the Tong Tiphon. The storyline imagines that Rajer had never died and that Dekka's own life took an entirely other course. The backstory of Dekka and Rajer is recounted in Episode #9 of this series, *His Hundred Million Sons*.

with some mild embarrassment) listening to the students talk about my book and ask me questions about it, but after a couple hours of this I was ready to move on. I still needed to suss out exactly why I was there, why me being there was demanded by a clairvoyant song from Colin and a picture from Ethan.

I guess because he knew that I had few hours to kill in between the morning seminar and the evening cocktail party for the seminar students, Matteo had arranged for me to participate in an enormous orgy with students in my huge on-campus quarters.

He caused several dozen lubricious lads of all colors and sizes to join me in my room to have sex with me and each other for a couple hours, and he supplied a buffet of snacks, drinks and drugs to assist as needed.

So that I could keep track of all their names and faces for my fuck-journal, I created an impromptu facebook for them to sign. They included:

Kamdyn, a slender red-skinned Kaseian senior who'd just passed his gay sex mastery finals and boasted of being a power-bottom (I double-dicked him with Tommy, a big-cocked white dude with red pubes);

Nowaz, a small Asian frat-boy-looking kid with purple spirals tattooed around his nipples and a barbell through his foreskin (a quick-cummer, I made him squirt in my mouth in under a minute, though he recovered instantly and had some form of sex almost continuously the entire time he was in the room);

Peyton, Odin and Nunen, a trio of black twink boyfriends whom I serially fucked and who all three jizzed on my face;

Kasmo, a blond white boy whose legs had been replaced from the knees down with prosthetic blades with an amazing weight-distribution tech embedded in them, who could literally stand in a crouch upon my abdomen with me barely registering his weight, while he put his dick in my mouth and took a piss;

Erikus, a chubby white dude with a super-thick dong who poled my ass on my back and shot his spunk inside me;

Tradyn and Michael, two maphs from Venus who wanted me to knock them up (and I may have, but no way to know for sure);

Justin, another red-skinned youth from somewhere on Mars whose fetish was cock-cheese and had come up with an innovative mad-science way of almost instantly culturing it by inoculating his foreskin with some kind of enzyme-enhanced concoction of wild yeast, milk, his own spunk and spit and sweat— he asked me if I was into it, and I told him that I was but didn't get much of it since (even though I have at least one uncut cock in my mouth pretty much every day of my life) my boys at the Home usually just keep themselves too clean to grow a whole lot of it. He had so much of it, I literally smeared some of it on a cracker from the snack buffet and ate it with a gulp of wine;

Tullum, Macro, Juan and Angel: a quartet of Latino dudes with matching tattoos on their cocks and nuts depicting a serpent wrapping their ballsacks and nuts. They seemed to form a gang together and I let them take turns banging my chute until they'd all jettisoned their loads;

Laird, a blasian lad from Nippon, who claimed to have enough of my DNA in his ancestry (thanks to the giant breeding program that I was subjected to in my youth and which still bears kids) that I could be considered to be one of his grandfathers, and I obliged his fantasy of having some his ancestral sperm up his ass;

Tamoh, Yig, Chagon, Dagen, Anh and Bairn, another ethnic "gang" (this time Han) who sort of set upon me *en masse* with kisses and gropes, a tangle of arms and mouths, and spent a few minutes sucking my rod and eating my ass until eventually cumming, all six of them, after a couple minutes of jacking off over on my face;

Taryn, Nguyen, Dash, Treble, Maxcard, Zach, Sulum, Cain — these eight young men of various colors and body types were all scat-fetishists and were involved in some shit-play in the enormous bathroom while I was otherwise engaged, but when they invited me to join. I wasn't in the mood for their particular kink right then, but I did enjoy a few minutes of mass-oral/anal fuck-play with all eight of them in the shower area;

Donny, a fat Latino kid with giant nipples that I sucked on and gently bruised with my teeth while he cried with joy, and a gorgeous long brown dong, sleeved in even longer foreskin, that I made squirt with a vigorous spit-lubed hand-job;

Rager, a tall hairy white dude, chest like a fucking carpet, with very pretty eyes embedded in a somewhat unfortunate acne-scarred face that I fucked with Donny's cum as lube;

Dial and Norther, a freshman boyfriend couple (both rather small femmy white boys with lush and greasy mops of pretty brown hair on their heads and no hair at all anywhere else, not even on their arms and legs) who seemed almost too shy to be ready to jump into a mass-sex party, and whom I jacked off on, spattering both of their faces while Dial fucked Norther at my request, and Dial spent a moment trying to blink my spunk out of his open eyes;

Fourchan, Dazzle and "Cocksucker", who claimed to be in a three-way marriage and whose bag was to invite other men to fuck Cocksucker while Fourchan and Dazzle watched and jacked off — I obliged and all three shot loads;

Tony, Morgan, Kevro, Toxyn, Axel, Hiro, Saddik, Bashar, Kamen, Toff, Rajesh, Kody, Harrison, another Justin, Ganesh and Henry (mostly south Asians and blasians by the look of them) who comprised a good percentage of the school's cricket players, and who showed up in uniform, but eventually all sixteen of them had shed at least their pants and jock straps and I am pretty sure I had at least tasted all their cocks and had mine in at least most of their mouths during my session with them;

Kilo and Kieran, who made an impression (a lot more about them later);

Beson, a little white dude with curly blond hair on his head and a lot of it in his ass crack and big bush of it around his cock and nuts, who (were it not for the ass-and-cock-hair) looked like he was maybe twelve or thirteen, though he said he was twenty-one, and whose fetish was getting fucked by "daddy," so I assumed that paternal role for a few minutes and nailed his boyish cunt...

...while Davros (stocky cute Jewish kid with a fat cut cock) and his boyfriend Leto (lithe and tall black twink, uncut, shaved pubes) watched me fuck Beson, jacked off and shot their jizz in my face.

This was, overall, a fine diversion but it was still a diversion: I had no more idea now than before as to what it was that I was supposed to discover here. But yet I felt a pull toward that answer, and it was undeniable, like an itch deep inside. And then I heard this: Colin singing in my head, that song that led to me to this point. And I heard this: *You need to see it, this thing that Ethan is doing! And you hear him scream: A-Star! Again and again.*

8.

A hard, rough dawn on Venus, and a stunning proposition for the lithe and lusty lads.

From Braden's journal...

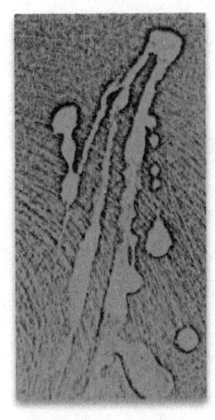

The next morning, we awoke quite seriously hungover, quite seriously annoyed with the tiny pink-plumed birds lined up on the sill of the open window, twirping at us. Austin Bajer offered us remedies for this discomfort in the form of jerkfruit mimosas made with a local prosecco, and also some pills...made, I assume, with some kind of medicine. "We cannot risk," said Austin with great gravity, his erect hair encircled in a blue corona of sunlit narco-whirl smoke, "that you fail to stop the Tong Tiphon's impregnation beam. If we assume that their technology is real, then this atrocity *will* happen to our world. But at least *some* of our people must be spared the stain of bearing Tiphon's zombie children."

"Uh, abortion?" said Patrick, still naked from sleep, hangover eyes bright and blue and bleary, blond curls awry and matted in snarls on the back of his head.

"Not socially acceptable on Venus," Austin said, "except in extraordinary cases. There are possibly a billion people who could be knocked up all at once, and even if they all decided that they wanted to abort, the demand for it would overwhelm the system. It would throw the whole world into madness, chaos, possibly even civil war. But that could happen regardless if this awful thing happens."

"So," Patrick said, "we should probably get our asses back to Earth and figure out how to stop this shit. Is that right?" He lit a cigarette and added, "And before you reply, have you people *heard* of phones? While it's certainly been interesting to see this place, was it really necessary to bring us all the way here just to tell us a time-sensitive thing that you could have said in an aethertext message?"

I said, "*Um*, Patrick is sometimes a rude-ass prick. Please excuse his mouth. Unless you want to put your dick in it. It works well for that, and that's about it.[12] We do appreciate your hospitality and I am sure that there is a great reason why we actually came to Venus

---

[12] From Braden Vaieux's journal during this period: "I talk so much mean shit about Patrick. Listening to me, someone would think that I am always arguing with him, always busting his chops about something, always insulting him, and maybe someone would think that I don't even like him or that he doesn't like me. But that's so opposite of true. It's hard for me to say it directly to him, but I love that boy so much, and he doesn't say it to me very often either, but I know that he loves me so much, too. If anyone else fought with Patrick the way I do or said the kind of things to him that I say to him, I'd beat the snot out of that sorry motherfucker, and I know he'd do the same for me. We can bicker and insult each other all day long, but he is the guy that when I am feeling badly about something or really bad about myself, I can go to his room at night and lie down with him and ask him to just hold me, and he does. He doesn't even try to fuck me. Well, last time I did give him a hand-job so he could fall asleep, but still."

other than just to get the knowledge of this beam." I still was so fucking hungover and sleep-deprived that I wasn't sure if this whole bizarre beam talk was possibly just a dream from which I'd not yet awoken. I gulped another jerkfruit mimosa and asked Austin if he had, in fact, ever told us why we needed to be there. It seemed like he was about to have done so last night, but all I really remembered anymore was going to bed with him and Patrick and I think I fell asleep while jerking off and while Patrick was fucking Austin. And I may have fucked Austin myself, but I wasn't sure if I actually did or if I just dreamed it.

"I didn't get to all the details," Austin said, "because you guys were so fucking wasted and I was pretty horny, so I just took you both to bed and told you we'd talk more this morning." He refreshed all our drinks and said, "The main reason I needed you to be here physically, aside from the fact that your bodies are beautiful and your faces are cute and I like having your pretty and dirty little Earth-boy penises inside me, is that my village here needs a whole bunch of sperm. It is our intention to get pregnant—*all of us*—before this beam hits so that we will be unaffected by it. You guys from Jace Dekka's house are known to be especially fertile and with almost impossibly short refractory periods after ejaculation due to all your fancy little junk-enhancements. So I think you guys could service us all in a couple or few days."

Patrick looked slightly confused. "But wait, can't you just, you know, do each other?" Austin and I both gave him the side-eye for a moment and then he instantly blushed and blurted out with, "Wait, wait,

wait! *Don't* say it! I just forgot! I know it's impossible. I'm dumb! I'm a poorly-educated man! So kill me!"

But I decided to say it anyway: "Dude, these maphs can no more get each other pregnant than you could get *me* pregnant."

"One thing I *do* know," Patrick said, "is that if you *could* get pregnant, you'd probably never leave the house! I bet Jace would keep you knocked up and barefoot full-time and every year we'd have a new black-eyed, lop-eared rugrat crawling around the house!" Austin laughed loudly at this. Patrick, quite pleased with this speculation and with Austin's mirth, grinned and winked at me.

"Maybe constantly pregnant," I admitted, "but certainly not barefoot: he often likes me to wear shoes when we fuck. Last week he even boned me while I was fully clothed. He just ripped open the ass of my pants and pounded away."[13] It occurred to me that

---

[13] Braden Vaieux comments on this in an earlier entry from his journal: "Jace took my ass in the greenhouse this morning. He didn't even undress me. He bent me over my potting table, cut open my pants with the razor that I use to make plant cuttings and jammed his pole in, just his preek for lube. He only pumped for like two minutes, came, pulled out, turned me around and pushed me onto my knees and jizzed again, this time all over my hair, which he then rubbed in really well. Then he blew me, my cock sticking out of my fly, and I unloaded in his mouth. This was pretty fun, some hot and fast greenhouse sex, but I was kind of ticked off that he wrecked my pants. I liked them a lot—lilac-colored linen capris, very tight-fitting around my crotch and cheeks, and they made my dick-package look awesome and made my ass look fucking cock-dripping delicious (I guess Jace thought so, too, since he couldn't even control his lust for it long enough to get me

this was probably the very incident during which he gave me the command packet.

Patrick said that since we were here anyway, he wouldn't necessarily object to knocking up a few maphs provided he was absolved of anything further to do with it later, but, he said, "How many of you are we talking about? How many people in this village?"

"One hundred and ninety-eight," said Austin Bajer, and we just kind of let that number hang in the air amongst us for a moment or two. In fact, I pictured literally like that: big, colorful blocky digits hanging in the air, drifting in the space between us, slowly rotating and eventually evanescing. "Though we can deduct one already: *me.* I was impregnated last night by one or the other of you already. I don't know which — you both shot loads inside — and I am not even that curious about it, and I suspect I will know immediately when the baby is born since the two possible fathers are so different in ethnic type. But if you would like to know which one of you fired the sperm that hit the target, we can do a little test and find out."

Patrick said that he actually wanted to know. "Just curious. I have never knocked anyone up before. The only other maph other than Colin that I ever had sex with I used a condom, and I have never fucked a woman in my life."

So we did the test. As Austin observed, there was plenty of our DNA lying around the place, and he could have swabbed some from our cumstains on his

---

naked before fucking me). Of course I ordered a new pair of these same pants — two actually, so I have a back-up ready in case he does this again."

sheets, but there was no way to be sure whose stain was whose. So he had us scrape around inside our cheeks with little demitasse spoons from his espresso set and then fill narrow little cordial glasses full of spit. It wasn't clear to me how he was getting the DNA to compare from his brand-new embryo, but he messed around in the kitchen for a minute, and eventually upended the shot glasses into his mouth and drank our spit. That kind of stiffened my pole because it was so much like something that Jace that would have done. But, however he ran this test, we soon we learned from Austin's tablet computer that Patrick was the father of Austin's embryonic child.

Patrick was really quite too pleased with this information: "In your *face*, bro!" he said. "My swimmers must be stronger! And they even got in there second!" I let this pass without comment beyond an eye-roll, though Austin thought it was quite funny, and he laughed rather too long and loudly over it.

Then through the open front door came someone pulling a hand-truck with cases of groceries upon it. He was a black-skinned dude with a wild crown of yellow hair, shirtless like everyone in this neighborhood. "Excuse the interruption," he said. I wondered how he had even gotten up there with all this stuff but then I noticed a big humming hover-board thing floating around outside the open front door next to the deck.

"Thanks for being so quick," Austin Bajer said.

"I must say," said the delivery dude, "that I can't believe you need a restock already!" He went about putting bottles of beverages and sundry groceries away in the kitchen.

"I have never in my life," said Austin, "seen people who can *drink* as much as these two Earth boys! Or *eat!* The cupboards are nearly bare!" Patrick and I looked at each other and silently agreed that we were very glad that this restock was occurring so that we could continue such prodigious eating and drinking. The delivery boy finished his unload and, walking past us with his now-empty cart, smiled at us and said that he assumed he'd be seeing at least one of us again very soon.

"So," I said, a few moments after the black/blond boy departed, "you seriously want us—just the *two* of us! —to fuck and knock up a hundred and ninety-seven people over the next few days? I mean, like, holy *shit*, brother! I can certainly cum a lot of times in a day, but this is going to take a while."

Patrick looked skeptical. "Can't we just," he said, "maybe shoot off a couple/few times in a cup or something? You swirl our little swimmer-boys together and then everybody gets a little dose of it and get it done that way? You could probably finish it in one day like that, and then if you need some more juice, we'll just make some more tomorrow."

"Again," Austin said, "we are dealing with some Venusian cultural norms, especially among maphs. We really don't like any sort of artificially-assisted methods of reproduction, beyond the fertility herb that we are all using to ensure our success with you boys. It's one of the many cultural residues of the Jihad.[14] We strongly feel — or at least most of us do — that the best and most ethically decent way to get pregnant is to have willing males ejaculate their sperm into us directly from their cocks during sex. And doesn't that sound like more fun, anyway? Better than jacking off in a *cup*, certainly!"

We could hardly argue with that logic, and later that morning, with our work about to commence, our bodies readied for a long day, we did the fecund deed.

---

[14] Here Austin Bajer refers to a decades-long political and cultural fugue that overran most of Venus about two centuries before the time of Braden and Patrick's visit. Commonly called the Jihad in Venusian literature, it was not actually a "holy war" in the way that Terrans usually use the term, but rather a period of multi-faceted political and cultural strife and social realignment which eventually reached a violent flashpoint when an interregnum government ordered the abortions of all maph fetuses as well as the physical castration of all queer male adolescents. While the order was violently rejected by the populus, many maph abortions were carried out before the regime was toppled, and the testes were removed from as many as half a million children and teenagers. While some of these victims later regained their nuts by way of cloned grafts, many remained eunuchs for life, and there exists a large body of literature, music and film about and by them, the so-called "Eunuchs of Amtor." The lingering effects of this period make the clades of Venus rather unusual among the humanities even now in having cultural norms that are very sex- and gender-positive while also being rather restrictive on reproductive choice. To this day, many of the cultures with the most restrictions on reproductive freedom also tend to be the most repressive sexually, but this is not so on Venus. It should be added, however, that Venusian conservatism on reproductive issues is not actually codified in any formal laws or religious mandates, but somehow adheres simply through tradition.

9.

Trace, Ando and Zane organize an orgy with students; one of Trace's partners shows him a strange piece of fiction and falls into an unexplained state; Trace experiences a vision that points toward the answer to a riddle.

From Trace's journal...

We invited a bunch of horny young queers to our suite. They were Nathan and Axel, a pair of roommates from across the hall, both tan white dudes with blond hair; Gunnar and Nikko, a chunky and muscular Nipponese boyfriend pair from another floor of the building; Hastur, a black twink with flaming red hair on both his head and around his prick; Tradyn and Michael, another boyfriend pair, pretty-faced maphs with wet snatches and cute cocks, Tradyn being very tall with long limbs and Michael being much shorter and stockier.

Zane had stocked a fine bar for us in the kitchen area and mixed martinis for everyone and passed around Erec-T for anyone who wanted it, and after a bit of drinking and smoking (narcowhirl-laced marijuana joints that Nathan and Axel had brought), all ten us pretty much just got naked and started having a nice orgy for a couple hours.

A couple of the guests—Gunnar and Hastur in particular—found it necessary to remark at some

107

length on the size of my pole after I released it from my jockstrap. It's true that I nearly always have the biggest dong in the room unless I hook up with someone else from my generation of former sex/sperm slaves. A lot us were given rather larger than needed dick-enhancements when we underwent the rest of the enhancements to our sex equipment [15], and I sometimes feel slightly embarrassed about it when a dude acts like he is almost scared of it the first time he sees it fully erect. But it's also true that it also kind of turns me on, kind of makes me proud of it. And it's not really *too* big to be useful. Maybe three or four times ever have I been with a bottom who just couldn't take it, but I am happy to be gotten off somehow else in those cases.

Partners were swapped, and I think I made time with each of our guests, including getting off inside both Tradyn and Michael—in their "girl" pussies, fucking one while the other ate my ass. They both acted like they wanted me to knock them up for real, and they wouldn't answer one way or another if they were on any kind of birth control. I didn't really care either way, so I played along since they seemed to get off on the concept of getting knocked up by me even if it was just role-play. They probably saw on my social sex media profile that I listed "mpreg" as one of my turn-ons. I play that game with Colin a lot at home. He is always on birth control because he

---

[15] Some of Trace's background as a breeding slave and high-end rentboy is depicted in Episode #6 of this series, *The Royal Rentboy of Kasei*.

doesn't want to have a kid, but we like to pretend that I am making a baby grow inside him when I fill his tunnel with my cocksnot.[16]

Later, I was lying around in one of the beds cuddling and making out with Gunnar after he'd blown me and after he'd jacked off on my chest, and he told me that he was a degree candidate in fiction writing and that his final project for the semester was what he described as a "literary sf porn novella" … about *me*. At first I misunderstood what he meant, and assumed he was just saying goofy bullshit about how he was going to write his next story about his sexy time with me. But then he said that his seminar advisor liked this novella a lot but gave him some good ideas as to how to improve it during revision. "Wait a second," I said, "do you mean that this thing is already written? [17] You just met me tonight."

"Oh," he said, "but I have known *of* you for years." He next unveiled that he was aware of my activities on Mars years ago, that he was obsessed with

---

[16] Trace relates elsewhere in his journals how this "mpreg" sex with Colin varied in its fantasy content. Sometimes they pretended to be simply a married couple, deeply in love, who wanted to make a baby. Sometimes the scenario was that Trace was being coerced or tricked by Colin somehow into getting him pregnant. Sometimes the scenario was reversed and it was Trace who demanded that an unwilling Colin receive his seed and bear him a son.

[17] The story that Trace mentions here is *Go Down, Trace*, published as a stand-alone novella by Gunnar Duncan a year after this encounter. It was nominated for the Nebula Award in the novella category that year.

"Ornate Martiana," a historical fantasy genre based on the history of Mars before and during the Kaseian Revolution. And then, he told me something that I already sort of knew: that I have been the subject of erotic fan fiction in this genre. I knew this already because of that magazine, its glossy paper pages warped and brittle with dried cum, that the angel-boy from Mars had brought to me when he translated into my room a couple months before.[18] But then he said it goes way further than that, that Wattpad is sick with fan- and slash-fic starring "me." And he wanted to prove it to me.

He got up from the bed, wandered naked and dick-stiff around the suite for a minute looking for his pile of clothing, fished his phone out of a pants pocket, grabbed us a couple beers, and came back to bed. He showed me on his phone the search results for "Trace Battle" on Wattpad. There were like thirty-thousand hits, item after item ranging in size from little fragments to epic-length novels, most of them with cheesy cover art based around the many naked pics of me that can be easily found on the web. In many of them, as Gunnar explained to me, this fictional version of me was a grand hero. In others, he was just some chick's (or fag's) high school crush, a new boy at school. In others still he was a pathological villain, such as in one story for which I only saw the lurid cover art, but which Gunnar told me was a three-hundred-thousand-word novel depicting me as a drug-

---

[18] These events are depicted in Episode #3, *The Spunk-Angels of Mars.*

addicted serial rapist of inmates in a concentration camp for juvenile male criminals who eventually falls in love with a heart-of-gold religious boy (after raping him, of course), and later swears allegiance to that pious boy's "Lord," and then becomes a televangelist, and then ultimately leads a theocratic revolution on Triton.[19]

But then he showed me this: *"Trace and Zach on the Sperm Asteroid."* This was the title of a story that he suggested I read in its entirety right then. At first glance I parsed "Zach" as "Zane" and was kind of weirded out. The thing's advertised word-count wasn't that long, so I read it while Gunnar gently played with my nutsack and my dong, as if trying to do the very most for me while I read porn.

The Zach character was the first-person narrator, plainly a "Mary Sue" stand-in for the author, and he depicted me as his father and lover. In this tale, we were on a father-son space-cruise that I had for some reason decided to take my son on before he left for his first year of college (because that's what one does, I guess?). Stuff happens on the cruise, a bunch of goggle-eyed love-making with the boy in a shower and then in his bed and he smiles and cries with big wet

---

[19] A few years after the events that Trace describes here, this particularly lengthy piece of fan fiction was professionally published to some critical acclaim, with the Trace Battle character renamed as "Brace Kamnotta," and it was later adapted into a long-running and fan-beloved telenovela titled *Dark Hearts of Triton*. The run of this series coincided with, and was considered a part of, a "new Golden Age of television," and it was notable even in its time for its many scenes of unsimulated sex and drug use.

eyes when he cums because he loves me so much, and on and on like that for a few pages. Then the cruise ship hits a space iceberg of some sort but it turns out that it wasn't an accident at all and that pirates had deliberately crashed it into the ship. Another character (named Justin Bieber) briefly appears — also a cute young college-bound lad like Zach *(might I have a hot and sweaty threesome with a lithe twink duo in my near future?)* — and he leads us to safety aboard a lifeboat, and it seems like Justin is going to be with us from then on, but he disappears after that one scene, and he is never mentioned again. But it's all been a ruse to capture me and my son, and soon we are so nabbed by the "Juice Pirates of Thulha" who seem to be some kind of criminal cartel but we have no idea what their deal is. First they suck us into a giant mothership and some more fucking happens with my son because he is afraid they're gonna kill us and he wants me to make love to him one more time, so I vigorously sodomize him again and tell him that I love him like he's "a naked singularity of love." But that luridly sweet moment passes and somehow we end up in a prison cell somewhere that reminds me of old alien abduction stories (reminds *me* really, while reading about it, not my dumb caricature in the story who is totally clueless about anything), and then there's finally a big reveal. This is the big reveal: Zach and I are to be enslaved into a vast apparatus that is literally milking hundreds of millions of queer males of their sperm for some unknown purpose. As our dicks are plugged into this machinery, our brains go dead or possibly into some kind of coma. It's not really clear. This happens to me first and Zach sees or feels it and sobs piteously and moans I-love-you-dad until he, too, moments later, goes brain-dead or into the coma (which begs the question of how a first-person narrator can tell this story credibly as there is no indication that he ever recovers from this condition, but whatever).

Something wasn't quite right here. Suddenly annoyed, I slapped Gunnar's hand away from my cock and asked, "Why did you have me read this anyway? For one thing, it's fucking terrible. I don't know if even a *good* writer could have managed this material. But there's some reason for it." I felt it deeply, that it was not an accident that this lamentable story was put in front of me by this goofy kid. "Tell me why."

Gunnar shook his head: "I don't know, man. I really don't! But you're right: it *does* mean something and there is some reason why I *had* to show it to you." His eyes lit up with tears. "But I don't know the answer to either one of those questions!"

I rolled over on top of him and pinned his arms to the bed and straddled his legs with mine. "I think you're lying," I said. "You know something else."

Fuck me and find out, he said, but he didn't really *say* it. It was more like I heard it somehow from *inside* as if it were beamed into my head from his. His eyes rolled back a little bit into their sockets and he grinned. This sounds — when you just say it like that — decidedly creepy and non-arousing, but somehow I found myself raging hard anyway and I needed to do what he said and I spread his legs wider and pushed his knees to his elbows and pressed into his cunt with my shroom-head and jammed my whole cock-length inside him and then this happened:

You are no longer in bed fucking this young faggot writer but instead in a vast marble-walled room lit by gigantic columnar windows rising twenty meters from the floor toward a coffered vaulted ceiling. It's filled with aisles of book shelves and, down the center, a long rank of heavy wooden desks, each with their own brassy, green-glass-shaded lamps. It's a library like one finds in an ancient college or somewhere in the past. A voice behind you: "Oh. It's you!" He steps around in front you, Gunnar, but now he is not naked but wearing a white button-down shirt and a her-ringbone-patterned vest and olive green chinos. Oddly, given the rest of his attire, he is barefoot and you look down and see that you are, too, but otherwise you are dressed similarly to Gunnar. "You are very late!" he says, and he grabs your right wrist and pulls you along behind him down the rank of desks. He stops at one where two young students, a boy and a girl, are seated at it and they are kissing and giggling. "Leave!" he yells, and they look up in horror, grab their book bags and scuttle away, leaving little fragments of their clothing and hair behind them as they flee. Still controlling your movements, Gunnar seats you at the desk and before you on its top is a large hard-bound book. Its cover art is abstract but it puts you in mind of a forest canopy and enormous cloud-scraping trees. Lettering in the lower third of the cover is at first unintelligible as if it is in the script of a language that you do not know, and this alarms you like a sudden pit opening in your belly because you know — or at least can make a good guess at — all human languages and their orthographies. "Look at it more closely," Gunnar says. "You're in a dream, but you can read it if you try." You peer more closely at the titling and eventually you see these words: "Ethan's THE A-STAR! Rendered by Ethan Komorford-Brace." Gunnar knows that you have successfully read the title and he tells you to open the book. The leaves inside open into huge panels many times the diameter of the shell of the book and each offers a new bizarre and beautiful painting or drawing and while they are not titled and do not have accompanying text, you give them titles as you examine them:

intersex boys of Venus
vampires of Phallos Vallis
the spunk beam
queer invaders from Mars
sodomites of Cthulhu
the punk exorcist
asteroid Sperm-X

The fugue ended when I lost my spunk inside Gunnar. He seemed to not notice. I think he may have fallen asleep—passed out drunk—before I was finished. But even as tired as I was myself, I was not going to be sleeping for a while. I could not un-see what I had seen.

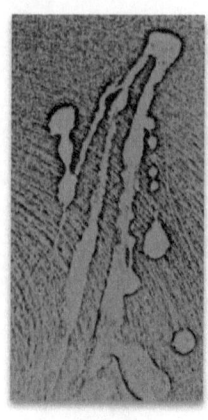

10.

Jace encounters a pair of slick young queers from earlier in the day, and he indulges with them in vigorous sodomy; one of the boys falls into a supernatural fugue and gives Jace a strange warning and new piece of information.

From Jace's journal...

I was quite entirely fagged and fashed from the long day of the seminar, followed by the sixty-way orgy, followed by the dinner and cocktail party — all of it heavily fueled with booze and narcowhirl — but I still kind of desired some late-night bed company.

I could certainly have called over Trace or Ando or Zane or all three of them from their dorm, but I assumed that they were having some sort of fun of their own in the famously boy-humid Edom Hall. But, as it happened, on the way out of the party and into the car that was to take me back to my quarters, I encountered young Kilo and Kieran, both of whom I'd briefly fellated that afternoon during the orgy. They seemed to be hanging back from the rest of the departing crowd and seemed to be watching *me* as I approached the car. *Yeah, what the fuck,* I thought. And I thought it *again* but in a deeper and more strange way: *They are supposed to be here right now. You need to walk up to them.* And I walked up to them.

"You boys have any plans for the rest of the evening?" I wondered. They looked at each other, grinned at each other, laughed, said, no, do *you* have any plans? I ushered them into my car, and we kissed, the three of us in a tangle, the two of them competing playfully with each other to get their tongues into my mouth, the whole way back to my rooms.

I love your suits, I told them as we entered the vast bedroom. They're very cute. But I still think boys hot as you shouldn't even be allowed to wear clothing, at least not until your thirty.[20] I asked them their names and years in school. Kilo was a senior and Kieran was a freshman, and they were brothers. Like, *real* brothers, both born of the same mother from sperm spewed by the same father. They were also desperately in love, they said, and married. Kilo said that he married his little brother when the younger dude turned sixteen. This startled me as it sounded on the face of it so much like the story of Zane and Ethan, marrying on

---

[20] Jace Dekka records elsewhere a recurring masturbation fantasy founded on the premise of a country where a strict dress code is enforced on "twink fags," enjoining them from wearing too much clothing or too many layers. For example, the subjects of this code may wear pants or underwear but not both; if they wear a hoodie, then there must be no shirt under it; etc. Cops are empowered to inspect these twinks for compliance, and chronic offenders are thrown into a prison where lavish corporal punishments and various sexual torments (such as chastity devices) are inflicted upon them. This idea was lifted by novelist and Dekka scholar Brad Lurian (writing as Penelope Box) as the basis of his novel *The Fag Boys of Block 8*, which in turn inspired a spate of "boys-in-prison" exploitation novels, comic books and movies.

Ethan's sixteenth birthday. But there were differences: Zane and Ethan had a very pressing reason other than their love for each other to marry, and they weren't actual brothers biologically, just raised as such for a few years before their passion fruited.[21]

I stripped out of my clothes and told them to do the same. I had to take a piss and asked if either or both of them were into drinking it or being hosed down with it. They both said they were, and followed me into the shower chamber. I asked them to kneel and look up, mouths open, and I opened the valve. I alternated my aim, first into the Kieran's mouth and then into Kilo's. I spattered their faces liberally and they swallowed what they managed to catch. Kieran grunted, dropped a log of shit on the tile and pissed upward onto his own belly. Kilo laughed at his brother, kidded him for not being able to control his bowel. The younger dude actually blushed.

Finished with piss-spraying them, I told him that it was not nice to make fun of Kieran for letting loose like that. "Go ahead and clean up after him!" I said,

---

[21] From Christopher Fletcher's socio-political tract *Idiots and Demigods of Utopia Planitia*: "In the Martian and Jovian anarcho-capitalist clades, we see plenty of history showing sibling marriage as being—at least in their context—a rational social, political and economic arrangement among the scions of the top stratum of these societies. It is, however, quite rare that these marriages also include sexual relationships. When there are exceptions to this general rule, they nearly always result in the sibling-lovers fleeing the clade, as we see in the famous tale of Kilo and Kieran Mass-Armada, the storied brother-lovers who fled to the Kuiper Belt and decades later returned to impose the so-called 'Osmium Terror' upon their former homeworld of Triton."

on a hunch, detecting something about Kilo that made think a turn-on for him was being submissive to the younger man. Kilo, grinning, lifted the chunk of shit from the floor, paused for a moment looking at it, and I wondered if he'd just remove it to the toilet or perhaps eat it, but he did the former.

I told Kieran to stand, hands against the wall, legs spread. I pulled a hose attachment away from the wall, started the water, and sprayed his ass-crack and fuck-hole. I inserted the nozzle inside him for just a moment and pumped a few quarts of water inside. Kieran yelped loudly and blew out the water immediately, soaking my feet. I gave Kilo a light slap across the face. "Finish cleaning him up," I said. He knelt behind his lover between his legs and licked the younger man's anus for a couple minutes, Kilo's slender but very long member standing upright, reaching past his navel. Kieran giggled as if this was a very ticklish spot on his body.

I lifted Kilo back to his feet and kissed him deeply, tasting Kieran's asshole on his tongue. I dried them off, took them both to the bed and we ass-fucked for about an hour in a variety of positions: me inside Kilo, me inside Kieran, Kieran and Kilo inside me individually and at the same time, Kilo and Kieran inside each other alternately. After we had all cum a couple times, I moved us to the open-air deck of the suite to smoke and drink some wine. I enjoyed the sensation of sitting bare-ass on the wooden deck chair, feeling their mixed brother-spunk weeping out of my hole.

"I can't believe," said Kilo, "that I actually got to fuck *the* Jace Dekka!"

"It's not that difficult a feat to achieve," I said. "At least once you get within my physical presence. You probably know — if you're a big follower of my life — that I will have sex with pretty much any guy who wants to do it with me."

"We're not special, dude," Kieran said to his brother. "This man's had more ass and cock than we can ever dream of."

But there is something special about you, I said, or maybe it was more that I *thought* it. But I thought it in a way that Kilo "heard" it, because Kieran looked at his brother and said, *"He knows. Don't fight it."*

You've been *sent* to me, I said-thought. *Don't be scared. Don't fight it. Just show me why.*

Kilo stood, shoulders arched back. His eyes rolled upward, and he vomited wine over his chin and down his chest. Kieran jumped up. "Help me!" he said, taking his brothers arms from behind. "We need to lay him down! He's going to seize!"

He was obviously seizing already, but I didn't want to drop him to the deck, so I picked him up and strode back into the room with him in my arms and put him on the bed on his back. He vomited some more, and I turned his head to the side and swept his mouth clear with my fingers and made sure he was not choking.

You know what's happening, I said or thought to Kieran. *Can you tell me, or will I have to hear it from Kilo?*

"Kilo's the only one who really knows!" Kieran said, undeniably out loud. He gasped, choked back a sob. "I don't like this freaky-deaky shit! But he insisted on it!"

I leaned into Kilo's face, looking into his eyes which remained open but still rolled back. "Kiddo," I whispered against his ear, "There's no way I'd ever hurt you or let anything bad happen to you, but I need you to come back to me now. Come back now, baby. Wake up." And I yelled it: *"Wake up! Give me your message!"*

Kilo rose from the bed and hopped off it, almost in one single water-like motion. If I had not been still rather drunk, I might have believed my perception that he actually hovered in the air for a moment before setting his bare feet to the floor. His eyes refocused and he spoke: *"Commander Jace Dekka, this boy agreed to be used to as a conduit so that we may speak to you without revealing our identity or location."*

The reader should know that this was less weird to me than it might seem to most people, but also that it rather creeped me out nonetheless, and I had to make an affirmative effort to not jump back from him as if he had suddenly become a scorpion. *Continue*, I whispered.

"You have an ally that you can trust. But we cannot make ourselves known to you yet because it will prejudice the outcome. You understand."

I considered Braden and Patrick on Venus, how I'd sent them there without them—or even me—knowing why. "I understand," I said. "But why should I believe that you are an ally?"

"The war is not over," said the Kilo-thing, *"as you well know. Our shared enemy is planning something extraordinary. You will piece it together soon enough. Using*

this boy's body as a communication tool, we have left what we know inside you. Inside you. Do you understand?"

A *command packet?* I wondered, considering that I'd received a load of Kilo-spunk inside my gut.

"Our bio-aethero-technology is not as sophisticated as yours, Commander Dekka," said Kilo, *"but what we have given you should persist in your bloodstream for at least a couple days. Get yourself home, back to your doctor, for an extraction. Your team will find something that will be useful. In your blood."*

As if a puppeteer had relaxed some strings, Kilo settled back to the bed, gasped a few times, and then seemed to return to a normal state. "That was fucked up," he whispered. "God damn! That was fucked up!"

After a short while, I put the lithe young brother-spouses to bed together, in a fresh bed without Kilo's vomit-stains or the stains and stench of our athletic sex together, and they quickly drifted into sleep, Kieren's white biscuit-doll face cuddled into Kilo's blackly hairy and deep armpit. I showered quickly, dressed for travel and returned to the deck to smoke another narcowhirl joint, to drink some more wine and to consider what I'd heard. It was three in the morning at this point, and while I was loathe to disturb the Unsuitable Boys—because I assumed that they were at such an hour either sleeping or fucking—I could not stand to delay our next move.

11.

Meanwhile on Venus, the Earth lads induce maximal libido in themselves with a chemical aid; they proceed with Austin's assignment for them; later Austin critiques them over their hygiene.

From Braden's journal...

Patrick and I decided that we'd dose ourselves very, very heavily with Erec-T, not only to keep our bodies horny as fuck all day and our nuts and other glands working in super-overdrive to keep the sperm flowing, but also in case we needed to fuck anyone that we didn't think was hot enough to be fuckable under normal conditions. All these maphs that we'd seen so far in that treehouse cabana village were pretty cute in their twinky-boy way, but there had to be at least a few fugly ones somewhere in the bunch. It just stood to reason. But, as totally raging boned as I was going to be from the drug, I could probably fuck anyone at all, even a hideous troll, and not even need to close my eyes. [22]

---

[22] A fact of which Braden seems unaware is that these maphs were similarly drugging themselves to ensure that they were in maximum "heat" for their sexual encounter with the Earth boys. Under these biochemical conditions, the maphs would have been exuding a tremendous volume of fuck-pheromone, an amount probably sufficient to have left Braden and Patrick with little conscious choice as to whether to breed them regardless of their appearance.

If this were Jace's story in his journal, he would probably list every last single person that he had inseminated by his name and age and appearance, but I can't keep up with all that data. I can't make lists like he can. I lack the eidetic fuck-memory that seems to be his special gift. There was just *so* much fucking, so very many of them, and in such a short time.[23]

Once we were ready, we went to Austin's bedroom and he started having them come to us two at a time. He did ask us first if we minded doing it in the same room (he only had one bedroom despite his status as the tanjong of his village) and suggested that one of us could have the bedroom and the other the back porch. We pointed out, of course, that not only had we fucked each other scores of times but that most of those times had happened when at least one other dude was in the room with us, and also that we had done it dozens of times on a live-stream that was

---

The queer Earth boys would have been literally fuck-drunk on the aroma of these Venusians. The heavy dosing of Erec-T, however, made it possible for their bodies physically to produce the volume of sperm and semen required for this extraordinary amount of mating activity.

[23] It is a fact that Braden could actually have retained a far more complete mental record of these sex partners than any that Jace would have been capable of had Braden opened his mind to their inner dialogues, but it appears that he closed off completely his touch-telepathy during this episode as he often did during random sexual encounters where he having sex for entertainment rather than to learn something from consciousnesses of his partners. Evidently he kept this ability closed off during his encounters on the aether ship voyage as well. If he had not, then one might expect his journal to contain some impressions other than the purely physical recollections recorded here.

viewed by millions of (probably) masturbating (probable) fags, so, yeah, we were cool with doing this in the same room with each other.

And so, fucking side by side, Patrick and I jizzed inside one cute maph after another. We cooperated with each other to time our loads reasonably closely together so that we'd finish with one pair at about the same time and be ready for the next a little while later so we could maintain an even pace, the idea being that we'd each do half of the total population. In most cases, we sucked their cocks as well and made them cum, but after a while I was feeling that long blowjob ache in my jaw. I don't think I have ever sucked so many dicks in one day before, and I'd definitely never swallowed that much cum—I was taking it in from their cocks and their pussies all day.[24] By the end of the first day, which didn't really start until past noon, Patrick and I had each fucked twenty-nine maphs, fifty-eight in total. Or a bit more than a quarter of our goal.

Though I'm not going to try to document each and every one of these fucks, there is a one that was especially perfect:

---

[24] Venusian maphs, particularly when in reproductive "heat," can produce copious quantities of a semen-like fluid from an organ inside their vaginas during vaginal orgasm, often several ounces of it during a sex session. Braden Vaieux has noted elsewhere in his journals that he is an enthusiast of ingesting this fluid while performing oral sex on maphs. While he doesn't speak at length about having performed an exceptional amount of cunnilingus in this account, it stands to reason that he probably swallowed as much fluid because of that act as from fellatio.

His name was Angel, and he was a lot whiter than most of the other Venusians, almost pale like Patrick, and he reminded me of Colin with his huge purple eyes and his crazy tangle of thick black hair tamed here and there with little bands pulling together little licks and tufts of it. Most of these maphs we fucked didn't have especially big dicks, but Angel did, and it was wide and thick and uncut (unlike any of the others we sucked that day, because maphs usually don't have foreskins) and he told me—after I commented on it—that he'd been a rentboy back in the day and had gotten a bunch of bod-mods like old-school CHOAM trade from before the Dirty War, mods like Trace's and Jace's. And he had a mod that I'd never seen before. Maphs have a sweet extra little organ inside their snatches, kind of like a mini-cock. You can feel it with your dick when you fuck them and rub on it with your tongue when you eat them out, and this usually makes them cum, and when they get off their inner cock spurts out goo just like a regular boy's dick does. It's not exactly the same stuff, but it looks and tastes a lot like it and they make a lot of it. When I do Colin, he fills my mouth with it. So I obviously knew all about this already, but Angel's was special: it had been enlarged, and so much so that he could push it fully out of his cunt and it was almost as long as my cock and kind of looked like a cock, too. I sucked him off, slurping on this organ while he beat on his actual penis. He told me that I'd need to make him cum first so his extra dick could go soft and retreat inside his slot if I was to have any chance of getting *my* cock inside him and pregging him. It wouldn't have been possible for me to get inside him with that thing in the way. When he came, the cunt-cock jizz flooded my mouth so hard that a lot it just sprayed out around my lips and drooled over my chin and I almost gagged on it, there was so fucking much of it! Angel pulled my head up and put his cock in my dripping mouth and came a second time. I was freaking out on how hard I was, how bad my nuts ached. I needed to get off so fucking bad: I begged him. *Please let me cum!* He said: *Do it inside me, you little Earth-boy fuck. Stick that cute little knot right in here. Give me a baby.* And I did. I jizzed so fucking hard in Angel that after I was done I felt like I was probably *done* for the day. Patrick agreed we needed a little break. He fed me some more Erec-T and made out with me and gave me a couple big fruit-juicy cocktails, and soon enough we were ready to resume our breeding duties.

I was so tired when it was time for sleep, that I just sort of collapsed into Austin's (kind of damp and super-filthy) bed with him and Patrick. And Patrick somehow mustered the energy to fuck Austin again, thrilled and ultra-aroused when Austin told him that it's good for the pregnancy to keep having sex daily throughout it. And Austin wanted to drill my ass. I agreed but I told him not to expect very much reciprocal energy from me until I got some sleep, even though the Erec-T was still flowing in my bloodstream and giving me a very hard, ready-to-squirt cock.

We got an earlier start the next day. Austin fed us a huge breakfast of eggs, tomatoes, avocados, jerkfruit, refried beans, salsa verde and roasted chicken (or some kind of feathered dinosaur that they call chicken on Venus). We popped a lot of Erec-T again and downed it with a bunch of mimosas and a couple shots of vodka. Before our first customers arrived, I needed to take a boozy piss badly but I couldn't knock down my boner much at all, so I made I big nasty piss-spray mess all over Austin's squat toilet and the surrounding floor. Patrick did the same, though while squatting over the bowl and dumping. His dirty prick was so cheesy I went down on it and cleaned him off with my mouth so he wasn't so disgusting at the start of our next round of mpreg dates[25], but as I finished

---

[25] From Braden's journal: "Though I have frequently teased Patrick with disparaging comments about his junk, I think he has the prettiest penis that I have ever sucked even when it's fucking filthy and cheese-caked. Among the cocks of Jace and the other Unsuitable Boys, Patrick's is probably actually the smallest. Trace's is stupid-big. Jace's is well above average. Zane's is as long as Jace's but not nearly as thick. Even little Ethan has a big long chunky snake in his crotch. Ando's isn't all that big, but he has that crazy super-stretchy sleeve on it. Colin, Tim and me all have basically average-size dicks, and mine is probably the smallest among those. But Patrick's might be even a bit smaller than mine,

that task, Austin entered the little bathroom looking rather dismayed.

"You dudes," he said, "are the filthiest motherfuckers I have ever seen in my life. You're both cute as fuck, but goddamned *dirty!* Get in the stall for a minute." He pointed into the lacquered shower chamber. He turned on the sprayers. Patrick and I both gasped a little bit at how cold the water was at first, but after a couple seconds, it felt good. Austin stepped into the chamber with us, pulled nozzles free from the wall by their flexible hoses sprayed down our bodies. "I'm not going to soap you up too much because I don't know if the herbs in my Venus soap will irritate your skin, and also because I actually *like* your sweet Earth-boy crotch-and-pit stench, but damn if you don't need at least need a rinse!" He cleaned both our cocks, and got under our dick-sleeves, and hosed our armpits and ass-cracks. He asked us to lean against the shower wall, back to him. He selected another attachment for his hose. I suspected I knew what was about to happen, but I didn't mind, and I knew Patrick wouldn't either since Jace does this to us a lot. He very quickly injected us each with a big load of water up our asses, which we both expelled quickly, and which made us both projectile-shit on the shower floor, even Patrick who had just emptied some of his out on the toilet. Austin told us to go to the bedroom and get ready to start our impregnation shift. "I'll clean up this mess!" he said, and grinned and winked.

---

but it so perfectly formed, so fucking tempting to the mouth. When I put it in my mouth, I'm obviously aroused, but I am also telling him that I love him, and I think he knows that."

He didn't *say* that he was going to clean it up by eating it, but I kind of wondered if he would.

12.

Trace sees a new piece of evidence in a strange image from Ethan; he and his companions return home by way of Zane's preternatural ability.

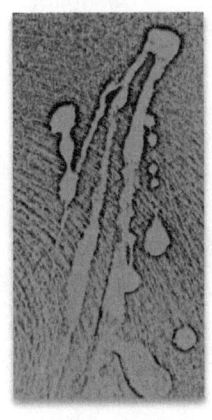

From Trace's journal...

The orgy had basically ended. Those dudes who hadn't gone back to their own rooms were all asleep, including the literary Gunnar, whom I'd gotten a little tired of with all his obsessive attention to my cock and how big and beautiful he thought it was. Yeah, bro, I wanted to say to him, I know I have a big fuckin' dick. It's not news to me! I pondered going ahead and asking Tim to do a reduction on it when we got home. I got out of bed, found another beer, and wandered into the main room — its every surface was littered with glasses, bottles, ashtrays — where Ando sat at the terminal looking at something. It looked like a big smear of colorful nonsense. I stood next to him, he looked up and said hi, and I kissed him on the mouth, smeared what remained of his pink lipstick, and he gave me a little squirt of spit. "What's that?" I wondered.

"Ethan sent this to me," he said. "It's a drawing that he was working on before we left. He's added something to it."

What he added:

A shambleau of static and haze, shredded by acidic streamers of light, and a couple of comic book speech balloons, one saying "beam!" and the other saying "asteroid X!"

I heard my phone dinging somewhere, wherever I had set it down before I stripped for fucking. Ando intercepted the call on his. It was Jace. He said, *"I'm leaving for home now. I don't know that it's imperative that you guys also go back immediately. But I'd rather you did."* Tickets for us appeared on Ando's phone—not for the civilized airship this time but rather for a jet. *Ugh, a fuckin' plane,* I thought. *Never a dull day.*

"It's okay," said Zane, who I had not realized was even in the room with us. I turned around and saw him lying on his back, eyes closed, on a couch under a window, bars of light from lamps outside striping his naked skin. *"Shhh…"* he said, *"don't worry about it baby-boy, I'm coming back soon."* He was talking to Ethan. *"Don't worry, baby-face, don't be scared sweetheart,"* he said. *"I'll be back soon."* I should clarify that this absolutely was *not* just sleep-talk. Zane was not *dreaming* that he was comforting Ethan—at least not in the way that most of us think of dreaming. He was actually talking *to* him and I believe that Ethan was somehow *hearing* it. *"I'll make love to you, baby,"* he whispered. Sleeping Zane cupped his nuts in one hand and gripped his now-stiff cock in the other. I'd seen this before, knew what I was going to see if I kept watching: Zane jerking off, squirming on that couch, in his mind fucking his sweet Ethan who would be in a similar state in his own bed back at the Home. But it gave us an opportunity, one that I felt we needed to take before too much more time slipped past us.

I replied to Jace: "Fuck that plane. Cancel the tickets. Get over here right now. We have a lot better and faster way to get home."

Zane and the fuckin' swimming pool, always back at it with the pool. I wish that just once he could land us on the deck, or better yet, in my bed. But the four of us materialized in the pool, under the water, thrashed around a bit getting our bearings and eventually surfaced coughing and spitting. My top priority was to get Zane to the surface and out of the water: he'd be weak from the transit and I'd never be able to forgive myself if he'd drowned after it was my idea to use him to translate us all back to the Home.[26] But he was fine,

---

[26] Zane Brace's ability to physically "translate" himself and others from one spatial location to another is entirely mysterious to science, and remains the only known example of such an ability in a human as it is described here and elsewhere in the annals of the Unsuitable Boys. Scientists who have studied this (from second-hand accounts only as Brace has never submitted to direct outside study) believe that he needs a "psychic anchor" at a "transaetheric node" which is a spatial location known to him prior to translation. In many cases, it appears that his spouse Ethan is that psychic anchor, and accounts of their relationship

and once out of the water, sat happily on the edge of the pool and asked for a cigarette and a drink, which Ando went to get for him. I got back into the water and swam around gathering up our bags of stuff — clothes, phones, other travel junk — that were floating all over. We'd at least had the sense to strip (or, in my case, just stay naked) before the translation on the assumption that we'd probably end up in the water.

"I want to see Ethan," I heard Zane say. "But I am too weak to get all the way up to his quarters right now." He sipped at a gin and tonic and dragged on a cigarette and kicked his feet languidly under the water. I floated up to him and saw that he did look very tired, almost limp, even though his dick was stiff. He's told me before that he always cums during translation, but he certainly looked like he was ready to go again if he had this time. Ando said he'd go upstairs and get Ethan. "But if he's sleeping," Zane said, "don't wake him up. I think I can feel him sleeping. I can wait to see him until later."

Jace told Ando to hold up, don't go get Ethan. Instead, Jace told Zane to set down his drink and his smoke, and Jace reached down and, with what looked like no effort at all, grabbed Zane up into his arms and

---

abound with suggestions that they can communicate with each other telepathically while one or both of them is asleep and in a dream state. But how this facilitates actual physical teleportation remains a total enigma. Dathan Arago's novel *Jaunter* is a magical realist imagining of Zane Brace's early life and marriage to Ethan Komorford in which this ability is explained as a form of folding space by means of a kind unconscious sorcery rooted in his love for Ethan.

held him aloft, cradled on his back like a child. I forget all the time how fucking strong Jace is. "I'll take you to him," Jace said and kissed his forehead. "I'll put you to bed with him."

I watched with Ando as Jace went inside the house, carrying Zane. He and I kind of wanted to discuss what might have just happened with us—and what might be going on with Braden and Patrick on Venus—but we decided it could wait. It was four in the morning.

13.

With the mass-impregnation complete, potent young Braden and Patrick learn clues to their next mission; Jace summons them home, but they select alternate transport.

From Braden's journal...

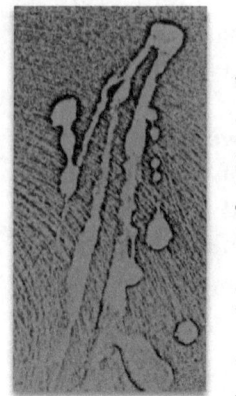

By the end of day two, we'd each boned forty-one more maphs or eighty-two total, but six of them were repeats from the day before who didn't successfully get pregged, so we increased our net only by seventy-six. This left us sixty-three more to do, barring no further repeats. We figured we could finish it on day three and then use day four to catch up on any that didn't take to our seed the first time. But when the morning of day four arrived, Austin reported that we had achieved a hundred percent success and our breeding work was complete.

I have to say that I was kind of relieved, and I think Patrick was, too. We obviously both like to fuck at least as much as any other healthy young gay man in his sexual prime, but the previous few days were perhaps a bit over the top even for us.[27] Many of these

---

[27] It's well known from their journals and from Timothy Arush's notes, that Braden and Patrick both were given some enhancements to their sex equipment including a several-fold increase in

dudes took pics of us so that they could remember what the father of their child looked like, and some said they wanted pics so they could show us to the kids later. These pics showed me as I was: naked, kind of sweaty, kind of flushed in the face and ears, hair a mess. I wondered what I would have thought of it had

---

the density of their seminiferous tubules, a fifty-percent increase in the overall size of their testes, a ten-times increase in the capacity of their urethral bulbs, similar increases in the capacity of their Cowper's glands, and various hormonal tweaks affecting their sex drives. These modifications, while intended mostly to increase their sexual capacity and pleasure for themselves and their partners during gay sex by wildly increasing their potential daily semen volume and the frequency with which they desired sex with other males as the preferred means to cause their bodies to release this excessive semen, these enhancements also had the effect of making them super-breeders much like Jace Dekka. This super-capacity is evident not just from their ability to achieve many ejaculations per day with very short refractory periods, but also in the actual sperm content of their semen. A typical unmodified Terran male may release anywhere from two hundred million to about a billion sperm with each ejaculation. Braden's output was measured by Arush near the time of these events as averaging ten billion sperm per ejaculation. While Braden suggests here that he and Patrick were rather tired of this work and glad to be done with it, it seems that their readiness to be finished was more emotional than anything else and related to their desire to return to their normal lives. But there is no particular physical reason why they could not have continued this breeding activity indefinitely had they wanted to, and had there been an indefinite number of subjects for them to have impregnated, as long as they had stayed well-fed and hydrated and with sufficient breaks for sleep. If the pace they set during this visit to Venus had been maintained for a month, it's possible that each of these young men could have caused a thousand pregnancies, a number a lot like the statistics we find in the records from Dekka's time in the forced breeding program.

I known my mother and had he actually shown me a picture like this of my biological father taken at the literal time of my conception. Like, "check out this pic, kiddo! I took this pic of your dad moments after he shot his load in me and got me pregnant with you!"

But our strange adventure on Venus was about finished and Austin finally gave us what he had promised in exchange for fucking and pregging his entire village: important clues as to the location of Tiphon's planned "spunk beam," and more importantly, a clue as to the location of Tiphon's secret slavery operation. "They call it," he said, *"Asteroid Sperm-X."*

We texted home. Voice communication wasn't possible with where Venus was in relation to Earth and with current aether weather. Jace answered: *"When are you coming home?"* I said this to him: "I think it's time that we do. I think we learned what we need to know here, but we don't know what it means yet."

Jace replied, *"Get back here as fast as possible."* Tickets for passage on a raggedy low-end fast-ship, a filthy iridium-mining vessel from Mercury, appeared on my phone.

I showed this to Patrick and he scowled and shook his head, and fuck no, he said and he kissed my mouth and licked my tongue. I deleted the tickets for the Mercury miner and Jace replied with an annoyed-looking emoji. "We're going back home on *Queen of the Aether*," I said. "The accommodations suit us better."

And Patrick and I—already back in our rooms aboard the cruise ship—took each other's clothes off and we crawled into the vast and downy bed together and we were so sleepy that we didn't even fuck, and we just cuddled tightly together and slept for a long time as the aether pulled us slowly (but fast enough) toward Earth and home.

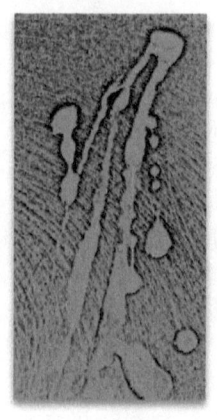

14.

An epilogue and an intimation of things to come...

Ethan crouches before his drawing table, both hands holding tools, in the left one a thick stick of charcoal and in the right one a magenta marker. He is naked and spotted with ink and chalk and paint and his cock his hard and he is deep into the topic of his drawing. For a couple minutes he does not notice that another boy has joined him, that Colin has knelt on the other side of the table, also naked, his glossy black hair awry in a great tangled crown over his olive brow. Ethan finally notices, looks up across the drawing table, when Colin says: "They've seen it, you know. What you showed them, what I sung to them about."

Ethan shakes his head, but not in a gesture of negation but rather one of wonder. "They are smart," he says. "All I can do is draw. But I can't understand any of it. But I am glad that I can help." Colin reaches across the table and grabs Ethan's hands, clasps them and the charcoal and the marker together, and he says: "You showed them almost literally what to look for and where to go to find it. Stop selling yourself short. You're probably the smartest one here."

But Ethan says, "You had the song. You did just as much." But Colin rebuts this, says that he the song would never have come to him had he not seen the drawing first. Ethan releases himself from Colin's hand-grasp and sets down his colors. "I don't know anything. I'm a fucking retard—a fuckin' aspy *retard*. I *see* shit but I *can't* see it, can't see what it *means*."

Colin comes around to Ethan's side of the table and pulls his body into an embrace. "Fuck you, Ethan," he says. "If you say that about yourself again, I'll slap you silly. I love you a lot, baby brother, and I'll beat you until you pass out if you keep saying such dumb shit about yourself. And I love you so much, you shiny thing. And fuck you, Ethan, and kiss me, Ethan," and Ethan does so for a minute and they love each other's lips and tongues and teeth for a long minute or two and eventually Colin sees something out of the corner of his eye and breaks away from Ethan's mouth for a second and looks down at the raging colors embedded in the rag paper and he somehow "sees" this, or somehow "hears" it, a thing that *will* happen:

You need to see this, this thing that Ethan is doing. In his room. On the desk and on the wall! You see it: a vast smear of paint, livid colors in swirls and jets against black, but there is the sense of something real in it: a crackling beam, blighting its own path, fire and vacuum. Ethan screams: A-Star! he shouts. And again and again, A-Star! A-Star! He is spattered in paint on every bit of his naked body. His hair is streaked and stiff with it, red and orange and violet. A cosmic green smear of it runs from his throat to his crotch and out to the foreskin-hooded tip of his stiff prick. A-Star! he gasps, and you pull him close, hands on his shoulders than hands around his back, on his waist, and you hug him into you. What, baby, what, baby, what does that mean? A-Star, he says again, but now it's a whisper, and he collapses into you and breathes softly, regularly as if suddenly asleep. You lay him down on his back on his bed. He sweats through the paint and smiles. He moans and spontaneously cums, long spurts from his painted pole. A-Star he says one more time and slides away into sleep. You don't know what that means, but someone else does...

TO BE CONTINUED

Years hadn't been kind to Carthoris. I knew he'd no longer be the same young man that he'd been when I'd sired a son upon him during my brief enslavement to his father, bloody Jalec, the jeddak of Kasei. But I did not expect this: the skin of his once-porcelain-smooth face was riven with keloid scars, and his once-lush black hair was chopped short, a patch of it entirely missing on the left side of his head.

At his side, hanging back just a bit, stood a tall lithe boy with huge dark eyes who looked a lot like Carthoris had when I'd met him, dressed in ornate leather courtier attire. Though I'd not seen even a picture of him in years, I knew who this boy was: Rajer, *our son*.

Carthoris told Rajer to wait elsewhere. "You can get to know Trace later. But I have business with him first." The boy exited slowly, backing his way out of the room, making long steady eye-contact with me until he was through the door.

"He's so tall," I said. "How can he be so old already?"

"He's a maph," said the Martian prince. "We grow quickly, and then almost stop aging altogether." That latter trait obviously did not adhere for Carthoris: he appeared twice his real age under those scars, in those dim eyes.

"Why am I here, Carthoris? And why couldn't you tell me why you needed me here before I left Earth?"

Carthoris lit two narcowhirl cigarettes and handed me one. "I need your help, Trace. You're the only one who can help me with this because you're the only one who knows the truth about us, about this place." Help with *what*, I asked, and it took Carthoris a long minute to reply: *"We're going to kill my father, Trace. Jalec needs to die."*

— from the journals of Trace Battle

- A glimpse into powerful Trace's bizarre and scandalous past...
- A deadly new crisis in the lavish royal courts of Mars...
- An incredible plot against the Unsuitable Boys thickens...
- Trace meets a son he never knew...

THE ROYAL RENTBOY OF KASEI

COMMANDER JACE AND THE UNSUITABLE BOYS EPISODE #6

COMING SOON FROM M-BRANE PRESS

ONE HUNDRED TIMES

Kyler FEY

M-Brane Press

Saint Louis

For Braden

For the poet, the world is word. Words.
Not that precisely.
Precisely: the world and words fuck each other.
—Kathy Acker

To say the name of your perfect erotic object is
always to say it for the first time.
—Samuel Delany, from
Stars in My Pocket like Grains of Sand

ONE HUNDRED
TIMES

Foreword

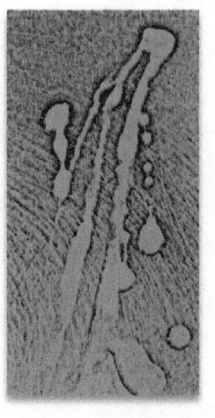

What is this odd little book by Kyler Fey? He doesn't it intend it to be considered as part of his *Commander Jace and Unsuitable Boys* series of erotic gay science fantasy stories and, indeed, it is not part of that series. But I think it's an interesting companion piece to it because, in the background of its sexually graphic narrative, is some insight into how those science-fantasy stories were created, how they were built out of their author's own queer sexuality. But more precisely: by his literal cock-behavior, by his peculiar writing process in which he exerted himself very deliberately to not jack off too much. He imposed such restraint upon himself to help foster and maintain the ongoing and unrelieved hard-on that he considered necessary to motivate him to write what he calls "an honest written gay pornography" at considerable length, at a length and depth far exceeding what one usually sees in the surfeit of short erotica available for e-readers.

To call *One Hundred Times* an erotic memoir is probably accurate enough — it's pulled from the thousands of pages of Kyler Fey's *"Fuck Record,"* his running journal of what he sometimes calls his "fagsploits." But it also reads like a novella with a simple

story. Is it non-fiction? The author would say it is "close enough" to true, close enough for its purpose. While it is clear that Fey has veiled (perhaps rather thinly in some instances) some details, and possibly entirely distorted some others to hide the identities of the real people described inside and to blur the actual timeframe of the events that he relates, it is also clear that he has allowed a lot of truth about himself to come through in a way that I do not usually see in most people's fuck-recollections. This book could also be considered a fifty-thousand word footnote to the volume on the A-side of the print version of this book, *The Intersex Boys of Venus.*

The story that Fey tells isn't complex. It's simply that of a recurring sex hook-up over a period of few weeks a couple summers ago, the bulk of it focusing on a single long day of continual sex play between him and a much younger lover. But it is also laden with asides about his thoughts about sexual concepts, and also with occasional intrusions from his fictional world: there's a complete short story late in the book which is set in alternate version of his fictional universe; he refers a couple of times to snorting a fictional drug from that world during scenes that otherwise seem situated in reality; the brand name of a masturbation lubricant is the same as one from the fantasy world; he claims that he met his lithe paramour through a website of which I can find no evidence of its existence.

Borrowing a phrase and a concept from queer writer Samuel Delany's *Stars in My Pocket Like Grains of Sand*—and he references Delany frequently

throughout the work, acknowledging the science fiction grand master and sex radical's deep influence upon him—Fey composes the ornate and semen-glazed picture of his "perfect erotic object," a young man that he calls "Braden," a nineteen-year-old twinky gay boy (only half Fey's own age at the time of these events) who worked at the grocery store that Fey visits nearly every day. He reveals that he had harbored a lustful attraction to this young queer for a long time, had been jerking off to daydreams about him for ages, and that this real-world Braden is, in fact, the "model" that Fey used for the fictional character of Braden, the touch-telepathic principal lover of Jace Dekka in the *Unsuitable Boys* books, an imaginary guy that he'd already created in that image by the time Fey got to know personally the Braden character's living physical template.

Fey tells of how he finally found an excuse to approach Braden in person, introduce himself as a compatriot in the writing of fantasy and science fiction, and then successfully attract this young man to him for sex. The rest of the story chronicles a series of fuck-dates between them, including one of great length and variety that fills most of the second half of the volume. This account could be interesting and perhaps arousing to certain readers (such as lit-porn-oriented fags like myself who get hard-ons and jack off while reading this kind of thing) in and of itself, but the other thing that makes it worth reading to my writer/editor mind is the running background detail related to Fey's writing and the way that he evidently continually edits his weird fictional universe in light

of new things that he observes or does in his real world. This process is going on even now: as I write this foreword, fully half of the *Commander Jace and the Unsuitable Boys* series' twenty-one planned "episodes" are in some state of major incompletion, and revisions keep getting added to the supposedly finished segments. This process by which Fey is simultaneously writing twenty-one novellas has caused me to revise many times the original publication plan for them. Instead of rolling the whole series out at once as I had dreamed of doing, when I'd envisioned it as a gang of short e-book quickies, I am instead going to present it in a few installments over a much longer period, with the first publication of any of Fey's *Commander Jace* work in the form of a print book in the *tetebeche* style of an old Ace Double. The following memoir-thing will be the second side of that print book, back to back with the fifth episode of the series, *The Intersex Boys of Venus*.

I think it is a good pairing because *Intersex Boys* was largely completed concurrently with the events that Fey describes in the following narrative, and it is the story that is mentioned the most frequently therein. In the Kyler Fey view of things, there is no problem with releasing the fifth Jace book before the first through the fourth ones have appeared (or have even been completed). But I fought this approach for several months, still committed to my plan of rolling out the entire series in one massive launch of twenty-one ebooks and one giant print volume. I have since come around to the idea that it doesn't matter that

much if we go more slowly and out of order, and *Intersex Boys* is sufficiently comprehensive of the basic premise of the series that a reader can start with that story and then later, if they wish, backtrack to the previous episodes as they appear.

Fey designed his series to be more or less like the original *Star Trek* tv show, or perhaps like the old *Doc Savage* novels, series with which one can start anywhere during their run and get the gist of them. But it doesn't have a "reset button" like *Star Trek* did, and there may be some references that won't make a lot of sense if one comes first into it in the middle or toward the end, but those do not render any single installment incomprehensible. The series does, however, contain a story arc that reaches a kind of sub-climax at about episode twelve, so it is still my intention to have the first twelve episodes released before the later ones. But I am somewhat captive to Kyler Standard Time as to when things get done. Today, for example, as I write this, it's become clear from a new manuscript that *Asteroid Sperm-X* is almost done. *Asteroid Sperm-X* is the twenty-first and *final* planned chapter of the series. Meanwhile, *The Lust Drug of Ephebos* — the *fourth* episode — is still missing about half of its content. But I am now wholly relaxed about it. It will be done when it's done.[1]

---

[1] I might as well mention that he slowed things down on the series considerably last fall — pretty much to a standstill, in fact — by detouring into a complete novel outside the series, though set in its universe a few decades after the events of *Unsuitable Boys* stories. That one is titled *FagJuv,* and it will see print from M-Brane Press later this year.

If one comes to this fuck-memoir first, before reading Fey's *Commander Jace* stories, one will get something of the flavor of what to expect from them (though that fiction is far more fantastical than this story as to what's possible in its realm of guys fucking guys) in that there is always a frankness about the way in which he tells the reader what he likes, what turns him on and what he does about it. There are no fade-to-black moments with lovers disappearing under sheets of imagination, and almost nothing in the way of gauzy sentimentality. You will not find characters, as you might in some m/m romance fiction, stewing for the whole book in juices of uncertainty, of first-timer jitters, of fear of their own emotional and sexual exposure. Fey, who calls himself an exhibitionist, likes to tell the reader what gets him off, and the entire reason that *One Hundred Times* was written was because he found a hook-up with another man who was a kind of kindred erotic spirit in that same way. Were it not for the happenstance of his affair with the real Braden, then I suspect that an item like the following would never have been written and that the fictional Braden on the pages of the *Jace* books would be a very different creature.

This text, like most of Fey's writing, is annotated with a lot of footnotes. He always seems to have a lot of shit that he wants to say that doesn't ever quite fit into the narrative. In his fiction, this serves to add a lot of supplemental information about the world that his characters inhabit and suggests a lot of additional possible stories that he'll probably never have time to write. The footnotes in this book clarify some items in

the story that might not make sense without them. I have added several of these footnotes myself. I have decided to proceed to publication without letting Fey see some of my own notes for fear that he would add to them further and make the whole book a big nest of footnotes. He has added at the very last minute his own foreword, a supplement and corrective to this one, which immediately follows.

—CF

Foreword
(the real one)

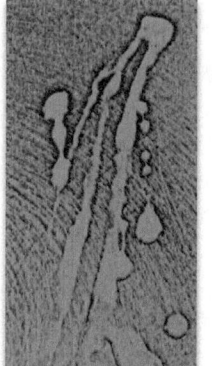

I persuaded F to come over to hang out and have dinner with me on Halloween. Both of our spouses were out of town anyway and we hadn't seen one another in some time. [2] Though we live quite near each other and have known each other for years, and have been collaborating on the eventual publication of my *Commander Jace and the Unsuitable Boys* book series for a while, we rarely meet in person lately. Our "day jobs" (as I still call mine) are rather similar positions in rival companies and we both experience concurrent wild seasonal swings of being stupidly busy with these jobs where all one wants to do at the end of the work day is gulp down a bottle of wine and fall asleep. But by the end of October, things usually lighten up a bit and I was in the mood for a guest and a friend, and I wanted to show him some things that I'd been working on. That, and the promise that I'd make enchiladas with a big brick of roasted Hatch chiles that I'd been holding in the

---

[2] I should note that our husbands are also friends and that his likes mine more than he likes me and mine likes his more than he likes F.

freezer from Danny's recent trip to New Mexico, lured him over.

He arrived at four that afternoon, bringing along with him a gallon jug of cider and a bottle of Fireball and a big lop-sided greenish-grey pumpkin that he said he'd carve into a Jack-o-Lantern to light up on my deck and a giant bag of candy that he said we could spill out on the front porch to appease the trick-or-treat kids without being bothered to man the front door.

It was a somewhat mild-weather day for Halloween here, and he wore just knee-length olive green shorts and a light hoody with no shirt underneath and a pair of white Vans with no-show shocks. The shoes and sock he removed at the top of the stairs, and I assisted him with carrying in his merchandise and his laptop bag. I hadn't seen him in person since earlier in the summer and he looked quite good — and maybe more rested and calm than I'd ever seen before — with a fresh haircut, newly blond, and he was perhaps ten or fifteen pounds lighter than I when I'd seem him last. I wondered if this was the result of a deliberate diet. I knew it wasn't from deliberate exercise. Like me, he is on his feet and running about at work plenty enough during the busy seasons, enough that any purposeful extra exercise would be regarded as preposterous. But, in any case, it would have been rude to have inquired, and so I didn't.

When he arrived, I had been in the middle of some preliminaries for our dinner — mixing tortilla dough, blanching some tomatillos, busting down a rotisserie chicken for its meat — so I told him to go grab my iPad

from my office and bring it into the kitchen and situate himself at the center island while I cooked. He got the iPad, returned to the kitchen, found a couple glasses and poured us each some cider and spiked it with giant shots of Fireball. We raised our glasses and wished each other a Happy Halloween and I told him to look at the open file on the iPad. "It's something that I am thinking about using as a footnote somewhere in the book."

He read the title and laughed: "'*Justin Bieber: Super-Breeder*.' Jesus Christ, dude!"

"Bitch, please! Do *not* act like you're not a fan of the Bieber slash! I *know* that boy rocks your big fat faggot belieber cock," I said, making that my-eyes-see-you finger gesture, and I gulped down the cider and poured another. "Read! You'll love it! I'm very proud of it! And it's also kind of in-universe with the Commander Jace stories. Or sort of in an alternate universe to that one, maybe."

He read for a couple minutes and then stopped and said something like, "A *footnote*? Kyler, this story is over seven thousand words long! If this is your idea of a fucking *footnote*, this book is going to look like *House of Leaves* by the time we're done with it."

But he fell quiet as he started reading it. He stood with the iPad, smoked a narcowhirl-laced clove cigarette, paced around the kitchen as he read, circulating around the prep island, pausing to drag on his smoke, stopping to ash it in the sink. It was kind of comforting and familiar, this agitated way that he stalks about as he reads things, and it made me feel like it was a proper Halloween afternoon. Occasionally he'd make

a quick comment: *this is fucked up...I like that phrase...what the hell dude, you're sick...fucking sweet!,* and I noted that he was evidently not wearing any underwear as he was pitching an obvious straightforward tentpole in his shorts as he consumed my sick-ass and sexy tale which features an alternate version of me as a trillionaire who grafts cloned copies of my big nuts into Justin Bieber's sack after a sadistic madman steals the poor lad's originals.

I smashed out some tortillas with an iron press, and he finished reading and set down the iPad. "It's very amusing," he said, "but I don't know if it has a future other than on a Bieber-fic fan-site." He paused and added, "Though it's way too sophisticated for that. You'd get such dumb hate-comments from the droogs. I guess it's one of those stories with no existing market. I guess you could stick it up on Wattpad and make a porny cover art for it."

"What if," I said, "we made it somehow an extra feature of *Twink Pop Star?*"

F frowned, then smiled, then looked skeptical, then waited for me to say more.

"The Jaustin Moss character in *Twink Pop Star* is obviously that universe's thinly-disguised version of Bieber. In fact, it *is* him. It's so fucking obvious on purpose. I barely even changed his first name," I said. "I could just change Justin Bieber's name to Jaustin Moss

throughout *this* story and it would be basically the same thing."[3]

Maybe, F said, and I stepped close to him and passed my hand over his still-stiff pants-bulge. I took him into the bedroom and insisted on playing a Justin Bieber playlist on the TV while we stripped each other even though he thinks fucking to music is a dumb cliché and I suspect that if he did want a fuck-soundtrack he'd be more of a Bauhaus dude. I picture him like David Bowie in the opening sequence of *The Hunger*, hunting ass in a freaky British night club.

After he was naked, I went back to the top of the stairs and fetched his Vans and told him to put them back on because I got this thing lately for fucking a faggot who is otherwise naked but wearing shoes and I like the way he presses the soles of them into my calves when I am going at it. And then we conducted a quick three-song fuck with me on top, with me first

---

[3] "Jaustin," while being similar in sound to "Justin," also happens to be a fan fiction tag for slash that ships Justin Bieber with Austin Mahone. I knew this already, and assumed that's why Fey chose that name for the titular Twink Pop Star of his story, but I didn't know why he'd chosen "Moss" as the character's surname, or if there even was a particular reason for it beyond that he just liked the sound of the two words together. To explain, he showed me a bunch of porn vid clips from a few years ago starring a skinny and pretty and vocally expressive mostly-bottom twink who shared Fey's first name—Kyler Moss. This Kyler also appeared in a couple movies playing a character based on Justin Bieber, which Fey also provided for my viewing. These were, of course, wholly ridiculous, and I didn't really buy Moss as a Bieber look-a-like, but that didn't dissuade me from jerking off a little bit while watching them, and I did enjoy learning about the thought-process on naming this character. –Editor

blowing him for a minute and then spitting into his fag-pussy and then eating it out for a little while and then drilling it really hard.

Even though he is a couple years older than me, he always seems younger when he gets his ass fucked. He makes this super-cute fag-boy porn-whimper/moan/cry when he is being pounded, which boy-noise somehow seems to strip a decade or two off his apparent age. I call him a cocksucker and a little faery and I spit in his mouth when I fuck him, and he likes this a lot and it makes him pant and moan louder and louder, and he yells my name again and again — which *I* like a lot. He's a good bottom for me because he likes to act submissive in that way, he is shorter than me, overall smaller, even though he has a huge uncut prick (like one of the biggest dicks I have ever seen in real life) with a lot of skin that he left tasting really sweet and dirty for me that day. [4] I got off quickly, pulled out and glazed his cock and nuts with cum, which he used as lube to jerk himself off in a few quicks strokes and he spunked out on his belly and

---

[4] Much of what Kyler relates in his account of this meeting deviates from reality, but it also contains enough fact that I am not going to dispute each specific deviation, and will instead accept his revised memory of things. It is true-to-life to the extent that one could conclude that he really is talking about me when he refers to "F," but I do not understand why he adheres to this wholly made-up description of my cock (he has characterized it similarly in many of his journal entries). It's actually circumcised, and it is definitely not particularly above-average in size. Indeed, his is a fair amount larger than mine. I asked him about this but his only explanation is that it's "hotter" to describe me thus. I'm not sure that I really like that answer. — Editor

chest. He didn't clean up with a towel or a shirt — he just smeared his cocksnot and mine into a fine film over the entire skin of his torso, wiped his hands through his hair, because he's a dirty fucker who likes to get sperm all over the place just like I do, and he hopped up from the bed and put his hoodie and shorts back on and kicked his shoes back off and declared that we needed another Fireball cider.

We drank some more and smoked some more and I continued dinner prep. He went back to my office and returned a moment later with my laptop. "I want to look at your sex journal again," he said. "Can I make my own entry in it for what we just did? I know you'll document it yourself later anyway. So you can correct with your own annotations what I say if you don't concur with my description and perception of that fuck."

He'd done this several times before, searched my journal for references to himself dating back over a decade, occasionally adding his own notes to those entries.

I gave him the password for the current volume's folder and he laughed when he opened it and saw that I had "officially" retitled my journal as *Kyler Fey's The Fuck Record*. "Seriously?" he said, laughing. He's said something like this about it: "As a title, it's as fancy and as pretty and as fucking arrogant as its author."

I explained that I stole the idea from my own fictional creation, Commander Jace Dekka, who calls his massive sex journal *The Fuck Record*. F looked at me, puzzled by this assertion. "You haven't seen that

chapter yet," I clarified. "It's mentioned in a footnote in *His Hundred Million Sons*."

"Seriously! Is that written already? Can I see?" I had promised him the installment of the series containing Jace Dekka's origin story some time ago. But it wasn't ready for him to see yet, so I turned his attention back to the journal. I stepped around to his side of the prep island. "While you're in there, take a look at this file." I pointed to an icon named **"Braden-PEO Super-Fuck."**

"Is this about the 'real' Braden?" He leaned close into the screen and peered at the icon as if he'd see something before even opening the file. F knew that I had based the character of that name in my *Jace Dekka and the Unsuitable Boys* saga on a real dude, a boy who worked in the produce department at the neighborhood grocery store upon whom I had silently crushed for a long time, and then eventually met and with whom I'd conducted several weeks of super-sex the previous summer.

"It's an entry that kind of got out of control," I said. "I recompiled all of my day-to-day entries about him into one long piece and added a lot of supplemental material. You might think it's cool because it kind of tracks with the writing of *Intersex Boys of Venus,* and I did feed some details from life into that story as I was revising it."

"What's PEO?"

"Perfect Erotic Object."

"Oh yeah. Of *course* it is."

He opened the file and checked the word-count and looked at me mouth agape. "Kyler, this shit is

over forty-thousand words. Do you really want me to sit here and read a novella-length piece right now while we are hanging out and making dinner?"

"Just kind of scan over it," I said. "You read really fast anyway. I can send you a copy of it later to consider in more detail."

He smoked and read for a few minutes while I started the process of making the green chile sauce for our enchiladas. After maybe ten or fifteen minutes, he said, "If you want to fuck again later, I'll definitely be able to get stiff for it. You don't necessarily need to make me read all the lurid details of your outlandish fuck-life all evening just for the sake of giving me another hard-on." But he kept reading and after another little while, he said this: "Let's use this somehow. As part of the series somehow."

But I didn't really see how. "But it's not in-universe," I said. "I don't see how you'd make it fit."

"It's a clear window into what's inside your weird mind while you're writing the stories. And what's in your fucking *body*, dude! Do you seriously not ever cum unless you are having sex with a guy? You don't masturbate at all? I don't believe it."

"I masturbate all the godsdamned time," I said. "I just try to stop myself from shooting a load. It helps me stay horny enough to work on all these erotic stories all the time."

"Yeah," he said, "I know that's what you say in this piece, but it seems incredible. I am a little bit older than you and I still pop off every morning in the bathroom when I am getting ready even if I just had wake-

up sex. Do you really go around day after day with an aching, raging case of blue-balls?"

"*Um*, yeah, pretty much!" I said, and squeezed my junk. "Though you just gave me some relief!"

"Glad I can help! Jesus Christ!" He continued to read for a couple more minutes and then said, "I think this could be some kind of introductory piece or fore-word to the series."

It would be an extremely long foreword, I said. It's longer than most of the actual stories in the serial. "And where would you fit it in anyway?" I wondered. "We are doing like twenty stand-alone ebooks. I guess it could be appended to the print omnibus volume."

F said that he wasn't sure yet, but that he felt strongly that we needed to use it somehow. "Go back at it," he said. "It needs some revision and embellish-ment and some unfinished scenes to be finished. Break it into chapters and give those chapters those funny long-ass Victorian-sounding titles like you did with *Intersex Boys of Venus*. And then send it to me."

We let that topic rest for the remainder of the evening, and focused instead on dinner, more drinks, the pumpkin carving and more fucking, but the next morning it was all I could think about, so I did what he said and a couple days later I sent to F the follow-ing book. It was his idea in the end as to what to do with it.

Any reader should be aware before looking at the following document that it ties in with my current work on my upcoming serial novel *Commander Jace and the Unsuitable Boys*, an erotic work with hundreds of depictions of gay sex acts strewn throughout, and therefore probably unsuitable for some audiences, though I think it may be entertaining for fags of pretty much any age and for queer-sex-tolerant readers who like science fantasy.

I have periodically included in my writing some erotic passages, and I have occasionally attempted to write in a fully pornographic mode, but I always found that I'd never finish anything. Inevitably, I would become too aroused by the topic, grab my dick, jerk off, drop cum on the wood floor under my desk, smear it around with my bare feet (a medallion of it has deformed the floor's finish over the years to my spouse's annoyance), and, during the natural refractory period that a male usually experiences after he drops his spunk, I would lose the most intense interest in the subject matter, stop writing about that and move on to something else.

In the planning for *Commander Jace and the Unsuitable Boys* I took as a valuable tip a comment from Sam-

uel Delany who, in his essay "Pornography and Censorship" (published in *Shorter Views*, Wesleyan, 1999) said that a part of his approach to writing his first published pornographic novel *Equinox* was this:

> "One of the self-imposed constraints on the writing of Equinox *was that I would write none of it unless I was actually in a state of sexual arousal, even for the nonsexual parts — an undertaking I'd advise only for the young and/or obsessive." (page 295)*

This makes a lot of obvious sense to me for a writer who wants ever to complete a very long piece of erotica, especially one with any sort of literary ambition (yes, I confess to having some small such thing even for my pulp sci-fi/porn undertaking). It makes sense to me that the author's arousal must be basic to the project of written porn — even when writing about things that might not necessarily be in that own writer's own bag of sexual tricks — if simply to sustain interest in the thing long enough to finish a work of honest written gay pornography. It's quite logical to me that a male writer of erotica would, at least much of the time, have a stiff cock while he is writing. So, I decided that I would work on my erotic serial, like how Delany worked during the drafting of *Equinox*, only while stiff and interested in imagining and perpetrating gay sex acts. But I also decided that I needed to take measures to ensure long periods of sustained arousal so that I could get a lot of this kind of writing

done quickly. So, I have been on a program of controlled orgasm-denial for months. More details on that will appear later.

The following text is derived from a series of entries in my private journal, some of them expanded and embellished upon, some of them presenting events in a somewhat different order than the way they happened, some of them conflating many events into fewer episodes for narrative reasons, and a few times I decided to just go with my preferred revision of a memory when it was prettier and more glittery than whatever I'd actually recorded in the journal.

— KF

1.

July 4. Some success with the Venus book project; recalling an auspicious first meeting with a lithe and lovely lad; and, later, the randy queers indulge their special kind of lust in the park.

Work is close to done on *The Intersex Boys of Venus.* I think I just need to finish up one scene with Braden and Patrick. For some reason the other day I detoured them into an enormous bathhouse on the aethership but never finished relating the details of their hot fuckery in there where they do the dudes from the lunch scene — including some piss-play in a trough — and later suck some big Latino guys' cocks. And I also need to fill in the information about a new and hidden ally that Trace learns about from the writer-boy during the dormitory orgy scene (which finally helps there be an actual reason for that orgy other than gratuitous fag-fucking, and also a plausible reason for Trace, Zane and Ando to even be characters in the story in the first place).

I've also been messing around with some cover art for this and a few of the other episodes. We are seriously thinking about making print edition doubles of

them, like the old Ace Doubles,[5] but I need perhaps more lurid-looking art than I have right at hand, and some cool tag-lines for the covers that feed right into the title. I am tempted to use this one:

**Two lusty young queers on a hothouse world
unlock a world-shaking puzzle
when they knock up…**
THE INTERSEX BOYS OF VENUS

It might be a bit much. I may need to work on that a bit more. Also, it screws up my plan for the title formats where they were each to have been in the *"Episode (number) Commander Jace and the… [whatever the main title is]"* style, such as *Episode #5 Commander Jace and…The Intersex Boys of Venus.* But I think I dig this new approach better, especially if we are doing print doubles with cool covers.

But, in much bigger and *vastly more important* news, I have finally, *finally* at long last achieved just yesterday my first hook-up with the "real" Braden. I have touched *his* body. He, of course, who works in the produce department at the grocery store that I go to everyday; he, of course, that polestar of lust in the shape of a boy that has made shopping for vegetables a special thrill these last couple years. I won't record his real name here—which I have long known from the name tag appended to his shirt—so I will just go ahead and call him "Braden" since his twinky body

---

[5] M-Brane Press has done one of these already, *The New People/ Elegant Threat* book (2010, by Alex Jeffers and Brandon H. Bell), and it's super-fancy.

and moppy hair and dollish pretty face are the actual "model" that I have had in my head ever since I came up with this character of the same name for the book.

I learned his age—he just turned nineteen a few weeks ago—and that he lives in the neighborhood with his mother and a younger brother. Because he lives with these people, he clarified for me that if we were going to "do something," as he rather cutely put it, we couldn't go to his house that day, and I knew that Danny wouldn't be thrilled if I brought him to our house. I'd shown him Braden at the store some time ago and had asked him if he could imagine having this boy join us for a three-way, but Danny wasn't interested—too young and too twinky for him. Which is to me, a wholly *ridiculous* objection (as if one could ever be too twinky to be fuckable), but there it is anyway.

And neither of us had a lot of time anyway so I asked Braden, very softly, a close whisper in the store next to a bin of fragrant peaches, if he could get into the idea of me sucking him off, of me slurping on his cock in my car. He grinned widely and stated that he was for sure up for that, so when his shift ended, I returned to the store and picked him up. He had ridden a bike to work, which I stowed in the back of the car. After the bike was secure, I briefly caressed its seat, a thing that supports Braden by his crotch and ass when he rides it. I imagined him riding it in the swampy July heatwave humidity, soaking sweat through his shorts, making that seat stink of his ass and his nut-sweat.

Fully boned, my pole pushing out the front of my shorts, I drove Braden into the woodsy park, astounded that I actually had him, the iconic boy himself, alone with me in my car. I almost cried out *"I can't believe this is really happening!"* like an excited teenager about to lose his virginity. And then there, deep in the vast park, I found one of my reliably safe spots for the kind of thing that I intended to do with him.

I unclasped our seat-belts and leaned into him and kissed him for a couple minutes. He is good at this and he likes it wet and tongue-sloppy, spit on our chins, just the way I like it. And then I undid his shorts button and zipper. I was very happy that he was wearing — if he must wear underwear at all — easy-to-open trunks, so that his boner just popped right out and up and through the open fly. He's uncut with a tight foreskin not quite fully covering his cock-crown. His dick isn't that large, but I wasn't really expecting it to be so since he himself is rather slight in build overall, but it's very pretty and decently thick. I reached inside though his fly and fished out his lightly fuzzy ballsack and squeezed very gently his surprisingly big nuts. He was very hard and ready to go, so I gripped his stick, spat thickly upon it and started blowing him in earnest. His dick-sleeve tasted so sweet and I inhaled his sweet boy-crotch smell like smoke. It didn't take him very long at all to spunk out — maybe two or three minutes. I caught all his jizz in my mouth, and he let me kiss him with some it, and let me push some of it into his mouth with my tongue.

I undid my fly and hauled out my pre-jac-dripping stick and gripped it tightly. I asked him he wanted to suck me off as well, but I added that if he didn't, I was cool with just jacking off if he watched me do it, as long as he kept his eyes on my dick until I unloaded. Sincerely, I really do not mind if a guy to whom I have given a blowjob doesn't want to reciprocate that service, but I do insist on cumming in his presence somehow, and I get just as highly aroused by being watched when I jack off as I do when I am getting sucked off. But he was fully into giving me his mouth-service, and he went down on me right away. He was perfectly good at it, like an enthusiastic and young but practiced cocksucker, and he was so fucking cute with my thick prick inserted into his bobbing head, his slender fingers wrapping my shaft and nutsack, so much like he looked in a few hundred jack-off fantasies that I'd had about him, that I think I shot off about fast as he did. He kept his mouth clamped onto my shaft until I was done squirting, until seven or eight pulses of cream left my crotch. He lifted his head, opened his mouth and showed me the thick load of white cocksnot that I'd put in there. He fed it to me with another long and sloppy kiss.

I drove him home and during the short trip we agreed to a second date. I unloaded his bike from the back of my car, and we kissed on the street in front of his house, each of us clutching the other's meat through our shorts, and I hoped that neighbors saw us like this, mouth-locked and groping. Our next date will be at his house because the rest of the family is going to Chicago for some reason. I have to go into

work for a couple hours Sunday morning, so the plan is that I will first go to his house early and hopefully pole his ass right there in his bedroom. He did indicate that he is fully open to the idea of ass-sex with me, and with me as the cock-insertive partner. But if he wants to top me also, that would be fine with me and probably really fucking cute, too: sweet young Braden panting over me, stabbing my cunt with his adorable dong.

2.

Recalling the means of meeting the comely young man; a coincidence of passions and a common artistic practice.

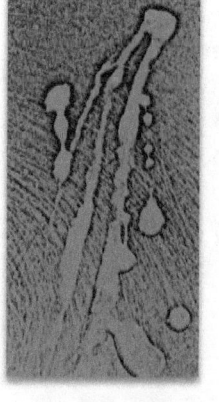

I should backtrack and relate the details of the awesome fucking coup of actually *knowing* Braden after ages of just fag-gazing at him at the grocery store and jacking off about him in the bathroom later. It was by way of the best luck that I have ever hit upon in the realm of my little writing and publishing life. I am one of the admins on a site that promotes and publishes work related to a shared-world science fantasy concept. I haven't spent a lot of time with it lately, but I get pinged when someone interacts with the site, and I started to notice a lot of posts from a writer using the handle "Jommy Cross" [6] who had written a bunch of interesting takes on some characters and situations from the shared universe including several short items in the erotica/slash section. They weren't *great* items, as they were sodden with teenage naiveté and overwrought emotion, but they showed a lot of good potential, some great language and some quite

---

[6] Which in itself got my attention. Jommy Cross is the young protagonist of AE Van Vogt's remarkable novel *Slan* which resonated strongly with me in a way that I didn't quite understand when I first read it as a kid. But I understand it a lot better now.

promising stuff from a young writer who would probably get a lot better later if he kept at it. Eventually I got interested enough in these posts that I spent some time trying to track down Jommy Cross's actual identity.

To make a very long and tedious part of this story a lot shorter, let me just say that a series of clues eventually led me to Braden's Facebook page where I was stunned to learn that the beautiful boy for whom I'd been merely lusting over from a distance, sometimes busting loads in the bathroom sink, sometimes spattering my body and sheets, was also Jommy Cross, this interesting contributor to the site. His Facebook page was sick with pretty pics of him, and he identified himself there as a community college student, a fiction writer, a science fiction and fantasy fan, an openly gay dude, a resident of Saint Louis and an employee of the very grocery store that I shop at almost every day.

I think it was probably for a very long time that I sat there and examined this information, sipping wine, thinking that it was just too perfect to accept at face value, too good to not decay under closer scrutiny or evaporate like a nice dream upon awakening. But, no: I had not only found my produce department boy Braden on Facebook, but I knew that he had also already been interacting with me indirectly in another way through his writing. Clearly, this was an obvious and perfect excuse to actually *talk* to him, and so I did, at the grocery store a couple days later.

And he talked back: "*You* are Kyler Fey?" he said, wide-eyed. "Seriously! I don't know. I was imagining

someone a *lot* older." This was the first and the last time that Braden would flatter me over the topic of my apparent age.

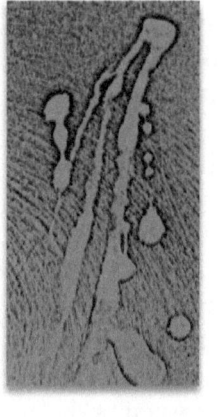

3.

July 7. The narrator perpetrates an act of early-morning sodomy with his beautiful ephebe; a second lover is revealed; recollections of two more intimate encounters.

Since I last wrote about my hook-ups with young Braden, we have met four more times.

I did indeed have my first ass-fuck with him last Sunday as planned. I threw some clothes for later in a bag with some rubbers and lube, and drove over there wearing just a tank top and fleece gym shorts and sandals. I didn't even shower before I left, just washed my ass and cock and nuts in the sink after taking a shit, rubbed some product in my hair and took off. I was so fucking horny and hard on the short drive to his house that I made a big wet pre-jac stain in my shorts. I usually leak at least a little bit of dick-drool when I'm stiff, but during this long period of denying myself solo orgasms, I seem to put out a lot more of it than was ever normal before.

When I got inside his house, I fell into a kind of erotic enchantment with his messy boy-smelly bedroom. The several times in my life that I have gotten to fuck a boy who is technically a fully-grown man but who still lives in the same bedroom in which he had spent his whole adolescence have always gotten

me so sweetly and crudely hot, dick-stiff and sweaty in the ass. This is why: it's because I imagine how he must have spent years beating off in there, sweating on his mattress, wiping constant and copious loads of cum off his body with socks and t-shirts and dirty underwear and stuffing them under his bed to dry and stiffen for the next time, making the closed room smell faintly like a box of sweat and sweet dried spunk.

Braden's room did not disappoint in this regard: it smelled entirely like a horny and not too overly clean young queer. His dark purple sheets — exposed, his bedspread and blanket kicked to the floor — were rumpled and dotted with obvious sperm-stains. Everything else about the room was very messy-young-man in character: dirty clothes on the floor including briefs and boxers probably stale with dried crotch-sweat, stacks of electronic paraphernalia falling over on his desk, a few bookshelves heaped with an awesome mess of sf and fantasy and other novels, his bike hanging from hooks on a wall that partially obscured a big Justin Bieber poster, the lovely Justin himself shirtless and clad in CK boxer briefs (which got me even harder if such was even possible, wondering if Braden ever lay on his bed and waxed his pole while looking at that picture[7]), the image somewhat hazed

---

[7] It is a very rare thing for me to jack off to fantasies about celebrities. I tend to go for real-life people that I either know or see around (like Braden for a long time before I introduced myself) or sometimes wholly fictional characters from my own writing and even sometimes fictional characters from books that I have read. But I do periodically beat off to Bieber. There are probably at least

---

a couple hundred instances of it that could be found in masturbation details recorded in my *Fuck Record*. These include jacking off to online fan fiction about crazy sex scenarios with Bieber. I read one a couple years ago, written back when the singer was a still a teenager, in which Bieber's manager conspires with a mad doctor to remove the boy's balls to stop his career-making voice from changing and to stop his ever more testosterone-fueled behavior from ruining the gravy train. The lad is duped into a medical examination in which he is fully restrained and, for some reason, given a hot soap-and-water enema. And, of course, since these sickos are going to deprive a horny teenage male of his nuts anyway, they may as well go ahead and rape his ass and piss in his mouth as a prelude to the castration. It is only after they have done all this sexual sadism and after the skilled surgeon has already excised Bieber's testes from his sack (evidently without the benefit of anesthetic) and replaced them with fake ones, that the boy's manager wonders what they'll do if Justin actually tells anyone what they did to him. But no worries, as the doctor simply erases the kid's memory with some kind of electric shock. And it is implied at the end that the two madmen eat Bieber's balls as a snack. There's shit-tons of erotic Bieber-fic online, not all of it anywhere near that fucked-up. I have written several stories in this genre myself, including a sort of sequel to the ball-removal one in which a thinly disguised version of me (simply called Kyler Fey in the story) manages to secure Justin Bieber in his compound and reveals to him that his nuts have been removed and replaced by fake ones, and then goes on to restore his body to normal using cloned copies of his (my) own balls. Danny thinks that my lust for Bieber is sick and stupid, though he did humor this quirk once by giving me at Christmas a Justin Bieber calendar and a book "by" him. For some reason, I think he is astonishingly hot in the body and super-pretty in the face and I am not in the slightest bit embarrassed to admit that when I see pics of him, or even hear his voice on the radio, I nearly always get a full hard-on. In fact, as I write this footnote, my stick is fully stiff and drooling pre-jac because I am thinking about him on his back on my kitchen prep table, me standing between his spread-wide legs, him on his back getting

and warped and blurred as if some kind of impressionistic filter had been applied to it.

Braden opened a dresser drawer and pulled out a bottle of vodka. "You want a shot? Do you like to be a little buzzed when you fuck?" Delighted, I accepted the offer, not mentioning that I'd already pounded a couple screw drivers before coming over there. We each swigged directly from the bottle. "I can get you stoned, too, if you want. If you like the weed. I'm not a big fan but I do it sometimes. My brother fuckin' loves it." I told him that I am not a big fan of it either, and that I'd pass on it this time. The fact of the matter is that it makes me dizzy and nauseated (at least while I'm drunk — which is often...very often) and it makes me feel like puking. I wondered if he had a fake ID for purposes of buying booze. He could probably easily pass for younger than his age of nineteen, but certainly not any older. "Dude next door buys it for me," he said. "I give him head once in a while."

We stood next to his bed and kissed for a minute or two. I pulled off my minimal clothing and stripped

---

piston-fucked by my thick drippy pole until he is literally crying from the ecstasy of it, sobbing with big tears and a snotty nose, until the force of my dick banging his prostate makes him finally and suddenly spray big ropey *yaoi*-cum streamers of his Justin-goo all over his smooth belly and chest, the sight of which makes me lose control and spunk out inside his cocksocket, filing it up with an impossibly giant and belly-inflating load of streaming semen that make's the dude looks like he's pregnant for a minute. Or, alternatively: pulling out and painting his pretty face with every drop of it and then smearing my cum over his entire face with my cock and then slicking some of it up into his hair. That's a pretty typical reaction for me when I see Bieber.

off his (he was only wearing a pair of flannel pajama pants, white with pink stripes, no underwear, just his naked meat and ass underneath) and we got to business. He was entirely enthusiastic about squeezing every inch of my penis into his tight rectum and after we'd only been naked together, exploring each other a little bit all over with our hands, in his bed for a couple minutes, he put a rubber on me, squirted a bunch of lube on my cock and mashed some of it into his hole and invited me to take him on his back, me on top.

I made it last as long as I could, but I hadn't cum since the blowjob that he had given me three days earlier, and he was so fucking tight and so very fucking cute, that I did not make it to the ten-minute mark (or, honestly, probably even to the five-minute mark), even with the rubber dulling the fuck-thrust sensation a little bit. But I had an awesome, staggering, double-orgasm. First I pumped out inside the rubber inside his body. I pulled out and had that rare but unmistakable post-cum sensation that I wasn't quite done. It felt like I needed to let out something else, something more. I pulled off the condom, spilled its contents on his cock and pubes, grabbed my cum-slicked tool and pumped it a few more times and popped off a couple more thick and ropey blasts of batter on his smooth boy-belly. It filled the dark dent of his navel. I lapped it all up off the soft skin of his abs and out of his belly button and sucked off his cute cock with a mouthful of my own cum. He came quickly, and I swallowed it.

We lay there together for a little while, kissed some more, and he told me a little bit about a couple other boys at the grocery store who are also gay, and

he admitted to having occasional sex with one of them that I'll call Ethan (also the name of a character in the *Jace* books). I knew exactly who he was talking about and I told him that I would also like to fuck Ethan sometime and maybe we could arrange a three-way.

I needed to get on to work, but we both got hard again so I gave him another blowjob, made him cum in my mouth again, and then I straddled him and jacked off. I asked him if it was okay if I dropped it on his face. He approved, and so I did. I was pretty happy that I managed to make another fairly decent load so soon after I my awesome double-jizz, and it looked sweet on his pretty cheeks and lips. He let me lick him clean and giggled like it tickled him terribly. That was, of course, very cute and made me feel very warmly toward him. But, time to go, so I put my shorts and tank back on, kissed him again, told him to let me know when he was available for some more fun.

I went to the office for a while did a couple hours' work, made myself a couple cocktails (Sunday morning when the place is empty except for me is the best time to be there), got horny again thinking about what I did with Braden. I stroked myself to almost-orgasm a couple dozen times, but held back because I was planning to write more on one of the book's chapters later and I wanted to stay fully aroused and cum-loaded for that.

I orgasm-denied myself until Tuesday when Braden texted me and asked if I wanted to take him to the park again and get blown in the car. Of course, I obliged. The next time was Thursday and Braden was feeling rather more daring. He had me find him at work during his shift early that morning. We arranged for me to go into the men's restroom. He followed a moment later and left a restroom-closed-for - cleaning sign outside it. We alternately stood and knelt in the stall and put squirts of cocksnot in each other's mouths in the space of less than ten minutes.

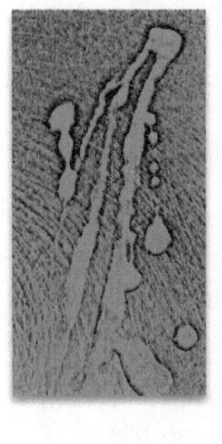

4.

July 14. A brief encounter with the pretty and glossy young man's other boyfriend; another act of earnest sodomy in Braden's bed; a lusty younger brother's most private pleasure is exposed; a cum-stiffened image invites closer examination; the narrator speculates about gay virginity and contemplates the pleasure of putting his ardent fluid on a lover's face.

Then this morning—Monday—we were back in his bedroom. His mom wasn't home, but his brother was, but Braden wasn't worried about that since the other boy was just hanging out in his own room with the door closed. And there was a great surprise when I got there: Ethan was leaving as I arrived. He greeted me with Braden at the front door, dressed in his grocery store work clothes and apparently on the way in for a morning shift (while Braden himself wore only black trunks-style underwear).

"See you later," Braden told him, and kissed him quickly on the mouth. Braden led me upstairs into his room and, like last time, we got naked right away and kissed for a minute. He revealed that Ethan had spent the night and that they'd had sex this morning. He looked like it, too: cute rumpled morning-fuck hair, flushed cheeks, and he smelled like it, too, like his own spit and sweat and the spit and sweat of another

boy on his body. But I wondered, is Ethan cool with this right now? He just saw me show up here. Does he know that the whole reason that I am even here is to fuck you? He confirmed that Ethan knew this, that it was fine, that they were not in any way exclusive with each other anyway, that Ethan actually has a girl-friend, and even that Ethan would probably consider my three-way idea sometime.

I asked Braden if I could drill him again. He agreed. But I decided I wanted to rim him for a few minutes first since I'd somehow skipped entirely eat-ing his boypussy the first time, and I greatly like to lick a cute young guy's cunt for a while before I slide my dong inside him. I also wanted to see up close if I could detect any evidence that his hole had been en-tered by that cutie Ethan. It was, in fact, quite pink and livid, like it may have been very recently dilated by another man's dick. He moaned softly as I went to work on it with my tongue. When I pushed in I tasted something that was quite unmistakable in its flavor. I pulled back and tugged his hole open just a little bit with two fingers and saw what could only be the shiny slime of some leftover lube and cum that hadn't yet leaked out from a very recent fuck.

"You were busy with Ethan," I said. "Please share every detail!" Braden admitted that Ethan had *just* fucked him and jizzed inside him literally just a cou-ple minutes before I got there. He'd been on his way to work and had asked Braden if he could stop by for a quick fuck. So right before my arrival, Ethan had just pulled his pole out of Braden's ass and had been wip-ing his cock on a shirt and pulling his pants on when

I got to the door and texted Braden that I was there. Ethan had just pulled on a shirt and shoes and zipped up his pants seconds before I met him at the door and he was headed off to work without washing up first.

I guess Braden could surmise what I was going to start wondering about and said, "But I still think you should put on the condom. I know him better than I know you." Of course I will, I said, but I figured that I'd have nothing to lose with this request: "But it would be really hot if I could get some of Ethan's cum on my cock." I proposed that he permit me to just very briefly insert my bare dick just long enough to get it wet with the other lad's goo. Braden decided that he liked the dirty kinkiness of that enough to agree to it, said that I was sick fucker, and let's do it. I didn't bother to lube up all that much since he was evidently already primed inside, so I just spit on his hole and on my cock, maneuvered into position and worked my way, very slowly, inside. I am surprised that I didn't just spontaneously shoot off within the first two seconds, and I probably would have if I didn't just stop, freeze in place, pole inside his chute, and let myself feel the hot slippery wetness that was proof of another spermy boy having been in there just ahead me.

"Are you okay?" I asked. He grinned, said yeah, just fine. I knew I was supposed to immediately get out now that I had gotten what I wanted — some residue of Ethan's nut-juice on my bare meat — but I dared a slow thrust, and then another and I asked him again if he was ok with this. He said he was, and I said I guess I need to get out and put on the rubber, and he said it was fine, just keep going. I don't need to be told

twice, so I did it, and all the way I bareback fucked him. I didn't last long. When it was impossible to not cum, I pulled out and cuffed it the rest of the way and unloaded on his chest and belly. He laughed a lot as I gently pinned his arms to the bed and licked blobs and streaks of my spunk off his chest and out of his navel, and I nibbled at his stiff nipples, and bit and licked at the skin and fur of his sweaty armpits.

His prick was fully swollen and I asked him how he wanted me to make him cum. "Do you want to do that to me, too? Fuck my ass?" Oh fuck yeah! he said, we and switched positions. I rolled onto my back, spread my legs wide, raised my knees and invited him on top. I handed him the lube tube from the bed-side table, and he greased up. I didn't ask him to put on a rubber. Can you see where you're going, baby? He fingered me for a few seconds, got into position, aimed his cockhead downward and pushed inside quite forcefully, basically one solid stroke piercing my ring with his head and plunging balls-deep inside. He fucked me quite rapidly and quite hard and my stick boned up again fully after a couple minutes of that dick banging on my prostate.

While he was boning me, my mind wandered over these thoughts:

1. It's hot that a kid half my age is fucking me and that he likes it; I'm well old enough to be his father; if I *were* actually his father, I would have pregged his mom when I was the age he is now; I remembered that Danny and I had recently reached our nineteenth anniversary of being partners, that I was as the same age as Braden is now when Danny—a man of twenty-six

at the time—wooed me, and that Danny and I probably had sex on the same day that Braden's father put into his mother the sperm with the Y chromosome that made this cutie a boy.

2. The next time I see Ethan at the grocery store, I will be seeing a young man whom I have never even touched yet but whose jizz I have tasted and which has touched my cock because I had condomless anal sex with his boyfriend minutes after he'd just done the same. I think this is a first: having cum on my cock from a dude who I haven't otherwise had sex with. I have several times in my life fucked a guy right after another dude shot off inside him, but that was always in some kind of three- or four- or five-way situation where the other dude was right there and I was having sex with him as well.

3. While the difference in our ages and experience basically makes it impossible for Braden and I to ever have a "real" relationship—this will only ever be using each other's bodies for sexual pleasure—I find myself feeling very affectionate and even protective toward him probably just because he is so youthful and cute, but possibly also because we have in common a love of the written word.

4. Braden is a mixed boy in his ethnicity, but I don't know what—maybe part white and part Asian or Hispanic—not sure, need to ask later.

5. I wonder how many times, before this summery fling is over, I will have sex with Braden. Since there is almost a whole year before his next birthday, I could possibly reach a hundred times with him before he turns twenty if we continue at the pace of the first

week or so of our relationship and maintain this relationship long enough. And if that happens then he will be one of only three dudes that I have had sex with a hundred or more times (the others: Jay (714 documented times) and Danny (1626 documented times to date)) out of 211 documented sex partners to date. But I wonder if we will get bored with each other long before we reach that milestone. Another data point: in the nineteen years that I have been with Danny, I have also jacked off over 10,400 times,[8] which puts in perspective how rare orgasm through sex with another man is for me compared to how often I do it with myself, and I suspect that's true for most men.

6. I wonder how old Braden actually was when I first noticed him at the store and started tenting my pants, commando-cocked, obvious visible public erection while shopping for produce. I assumed eighteen or so, but now that I know he just turned nineteen a few days ago, that must be wrong because I know that I have been noticing him and beating it to fantasies about him for far longer than just a year. [9]

---

[8] Not counting the way I have doing it lately during the cum-denial regime. This number refers to times when I jacked off fully and shot semen from my cock.

[9] Later, at home, I would find via a keyword search of my masturbation log [produce-grocery] that the first time I jacked off using him as fantasy material was about three years ago, and my journal reminds me that I stood at the bathroom sink after shaving in the morning and pulled on my pole while imagining him naked and on his knees and slurping an impossibly huge amount of spunk out of my dong, and so he was evidently only sixteen during his appearance in that fantasy.

And that's about when he came inside my ass, and I loved the wide-eyed, wet-eyed look of his face as he had his lengthy orgasm. It's fantastic and beautiful how vulnerable a pretty male looks (and actually *is)* when he cums. The whole lead-up to it is voluntary in the sense that a dude enthusiastically chooses to do something—or chooses to have someone else do something—to his dick for the implicit purpose of eventually cumming, but when the actual orgasm happens he is more or less helpless. The orgasm is involuntarily, his body is doing stuff outside of his control, and he is fully exposed to his partner at that moment, and that's probably why I almost always find sex even during a one-off hook-up to have a sweetness and beauty to it. Because when a guy cums with someone else, he is at his most naked. He is totally exposed, nothing is hidden. Totally naked Braden panting on top of me, emptying his nuts into me, was sweet like that. A lot of guys automatically close their eyes during this moment of extreme pleasure and extreme nakedness and exposure, but Braden didn't. I liked that a lot: he made total eye contact with me while he was cumming, hazel eyes that said *look at me and what I'm doing to you, what you're doing to me.*

After he was done, he climbed off me, stood next to the bed and wiped his cock off on a t-shirt that was lying the floor and then got back into bed next to me and kissed me for a little while. Very quickly my dick was stiff again and I was thinking about which method to use for a second rocking-off with Braden, but I needed badly to take a piss. He advised that the bathroom was just to the right at the end of the hall.

When I moved to put on my shorts, he told me to not bother. "Just go naked," he said. "No one will see you. I do it all the time. And Eric's the only one home anyway (Eric, his younger brother). It's no big deal if he sees you anyway — he totally knows what I do in here when I have visitors."

This bathroom was evidently used and maintained just by the boys — no sign of any kind of feminine touch or motherly fussiness in that room. It was in about the same state as Braden's bedroom, with some dirty boy-clothing on the floor (including a black tank top and pair of men's size small green camo briefs, and I wondered if they were Braden's or Eric's), a pair of slightly damp towels hanging on the back of the door, twin tooth brushes standing in a glass next to each other, lots of tubes and tubs of hair products and shaving products and cleansers and acne remedies. There was a can of body spray, which I assumed to be Eric's since Braden never seemed to smell like anything other than his own body. A caddy hung in the stall shower with a couple bottles of body wash and

shampoo and, to my great approval, a tube of Stroke-Z.[10]

Evidently at least one of the boys was in the habit of jacking off in the shower, liked doing it with lube, and was out in the open enough about this practice to leave his masturbation product in plain sight in the shower. I wondered if it was Braden or Eric who used that lube, or was it both? Did Braden ever dildo-fuck himself in here? I liked the certain knowledge that — even though the details remained unknown — that there were expressions of young male sexuality going on in this room on a regular basis. One can assume that a bathroom used by teenage boys is the site of routine self-pleasure, but it got me dripping hot to see the plain evidence of it in there in the form of that lube.

I stuck both of their tooth brushes in my mouth and held them there, spit-soaking the bristles, while I pissed in their sink. I wiped off the last couple dribbles on that underwear that I'd seen lying on the floor, smelled the briefs to confirm that they had the scent of having been plastered over a dude's ass and junk for at least a day, and then rubbed that fabric all over my nuts and cock and into my crotch and ass-crack, kind of enjoying the fact that I didn't know whether I

---

[10] Editor's note: In Fey's novel *FagJuv*, this masturbation lube product shows up in a scene during which yet another iteration of "Kyler" uses it to lube a dildo during sex with his new step-brother, but it's described as a product widely marketed for its intended use to teenagers *on Earth and on Mars*. This leaves me unsure as to whether this entire event is imaginary or if he's just decided it's more fun to call KY or Astroglide "Stroke-Z."

was molesting Braden's shorts or Eric's. I opened the door a crack and looked out to make sure the younger brother was not, in fact, out of his room and in the hall. Since we hadn't met yet, I didn't think his first sight of me should be of me emerging naked and with an erection from his bathroom (and right after I had possibly just sexually assaulted his underwear and definitely soaked my spit into his toothbrush).

I slipped back into Braden's room and found him lying on his back with a book open, reading. It was a trade paperback of Murakami's *Kafka on the Shore*. I was very impressed to see him reading this book. I figured he was a good reader simply because I knew he was a writer, and because he had so many books in his room, but I hadn't investigated far enough into it to know much about what his depth and breadth in reading material was. *Kafka on the Shore* is one of those great books that is probably best appreciated by a reader a bit older and more experienced in life (like me), but it's also a great book for a young man his age because of its very sympathetic and brainy and horny teenage protag, and one that he can go back to in twenty years and enjoy again in a different way. He set it down on the bedside table. I like, I said, that book a lot and that you used even that short time that

I was away to read some more of it. "Never waste a minute!" he said.

I asked about the Stroke-Z in the shower stall, and Braden confirmed that it was Eric who liked to beat off in there. "I prefer, however," he said, "to just do it in here and cum on the sheet or on myself and just wipe off with some clothes. Eric's a lot cleaner than me, I guess, so he does it in the shower, and his bed doesn't have nearly as much sperm all over it." I told him that I don't much like jacking off in the shower that often either in part because I don't like how my jizz just immediately runs away down the drain in a torrent of water. I told him that I thought it was cool and very healthy that his bro wasn't in the closet about his jacking off practices and that he just stores his lube in plain sight in their shared bathroom.

Braden told me that a few years ago they had a cousin who lived with them for a couple years. They gave that relative Eric's room and so Braden and his brother had to share this room for a while. This was a couple years into Braden's adolescence. "I'd been jacking off in bed for like two or three years already," he said, "and I wasn't going to stop just because Eric was living in here with me, so I was very up front with him about it that I jack off a lot and that he might catch me or hear me doing it and that I don't care if he does, and he needs to plan on getting used to it. We had a bunkbed in here back then and he slept on top. And I told him that I am not going to be shy about it or try to hide it and that he shouldn't either. I didn't even know if he was doing it yet, but he told me that he did it a lot, too, but usually in the shower. I think it kind

of turns him on to leave his lube out where people can see it when they go in there. It's like he's announcing to whoever sees that tube: yeah, I'm a horny dude and you can assume that every time I am in this shower stall I am probably waxing my pole and pumping out a load."

During the time that they shared the room, the brothers were in the middle of their teen years. It was a sweet turn-on to imagine them both in here on their bunks beating their meat (even though I had just been told that in-bed masturbation had never been Eric's preference).

I inquired further into what he meant exactly by Eric *knowing* what he's doing with other guys in this room, and he told me that he has been openly gay to his family since he was fifteen. Eric was always cool with it, but it took Mom a long time to come around. She's very "traditional," he said (and I learned that she was Vietnamese-born, once married to a Caucasian man, and got my answer to my speculation about Braden's mixed ethnicity). Apparently she had accepted the fact of her son's sexual orientation as something that she just couldn't do anything about, but she was also adamant that he not emphasize the point all the time by actually having men in his bedroom for sex, at least not to where she would become aware of it. Eric, he told me, says he is "probably" and "almost totally" straight, but that he is also open "intellectually" to the concept of "trying some gay sex" someday if the opportunity arose. I asked if he knew if his brother was sexually active yet. He confirmed that Eric had just recently lost his virginity with a girl, who

had been his girlfriend for a year or so already. "But she only blew him or gave him hand-jobs for the first year."

Male virginity is a weird concept to think about sometimes. If this boy had been getting off orally and manually with a partner for a year, was he really still a "virgin" up to the point when he finally got leave to insert his cock into her pussy? Is the magic and mystique of that particular act alone what finally releases a youth from his virginal innocence even if he has been getting his knob polished by other means for a long time? And, if so, what then constitutes the loss of virginity for a *gay* boy? Do those first blowjobs also not count toward it, as they don't seem to count for straight boys? Does a gay boy stop being a virgin when he fucks another dude in the ass? Or does he himself have to be fucked by a guy to lose his virginity? Or is it both? Can a gay dude be a "half-virgin" if he has just been fucked but never been the top? What about a dude who never has any anal sex at all but constantly sucks cock? I thought about a guy I hooked up with on Craigslist last year. He was twenty-nine and claimed — and I had no reason to doubt him — that he had never even once had anal sex though he had been sucking on cocks since he was fourteen, and he estimated that he had probably blown like fifty dudes before me. Was this guy then a twenty-nine-year-old "virgin?" Well, if so, then he wasn't after I was done with him since he consented to getting drilled by me. So, he was at most a half-virgin afterward, I guess?

I asked Braden if he had ever jacked off to that Justin Bieber poster.

"I've jacked off *on* it, dude," he said. "Like, a *lot!* Go look at it, up close. Take the bike down so you can get a better look." I got up and pulled down the bike. He said, "I stand on my desk chair so I can get my cock right up against his body, so I can squirt on him." Up close, it was obvious, the thick paper slightly bubbled and warped as if it been repeatedly wetted and then left to dry. "I shot all over him and smeared it smooth on his face and chest and on his dick-bulge," Braden continued. "His underwear has like ten trillion of my dehydrated sperm on them." I ran fingers over the surface, crackling over the brittle cum-infused image. "I did it so much, it's soaked through." The damage to the paper was so severe that I was amazed that the image printed on it was still so legible. He told me to release the tacks that were holding up the upper corners of the poster and pull it away from the wall. "Take a look," he said, laughing.

Carefully, I detached the picture from the wall and it moved like a rigid board that could possibly stand up on its own. The paint on the wall was stained darkly where Braden's ball-juice had evidently soaked through the picture, the two biggest medallions of it located behind where Justin's face and his

dick were located in the image. "You can probably taste it, kiddo," Braden said, "my boy-milk on his face. Lick it. Give him a kiss. With your tongue." I pressed my tongue against the image of Justin's lips and held it there for a few moments. When I was a teenager I kept a t-shirt in my underwear drawer that I used daily to wipe cum off my body after jacking off. Sometimes, when I was fucking my fist, I'd stick that fabric, gluey with dried jizz, in my mouth and suck on it, my spit rehydrating weeks and months of old spunk. Braden's Bieber poster tasted and smelled like that. I liked this kid more and more: he had created a flat sheet of desiccated semen in the form of a Justin Bieber poster and let it hang on his wall and was proud to explain it to a guest.

"I assume you'd let Justin fuck you if the opportunity ever arose," I said.

"Dude, you don't even know!" He rose to his knees on the bed and gripped his stick. "I'd let him fuck the shit out of me for as long he wants. I'd let him fill me with a gallon of his baby-batter. I'd let him choke me all day on that fat cock. I'd let him put me in a harness and handcuffs and beat my ass with a paddle until it's a giant fucking bruise. I'd let him piss inside my gut, spit in my mouth and make me wash his ass with my tongue after he takes a dump." He grinned, still holding his tool and added, "Or: if he ended being a bottom-boy, I'd do all that shit to *him!*"

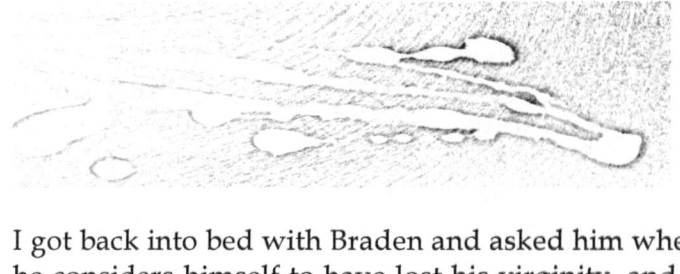

I got back into bed with Braden and asked him when he considers himself to have lost his virginity, and if it was with another boy and if he had ever had straight sex. He said he has never had straight sex and didn't suspect he ever would. He said that he gave head the first time when he was fifteen, and did it to a considerably older boy (who was a twenty-one-year-old college senior at the time, and who also sucked Braden off during their several encounters). "I guess I always kind of like *older* and more experienced dudes," he said, grinning at me, very kindly reminding me of my advanced age. I tickled him for this and he giggled furiously.

He summarized some of the rest of his sexual history to date: a couple more years of blowjobs and hand jobs with several other dudes, some his own age and some a lot older. The first dude who fucked his ass was in his thirties when Braden was seventeen, "nearly as old as *you*!" he said, and slid his tongue into my mouth for a couple more minutes. His first time putting his dick in someone else's ass was about a year later, and that was with a dude he met at school (he's been taking classes at the community college, and wants to go on to what he calls "real" college soon). He estimated that I was probably about his twentieth sex partner.

I asked him if he keeps a journal of it. I explained that I have always documented my sex acts — even every time I jack off — in my journal, so that I can always know exactly what I have done and with whom. This journal goes back so far that it records the details of my first sex act with another person, a blowjob given by me to Jonny Petersen when I was the youngest freshman in my high school (I skipped grades twice). I did that dude seventy-two times before he got a girlfriend and swore off getting sucked by boys. He never reciprocated but he'd watch me jack off after I swallowed his load (he insisted that I swallow because he didn't want to get it on his pants, which he never removed or even lowered, but rather just unzipped to let out his prick), and when I did him in his bedroom he'd even let me catch my white mess on his own cum rag, a thickly jizz-crusted, dead-semen-stinking red t-shirt that he stored under his bed. Though he wouldn't service me, it got me hot to mix my fresh sperm with his dead sperm in this way. One time I asked if I could put a chunk of that shirt in my mouth and suck on his dried spunk. He permitted it, though he said it was "gross." But, really, how gross could it have been? I'd just swallowed a glob of the same shit direct from his dick.

"That's very cool," he said. "Maybe I should start doing that. I write in a journal a lot but not that much about sex. It's mostly for my creative writing. I can't see actually writing about it every time I jack off though. Between the jacking off itself and then *writing* about it, I don't think I'd have time for anything else!"

60

He asked me if I had written in my journal about doing him. "Of course!" I said. And I revealed to him to I had been checking him out in the store, tent pitched in my pants, and jacking off while thinking about him for years, and that I'd never have worked up the will to speak to him, to actually attempt to get him naked in bed with me, had I not found out that he was "Jommy Cross" on the website. He said that he thought this was all very cool, and he kissed me some more.

He stated this opinion: "Some people think kissing is just a kind of *love*. But to me, when I'm doing it to a hot guy, it's a kind of *sex*. When I kiss you, when I put my tongue in your mouth, I am doing a sexual thing to you by kissing you just as much I as would be if I was putting my dick was in your mouth." I appreciated the honesty, the boyish aggression (kissing as a thing that he is *doing to* me), and the lusty truth of his conception of sex, and I agreed with it.

I decided it was probably about time to leave—I needed to get a little bit of work done today—but offered to indulge in some more cock-focused sex with him again if he wanted to cum one more time before I left. He asked for a blowjob and I asked if I could jerk off on his face again like last time. We consented to each other's wishes.

An aside...
Facial cumshots are, in my experience at least, far more common in porn than in real life. But I love it as a sex act—both delivering it and receiving it—and I

really dig a dude who is cool with it, because so many are not.

Danny hates it. In the nineteen years that we have been together, he has unloaded on my face maybe ten times. He has let me do it on his a few more times than that, but it is always over his objections. We have been together so long and have such a level of love and trust with each other that we can occasionally do something "non-consensual" to each other without it being a big deal. While with another guy, like Braden, I always carefully ask for consent to whatever sex act I want to perpetrate with him or upon him, with Danny I will sometimes just tell him to shut the fuck up and deal with it when I am determined to jizz on his face.

It's just cum. It wipes off, and I am always happy to lick it off. I am not sure why I like this so much, but I think it is somehow, in my sexual psychology, a highly affirming thing for my masculinity and my particular expression of my gay sexuality. It feels like a very purely queer thing to do to spatter my partner's face with my semen, and it makes me feel like my partner is accepting me at my very most naked and vulnerable — because you are totally naked and vulnerable while cumming — and accepting my sexuality for what it is with all its little Kyler-kinks. It feels like a very loving and even romantic act in a weird way when a guy says "yeah, you can cum on my face." Because he is saying, "Yes, I like you enough (or at least like having sex with you enough) that I want to let you do the thing that makes you feel good." It might develop over time, if I keep on having sex with

Braden, that I will feel that his consent for this act of spurting on his face is implied and that I do not need to ask him for his permission every time, or he may even tell me to not bother asking anymore and just do it when I want to do it.

But I might still ask anyway, because that in itself is fucking *hot*—literally asking out loud if I may please put my cock inches from his face, jack off and shoot my load at his eyes and nose and mouth. It's hot to say the words, to state honestly my desire to do this thing even if the answer is sometimes no. And I love the way Braden behaves during this. He smiles and he keeps his eyes open even as I am cumming and he doesn't care at all if I get some of it in eyes. Pretty much every other dude to whom I have done this has closed his eyes either during the entire event or right as I was shooting off. That's common behavior in porn, too, but it seems dumb to me: I want to *see* the juice when a guy gets off, and I want my partners to see mine as much as possible. I would never consider turning away or closing my eyes at the very moment when a guy is going to unload his cum. While I thought that it was very sweet when Braden launched it inside my gut, I kind of wished that he would have pulled out and shot it on me so I could see it and probably dab it into my mouth with my fingers (I'll probably ask him to do it that way next time).

5.

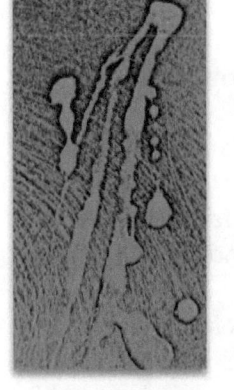

July 14 Writing while naked and aroused; a visit to the store and a brief interaction with the other lover; a pleasant dinnertime conversation with the spouse; observations about the practice of cum-denial.

I went home, did a little work on editing the *Spunk Beam* chapter, the eventual resolution to the Venusian problem in *Intersex Boys*. Danny was at work, so I took advantage of being able to sit bare-ass naked on the wooden stool at my desk while working. I should, by rights, be able to do that whenever the fuck I want to since it is my work room in my home, but Danny thinks it's all just too weird, and he thinks it's bizarre or possibly even creepy that I am often erect when I am writing and that I occasionally pull on my bone during it, but he doesn't get anything about my writing hobby anyway, and is he totally mystified by this multi-book erotica project that I have been working on for months.

Sitting in my office naked was especially nice to do today. It was a warm day, but not hot, and we had all the windows open. There was a breeze but it wasn't *too* breezy, and the air felt awesome on every piece of my naked skin. I could kind of tell that I probably

still smelled a lot like sex with Braden, but that turned me on and I decided to not shower at all today.

Before doing anything that I really wanted to do, I decided to peruse the dreary work calendar for the following month in hopes of seeing some things that could be deleted. During one especially clustered series of day, one thing jumped out at me: *"Cade's fucking birthday, at long last."* My dick kind of jumped at this.

Cade is a next-door neighbor, a very cute and demonstrative young faggot, who I'd met at a house party thrown by his rather bohemian parents last October shortly after they'd moved onto the block. So forward-leaning is he in his drive for sex with men, and so good was his instinct as to a potential partner that night, that he managed to identify me quickly and correctly as a horny queer with a refined taste for twink meat.

He isolated me from the group for a while, as such a seducer does, and he charmed me into slipping him drinks and smokes. I remember that he was wearing a black sleeveless hoodie (no shirt underneath) unzipped almost all the way down to his navel and very tight purple capris pants and green Crocs and a Sussex cricket cap atop his shaggy brown hair and he looked like a youth catalog model if there had been old-timey Sear's-style Christmas catalogs of slutty teenage twinks, or maybe he looked like a straight-up rentboy or maybe like someone from a twink porn vid getting fucked while licking on a big coiled lollipop, and I wondered what his parents' assessment of his plainly prick-provocative appearance might be, and

eventually he issued to me a very blunt fuck-proposi-
tion which would have involved me giving him a
hard and bareback boning in his bed and busting a
nut in his gut. He even opened his pants (no underwear beneath) and showed me his very thick and stiff
stick and his stubble of shaved pubes. But as much as
I wanted to suck on his fat fag-phallus until he milked
out in my mouth, I had to decline with great sadness
(and titanic self-restraint given how drunk and horny
I was), when he revealed his age, and he was disappointed as well, but he understood that he probably
wasn't worth the opportunity of jail for me, and I told
him to put that cute dick away and that I will deny
that I ever saw it if asked. But, right then, I asked him
to tell me the truth about when his birthday is and
made him prove it with his fresh new driver's license
(and I did not remark to him upon the ridiculousness
of a boy that like being legal to drive a deadly car
around the city but not legal to fuck), and I added his
date of sex-legality to the calendar on my phone and
we agreed to confer again upon it later. Though I have
not been able to enjoy him in the flesh yet, I have a
recurring early-morning masturbation fantasy about
him. It goes like this:

*I awaken in the middle of the night and go naked out-
side to the back deck which is just a few feet away from
Cade's back deck. Using an agility that I don't possess in
real life, I leap like a cat from my deck and onto his. He has
left open his bedroom window — both glass and screen — and
I slip through into his bedroom where the boy lies naked
atop his sheets, sound asleep. I get into bed with him and
awaken him with kisses on his sweet rank foreskin, his stiff*

nipples, his smooth chin, his pouty mouth, and soon he is kissing me deeply, filling my mouth with his spit. I make love to the kid for an hour, and I destroy his fag-virginity (though I don't think he is anywhere near a virgin in real life) first with my prick in his ass and then with his in mine. Once my mission of ending pretty Cade's queer sexual in- nocence is accomplished, I leave him to go back to sleep, sweaty and cum-spent, his sheets a stained mess, and I leap back across to my house and return to my bed, but my arri- val back in bed awakens Danny. "You smell like a boy," he says softly. "But I am a boy," I say, but he clarifies that he means, of course, that I smell like a boy that I had just snuck away to fuck. I admit that just minutes ago I took young Cade in his bed, and then Danny takes me with great force. He pins me face-down and pushes into my hole — he doesn't bother to use any lube, but none is needed since I am still weeping a thick slick of Cade's boy-batter from my asshole. It's a typical Danny-style punishment for unauthorized fucking. I tell him that I won't get in bed with Cade again (even though I fully intend to do just that tomorrow). In a few minutes Danny is done with this rough drilling, he has filled me with his juice, he has re-marked me as his wholly- owned fuck-property.[11]

---

[11] I think that the part of the fantasy where Danny perpetrates this punishment-fuck, this type of spousal rape, upon me derives from a memory of reading something about how the evolutionary rea- son that penises have mushroom heads is so that men can use their cocks to pull out of vaginas the sperm from competing males. In this fantasy, as he vigorously fucks me, Danny is also displacing young Cade's cum. This is purely a feature of the fan- tasy: he has never done this to me, and it would be highly out of character for him to do so.

I added a new sex scene into *The Spunk Beam* (a spanking scene involving fictional Braden and Ian-Adam, Braden beating a bound Ian-Adam with his hand, with a paddle, with a whip, before fucking his ass with a dildo and then his cock), got ultra-horny again, decided I was hungry, decided to go ahead and get grocery shopping for the day finished.

I knew that Braden wasn't working today, but it was possible that Ethan was still there depending how long his shift was this morning. I liked to imagine that I still—since I had never washed up—had some microscopic residue of his cum-DNA on my cock from having fucked Braden minutes after he had fucked Braden. And it would turn me on a lot if I actually saw him in person right away, so off to the store I went, after selecting my thin linen shorts that I got for our trip to Curacao last summer and which leave

---

I should mention also that a few weeks after this passage was written, I did end up fucking Cade. A few days after his birthday, after the long nightmare of him being "illegal" finally ended, he skipped school and spent most of a morning with me. We had sex first in my house and then, since his parents weren't home, I persuaded him to take me next door to his bedroom so I that could nail him in his own bed like I did many times in my fantasy over most of the previous year. As I suspected, he was in no way virginal at the time of this encounter, claimed to have had a couple dozen dudes before me, and he was very skilled at being an accommodating bottom-boy in the way that some practice provides. I invited him to top me also, and was surprised when he took that offer and did it with great energy. He isn't quite as pretty as Braden (and maybe only like ten percent as smart), but he is very pretty nonetheless and he looks so sweet in the face when he loses his spunk.

no doubt about what's happening if I get a hard-on in public (and which do a pretty good job of showing my meat even in non-erect state).

Ethan was still on duty in produce when I arrived. He was carefully placing big grapefruits in a display. I got close enough to him, approaching him from behind toward his left side, to notice that he had quite large but very slender hands, each one wrapping almost all the way around these fat pink grapefruits as he placed them one by one. He's almost as tall as me, though a fair amount thinner. He has very dark brown hair kind of slicked up into a short pompadour. He looks like a typical Hill Italian kid with dark pretty eyes, big lashes, slightly olive-tinted skin. He used to be clean-shaven but lately he has taken to wearing a thin line of beard on his jaw. It's a very cute affectation for a boy as pretty as he is, especially if he thinks it makes him look older and more mature than his eighteen or nineteen years (it doesn't).

I decided to buy a grapefruit, and said hi to him. He smiled, said hi, and that was about the extent of our interaction, though we did have a fairly extended moment of eye contact while smiling at each other. I was disappointed in myself for this lack of interaction, but I don't know what I *expected* to happen. Did I want

him to ask me right there in the store about what kind of time I had in Braden's bedroom this morning, right after he left it? Did I want him to ask me if I enjoyed fucking his boyfriend and then ask me for all the details? I wanted to tell him somehow that I'd fucked Braden condom-free, my stick lubed with his Ethan-goo, and even that I'd licked some of it from Braden's tight ass-pucker. *I have*, I wanted to say, *already had some of your sweet sperm on my tongue and on my cock and there's probably still some your DNA on my tool right now, you cute young fuck.* I wanted to tell him about the fantasy that I was having of pulling off his pants, stripping his body naked and bending him over the pile of grapefruit and eating out his boy-cunt with a quart of spit and then piston-fucking his cute head off right there in the store in plain sight of all onlookers, how I wanted to fuck him so good he'd spunk out all his boy-batter all over those red grapefruits. But obviously we couldn't have had that conversation there in his work place and my daily shopping place in earshot of his co-workers and customers. So we just smiled at each other, I selected my produce, finished my shopping and went home, pretty much with a raging boner the entire time.

Danny was still going to be gone for a few hours after I got back and fed myself some lunch, so I stripped back down to bare skin and decided I'd work some more on the book. I considered watching porn and masturbating for a while or seeing if I could jack off with someone in a chat room, but that's such a waste

of time when I could be writing, and I was still committed to orgasm denial unless having sex with another guy. If I were to go online in vid chat, some dude would want to see me cum. If I just did phone, I could fake it easily enough, but I ultimately decided that I needed to do something more productive with my arousal, like working on the book some more. Though I did spend a few minutes looking at pics of twinks who had spunked out in their underwear, and I watched a video starring a pretty Russian twink with huge brown eyes and a sweet smile who sucked and got fucked by another dude.[12]

I sipped a few vodka clubs though the rest of the afternoon and worked on the long "first Ethan" scene. This is an account of the first time Jace and Ethan ever have sex, immediately after the boy is brought to the Home, and I am using it to fill in some back-story on Zane for the *Center of the Earth* episode.

---

[12] The other dude had a nice dong and what one could see of his body looked nice but he never showed his face, keeping the whole focus of the camera on his cute bottom boy. I stroked my tool while watching this and just barely denied myself an orgasm because I was profoundly turned on by the style with which the top dude was using this pretty faggot to get himself off. The twink kid sucked the top's fat cock for a little while and then lay on his back and got vigorously cock-drilled. The top hand-jobbed the bottom dude for a minute or two but didn't make him cum. The kid finally came by jacking himself off and blasting a white cream-load onto his smooth belly at about the same time as the top rocked off, spurting sperm in the twink's crotch and on his smooth nuts and jamming some of it into his hole with a bonus post-cum thrust.

I finished the scene, which aroused me intensely, and then I spent a few minutes daydreaming, resisting cumming to this recurring fantasy:

I'm a billionaire super-being cum-pump like Jace Dekka and I spend a lot of time fucking a long wait-list of virgin gay and curious straight dudes who need their first time with a man. A lot of the gay ones I marry after I take their innocence, and I have like a thousand faggot husbands. All of the straight ones get their nuts replaced with cloned copies of mine and they impregnate thousands of chicks who have volunteered to get knocked with my super-sperm and bear my sons. I even join them sometimes, willingly fucking some females in mass orgies with these dudes who are all armed with my enhanced nuts. Some mutations happen and some of my sons as born as maphs who can get knocked up themselves and they are all queer.

My inner circle plots with me to eventually turn my offspring into a fag warlord army that will dominate all the planets of solar system. One of my chief lieutenants brings to me one day a few years ago a trio of newborns for naming, identical triplets that I dub Kasmo, Magnus and Draco. I am told that these three will undergo an amazing procedure that will enhance their intellects and physicalities at amazing speed. I forget about this over the next three years of spreading my seed, during which the number of my offspring explodes and while some of my oldest sons are already fucking and generating some of their own, building a next super-queer generation. I awaken to a message early one morning that I am to have visitors in my bed chamber. I don't know if you remember the triplets from a few years ago, the message says, but you won't recognize them now anyway.

They arrive and I am stunned to see Kasmo, Magnus and Draco again (in this latest iteration of the fantasy they look exactly like Braden). *Just a few years ago they were newborns but now they are grown men. I rise naked from my bed to inspect them. They remove their clothing and stand before me, their identical bodies those of fully-developed males in their early twenties with patches of black glossy pubes and trails of hair from their navels to their very thick and long cocks and I see the thatches of man-musky hair in their armpits and the shadowy scruff of a couple day's unshaven beard on their identical jaws and chins. They smell like they've just come the gym or fucked some men right before they showed up here and I suspect I do too since I haven't bathed since last night when I had a dozen assorted dirty men and twinky boys in my bed for an hours-long fuck-orgy.*

I grasp one of their stiff cocks and pull back his foreskin and expose his dirty cheesy shroom-head. I get to my knees before the dirty hard-cocked boy and raise his rod and see that on the underside of it he has a tiny tattoo of his first initial and I know that this is probably Kasmo whose prick I take into my mouth, slowly sucking and licking away the clotted glaze of dick-smeg and he moans softly and drools pre-jac over my lips and chin. I turn to the next of the brothers, "D" for Draco, and eat his cheese and dick-drool as well and then, finally to Magnus and his even dirtier dong and he whimpers as I suck him and he cries out softly and he spills his semen on my tongue in thick hot pulses.

His brothers laugh at him for cumming so prematurely and he tells them to fuck off and that he's got plenty more of that wet man-fuck where that comes from even if he can't control when he shoots it. But Draco decrees that since

Magnus lost control of his body and came first (and so quickly) that he should also be the first to get his ass fucked by me.

He and Kasmo pull their brother to my bed and push him onto it and tell him to get on his fucking hands and knees for me. I kneel behind him and spread his tight thick ass-cheeks and mash my open mouth into his funky crack and he groans and whimpers and I eat out his cunt shoving my tongue into his sweaty cum-leaky pucker and I can taste that this won't be his first fuck today and I wonder if his bros put their juice in him or if they gave him over to another man like they are doing to him right now. He's such a hot sloppy young slut-fuck that I decide I don't need to give him any lube and I spike his hole hard with my dripping stick and he shouts a loud oh fuck Kyler! and I jam him again and again with it and he keeps shouting my name and his brothers urge me to give it to him harder and harder, fuck him harder Kyler! Kasmo and Draco laugh when my drill-pumping inside Magnus makes him squirt jizz again, adding more wet blobs to the bedsheets, still damp and cum-and-sweat-and-ass-reeking from a few hours earlier.

I roll the boy onto his back and straddle his waist and pump on my post a few times and blast white spew all over his chin and chest. Kasmo announces that now that Magnus has been "punished" for being a premature ejaculator it's probably time to give him a reward. The notion that a hot young dude should be punished for releasing his cream — since it's actually one of the most praiseworthy things a boy can ever do — seems absurd but I like the concept: Kasmo proposes that Magnus — and, in fact, all three

of them — take a turn fucking my ass. You made us, Kyler, Draco says. Let us show you how awesome your work is!

But I had to stop there at that point in the fantasy where my dirty and hung and super-powered triplet sons start taking turns fucking my faggot ass because I needed to deny myself the orgasm and it was so close to happening spontaneously, and a lot of pre-jac had already drooled onto the floor wetting the dried cum medallion under my desk. I took a deep breath and went back to work.

I was still writing and still naked when Danny got home, and I thought he'd be annoyed with me for being naked and kind of buzzed on booze at 4:00 pm, but he was in a good mood and had even planned dinner already and brought home some groceries for it and was ready to start cooking with me.

I put my dirty pre-jac'd and piss-stained carpenter shorts back on, but didn't bother with a shirt. I joined him in the kitchen and he kissed me and remarked that my pits stank like rancid boy-fuck but he didn't request that I wash up. We spent a nice couple of hours having some drinks, smoking a narcowhirl joint and cooking dinner. I told him about my morning fuck-session with young Braden and my brief encounter with his other sex partner at the grocery store. I

assumed he would be bored by this because he is usually bored by my stories, but he was fairly impressed when I related the details of barebacking Braden minutes after the other dude had done the same.

"That's very hot," he said, "but I really wish you wouldn't do that without knowing for sure if he's clean or not." So I left out the other part of it—Braden emptying his nuts inside me. Danny was wearing loose gym shorts and I could see that even though he said my account of the morning was "very hot," it evidently wasn't enough so to make him pop a full boner but he might have been half-staff under the black nylon.

Danny is still stunning and hot: he stands slightly taller than me and is in really good physical shape and he looks a lot younger than he is because his face is still smooth and unlined and he has deep blue eyes and thick lashes. His hair, neatly short with a little swoop over his brow, has gone mostly grey but he distorts this with blond bleach highlights. His ass is a pair of taut bubbles of muscle and he has a huge fucking cock. Mine is above average in size[13], but his is fucking ridiculous. He has always refused to take a

---

[13] My somewhat unscientific data to support this claim comes from my *Fuck Record* where I always document my assessment of the cock-characteristics of dudes with whom I have sex. As of this writing, mine is in the top ninetieth percentile size-wise of cocks with which I have had personal contact. But Danny's is much bigger. It's like in the top one hundred and tenth percentile. It's like a fag-pole turned up to eleven. He really should get a side job in porn—at his age he could be the hot "daddy" in some dad-disciplines-stepson-themed shit. I'd totally go on PornHub and watch him dick-punish his poorly-behaved kid.

measurement, and has always denied ever having measured it — he says it's a dumb dude-bro thing to do — and has denied my every attempt to take a measurement of it but it's got to be ten inches when fully hard because it dwarfs mine which is eight, and he is more of a show-er than a grower so it hangs to great and tempting length even when flaccid. He is welcome to fuck me with it whenever he wants, but he really doesn't want to very often, and that's fine because he gives me a lot of love in other ways.

I am not quite sure when the change happened where Danny became totally fine with me fucking around with other guys without his presence and involvement in it. Early in our relationship, we established that three-ways or groups were cool, but the rule was that we both had to be two of the participants in any such thing and that we had to agree with each other that we both wanted to do the prospective additional partner. And supposedly no behind-the-back secret sex was allowed (but I broke that rule a lot, I must confess).

I think it's part of an evolution in our relationship, and in him, where he is just a lot less interested in sex in general and in sex with me in particular. But he is generous enough to accept the reality that I am still quite libidinal and possibly even a sex "addict" (as he asserts now and then), and that random hook-ups with strangers turn me on. He is older for sure, but I don't think of him as being as old as he sometimes acts. (I turned thirty-eight the year of the events detailed in this book, and he turned forty-six.) Is forty-six old for a dude? Do you just not want sex anymore

by then? Do I only have a couple/few years left of my active libido? Checking my journal, I find that the last notation of penetrative sex with Danny was five months ago. He woke me during the night when he pulled my hand to his cock and encouraged me to stroke it. I eventually got my sleep-dry mouth wet enough to blow him and did that for a while. Then I sat on his pole and took his whole length up my fag-cunt for a couple minutes. Then I rolled off him onto my back and had him sit up, straddle my belly and jack himself off. I put his dick back in my mouth at his moment of climax and swallowed his load. Then I beat off, lying on my back, and popped off on my stomach and chest and annoyed him mildly by executing a full body-roll and smearing my spunk on our freshly-washed sheets defying his wish that semen, once it leaves one of our bodies in bed, needs to be contained inside the other body. Since that occasion, I have had twelve sex encounters with other men (Braden being the only repeat cock-customer, with four times to date), and basically no real orgasms from jacking off because I have been practicing cum-denial that whole time.

Note on denial: it has been typical that sometime in the morning, after taking a piss, I will feel that special sensation that something other than piss needs to leave my body. I get quite aroused, grasp my shaft in my right hand and hold my left hand, palm open, under my cockhead and drip out some male fluid into my hand. Sometimes it's kind of thin and clear like a big flow of pre-jac, but often it's white and spermy

and fills my palm like a full-blown load of baby batter as substantial as it would be if I had truly jacked off to orgasm. I often always lick this from my hand and enjoy its flavor. Sometimes I smeared it over my entire dick, lather my tool with it and enjoy the knowledge that all day long my cock is coated in dried cum.

And it feels so hot, this involuntary release, as if I did orgasm but without the refractory period afterward. I always stay hard for a while and often stain my pants with some more leakage. In this way, I have for months been experiencing routine release of semen from my body but without the after effects of a real solo jack-off orgasm (namely temporary loss of interest in sex and therefore interest in writing porn, which is just bad for business if I am going to be a gay porn writer at least for the duration of the Commander Jace project).

Some days, during age of this denial, such as this morning when I am incredibly aroused, I occasionally reach a state where my dick is tenting my pants and the action of walking around with a hard-on quite nearly stimulates me all the way to orgasm without actually grabbing my pole. This feels especially possible when I am having certain thoughts about things I'd like to do with young men, and especially when I am having a period of occasional hook-ups such as this one with Braden where he is causing all my recent full-on normal orgasms. A couple weeks ago, I was seated on my stool in my home office, writing and masturbating. I intended to continue denying myself a cum-release, but then I wrote this phrase: "long white ropes of my dick-snot on his smooth belly," and

I just kind of lost control. I ejaculated a ton of spunk on the wood floor under my desk. I smeared my bare feet in it, rubbing it into the stain on the floor that I've been building for years. I was kind of annoyed with myself for losing my juice right then because I did not want to have post-cum refractory period right then while I was trying to write, but I persevered, looked at a bunch of twink porn, and was soon enough quite hard again.

6.

By way of contrast, a reflection on a previous boy of summer, one of a much different flavor than that of the current season, but with a common point of creative interest.

Two years ago, almost exactly, I had another recurring summertime hook-up with a much younger man, and one with a writerly bent somewhat like Braden. This was an eighteen-year-old named Nate who also lived in the neighborhood with his father.

I should back up a moment and mention that he was my "student" that summer. For the last three years, I have run a summer advanced course for creative writers at a very expensive local private high school. I took this on as a hobby, an activity to distract myself from my day-job for a while and to do something artistic in a controlled way, something that makes me feel like a "real" writer for a few weeks of the year. I got the job, I think, just because I applied for it and because no real pros in fiction or editing or publishing would have wasted their time with it, and I actually have a few legit writing, editing and publishing credits as a well as a couple of degrees that seem fitting with such a thing as this class.

The course is open to kids going from junior to senior year and from senior year to college. I don't

know how the students who get to take it are selected—they just bring me in to run the class, and for
six weeks each summer I have had about a dozen of
them work-shopping their short stories with me and
their classmates.

Danny thought that this was a singularly bad idea
when I started doing this. "You will," he said, "inevitably think one of those dorky misty-eyed Dead Poets'
Society college-bound boys is just too fucking cute to
ignore and you will do or say something inappropriate to him and then you will invite a shit-storm upon
yourself. There will be scandal, accusations, lies, tears,
a cold meeting with the principal, and your career will
be over!" I reminded him that this school was only
paying me six hundred dollars for the entire course
and that if I got fired from it then it wouldn't very
much impinge upon our lifestyle. At my "real" job,
nobody even knows that I am so fucking literary anyway, so that income stream is probably secure regardless what kind of scandal I embroil myself in at the
school. We'd still be able to afford wine.

So, there was this kid who I'll call "Nate," an
eighteen-year-old "dorky misty-eyed Dead Poets' Society" dude. The students and I met in a classroom
where we sat around a big table with me at the head
of it, and he sat closest to me at the corner to my right.
For this, the second year of my "teaching" at this
school, I changed the format a bit. The first year, we
just workshopped already-existing stories that these
kids had submitted as part of their application to their
class. But it seemed obvious to me that newbies like
this can be inhibited in their work if they are not ready

for what they have written to be read and pulled apart by a group—and most particularly not a group of their fellow students.

So I emailed all of them before the course started and told them that I would like to see a second story that would not necessarily be workshopped in the group, one that I would work with them on individually. It was an experiment to see if any of them came up with anything more honest or interesting than their workshop pieces (most of which were depressing in their dullness).

Some major writer—I can't remember who it was right now—once said something to the effect of writers needing to write a million words of bullshit before they are practiced enough to write something "good." But the thing with these school kids in my class is that—even if they are innately talented or can learn that talent with practice—they just haven't lived long enough (nor usually experienced enough of life) to have banged out their million words of bullshit by the time they reach a seminar taught by a Real Author. So a lot of what they turn in is naive garbage painfully calculated to receive acceptance from their classmates and their teacher. That is to say, it's worse than the bullshit that I think they'd crank out in private as they accumulate their million words. So I wanted to see, just to confirm my hypothesis, if any one of these kids would show me something privately that was any different from what they were forced to show to all their classmates.

One kid, Nate, did just that. The story he sent me was titled "What I Was Thinking While I Gave Him

Head." That title stopped me short because I was certain that I had heard this title somewhere before but I couldn't place it, but then a few pages into reading it—with its drugged and rather affectless main characters—I realized that I was reading something by a boy who had been infected by Bret Easton Ellis (as a lot of boy writers over the last three decades tend to be at one point or another, especially ones with Big Literature hopes and dreams), and the story seemed to be an attempt at an Ellis pastiche, an effort at making something that could live alongside the short stories that make up *The Informers,* almost a fan fiction. And so I finally got the reference. In Ellis's *Lunar Park,* the protagonist (who is simply Ellis himself in an alternate reality) teaches a creative writing seminar at a liberal arts college and he quips with some despair about being bothered by his students who want to know if he has read their stories yet, and the risible example of one such story's title is the same thing as that of Nate's tale (Nate subbed "While" for "When.").

The story itself was a pornographic horror fantasia about (what may be) a teenage male vampire hunter who has fallen (possibly for real, possibly not) into captivity by vampires, who (it seems) eventually sexually thrill him, then sexually mutilate him, and (it is implied) rape and murder him. But it's not quite clear what actually happens at all because the narrator upon whom he hangs this tale is very carefully unreliable. But Nate showed some great facility with language and sensory detail, and he described his homoerotic content in a good enough way that I jacked off

to completion over one of the scenes (literally: I jizzed-soaked a print-out of it).[14] As one might imagine, Nate instantly became my most interesting student.

But I did *not* flirt with him. I adamantly did *not* cruise him for sex. I did *not* favor him like a pet in class discussion, I did not handle him like a bowl of cream in front of his peers. How the sex finally happened was a coincidence perhaps as amazing and even more random than the one by which I finally scored Braden: we accidentally hooked up via Craigslist. He answered my post, we exchanged the obligatory face and cock pics and realized that we already knew each other. "I don't think this is too weird," he said in his email. "If you don't have a problem with it, I will totally do you."

Our first "date" consisted of him coming over to my place one drunken afternoon when I was home alone and we sucked each other off. He was somewhat unconventional in his good looks: oversized ears, a kind of fat stubby nose, totally unkempt reddish hair (Danny would have dismissed him as a "fuckin' ginger"), and his hygiene habits weren't great (though that didn't bother me). But he also had very pretty green eyes with big lashes, dimply chin

---

[14] Earlier this year, I bought from Nate a substantially reworked version of this story for a speculative fiction "fagsploitation" anthology that I am planning to put together, so it may appear in print soon if I ever get the book done. I badly want to retitle the story as "'Suck the Spunk of Jadu!' Said the Blood-Lord," but Nate remains set on his original title. He thinks my alternative is "just too much" (as if "What I Was Thinking While I Gave Him Head" is subtle in its flair).

and cheeks, a slender and decently muscly torso with a few stray hairs around his nipples, and a short but very thick circumcised dick. Our next date the very next day was at his house in his nicely smelly boy bedroom where he agreed to be fucked by me in his ass.

He asked me to come back a couple days later for some more fun and I was surprised to find another man home, this being Nate's father Derek. At thirty-six (my age at the time), I was the same age as this guy who'd evidently sired his boy half his own lifetime ago. I was astonished, albeit delighted, that he already knew that I was Nate's writing "teacher" and that I was there for the purpose of sodomizing his son, and that Nate had told him all about our hook-ups, and that he had no problem whatsoever with me coming by to see the boy and doing him in his bedroom as long as I was "nice" to Nate. This is obviously a huge contrast against what I'd later run into with Braden and his mother whom we needed to keep entirely unaware of the amorous and spunk-soaked ravages that I was perpetrating upon her pretty gay son, upon his perfectly-formed queer body.

I learned from this unusually relaxed father that he had "known that Nate was queer before the kid understood it himself" and that he had always been very supportive of this "because it's his nature and none of my business really what kind of sex he wants to have." We had this uncommon conversation in the kitchen of their home while drinking some wine and smoking cigarettes — and Nate partook of both treats as well, and seemed amazingly nonchalant about being present in the room with his father, and with his

most recent sex partner, and with his own sexuality and his actual sex life being the topic of the conversation. Eventually, Derek announced that he needed to leave because he had a dinner date with a girlfriend of several years, and on his way out encouraged Nate and I to carry on with each other and have fun. There was something amazingly arousing about the fact that I was having sex with Nate being known to the kid's dad and that he was aware that we would be doing it within minutes. This turned out to be so unlike Danny's warning against scandal and lies and tears.

I came with him three times that day: once while fucking his ass, a second time while jacking off and dropping my load into his open mouth and a third time while fucking him again. He came from me jacking him off while fucking him and again from a long wet blowjob.

The following week, I was invited by Nate to hang out and eat dinner with him and Derek. They had a deck behind the house with an aboveground swimming pool adjacent to it. I was again surprised by Derek when encouraged me to get into the pool naked. "If it makes you feel weird, you can wear trunks or your underwear or something," he said, "but Nate and I don't, and I always thinks it's kind of ridiculous to wear clothing in a swimming pool, especially if it's just guys around." And there was a decently high privacy fence around the lot. He clarified, just to be sure I understood, that there was nothing "gay" or "weird" about this in his mind, just that it was sensible to be nude while in water.

He was completely correct, and for the first time I realized how silly basically all swimwear is. Since I wasn't wearing underwear anyway and agreed with him that getting into water wearing my pants or any clothing at all would be silly, I went ahead and stripped. I buttoned and removed my shirt first, laying it over the back of a chair. I shucked off my sandals and then undid the belt and fly of my carpenter shorts and dropped them, all the while trying not to make too much eye contact with either Derek or Nate and hoping that I could actually strip in front of these guys without boning up. Once naked, and blessedly not overly erect, I slid quickly into the water. In the pool, I drank a couple beers with Nate and Derek and chatted about an array of random topics. After a while, Nate decided he was going to fire the grill and cook some stuff for us to eat. He got out of the pool and toweled off. I wondered if he would remain naked from this point onward, but he pulled back on his cargo shorts. Evidently it was sensible to be naked while in the pool (with his father and his lover) but once out of the water some clothing was necessary. I was glad that he stopped at the shorts, however, and remained shirtless. I should mention that it was simply not possible for my cock to not be in some state of erection during most of this, but I decided I wasn't going to worry about whether Derek saw it through the water or not. It was simply out of my control.

Nate went inside the house for a few minutes to gather his stuff for the cook-out, and Derek took this opportunity alone with me to make a rather astonishing statement: "I should tell you," he said, "because I

think you're a good dude, that you need to be careful not to get too caught up in Nate. He's no good for a relationship. Not now anyway."

I was a bit confused because thus far it seemed that there was no problem with the dad as far as my attentions to the son, and I wondered if he was now reversing this position and suggesting that I back off. But that wasn't it. *This* was: "He likes you well enough to use you for some hook-ups, and it's a bonus to him that you help him with his writing. But it's just sex to him. So, I hope you don't start actually liking him *too* much, like a real boyfriend, because you'll probably be disappointed."

Somewhat relieved — if still a bit weirded out by this situation — I assured Derek that he should not worry, and that at this point it was "just sex" to me as well. I elaborated that I have a long-term partner that I expect to be with probably forever but that it's irresistible to me to seek out sex for fun with other dudes, and that's why I met up with Nate in the first place (sex for fun). So, I continued, it's fine that he is "using" me for sex because that's what I am doing with him as well.

I wondered if I had gone a bit too far when Derek, who had previously seemed impervious to any sort of embarrassment, blushed bright and clapped his palms to the sides of his head in a hilarious "too much information" pose. And then he laughed. "That's so cool!" he said. "I am glad you are both on the same page." Derek was a good-looking dude, more or less an older version of Nate, and he looked young enough for his age that he could probably pass as the

boy's older brother. I exerted myself not to look at his penis under the water, but I was curious if it was as thick as Nate's when hard, though I had no expectation of seeing it in that state anyway. This thought passed through my mind: when Derek was Nate's age, he put his hard-on inside someone, spewed out some sperm and created Nate. That thought stiffened my pole, and I hoped that Derek was also making a point of not seeing my cock. But in case he did notice, I made a secondary point of gazing for a few moments at Nate who was now back outside and attending to his grill. If Derek noticed my arousal under the water, it would certainly be attributable to my sexual attraction to Nate and completely expected, or so I assumed.

The next week was the last of the class and Nate and I moved on to other things, but he still shares his writing progress with me.

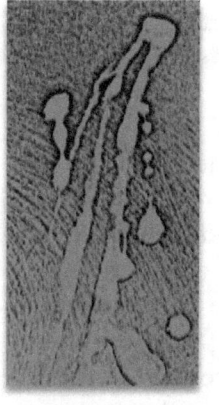

7.

July 21. Recounting several more acts of homosexual lust between the narrator and his lithe paramour; a plan is hatched for a full day of unrestrained sodomy; The narrator considers how to endure a day of passion with a much younger man; speculation as to what constitutes a "time" of having sex; a conversation with a pleasant neighbor; awaiting the arrival of the queer and comely lad; the priapic youth arrives for a day of buggery, and a fermented delicacy is served upon his prick.

I'm typically off from the day job on Mondays, and I value the alone-time in the house when Danny is at work. Mondays for him are usually a very long day and he generally is out of the house from 6:00 am until 5:00 or 6:00 pm, and I tend to get a lot of writing done, at least lately, because of solo-orgasm denial. Under these strictures imposed by my writing demands, I can't spend as much time jacking off as I might otherwise.

Though I shall confess that my regime of denial has hardly been too onerous lately since I have been having one kind of sex or another with Braden nearly every day:

…last Tuesday we sucked each other's dripping cocks in the heat of the park

…and did so again on Wednesday

…and on Thursday, we risked getting out of the car amidst the trees and the hundred-degree heat and I fucked him as he leaned with his hands pressed against a tree, my cock out through the fly of my shorts and snaking up into the raised leg of his mesh shorts

…And then it was Friday. I picked him up from work and took him to Target where we pretended to be shopping for clothes. I asked him to pick out some things that he really liked, that he might really want. "I'll buy you something," I said. "I would like to do that." In the middle of the men's clothes department, he said "thank you, kiddo," and stood on the balls of his feet and gave me a quick kiss on the mouth. This was like a thrilling wet dream: this pretty dude kissing me in public like we were two cute faggot boyfriends on a shopping trip. I don't know if anyone else even saw it as the store was rather sparsely attended that afternoon, but it stiffened my dick instantly: me being seen kissing a much younger boy in public is fucking hot because it makes me *feel* hot about myself when I do it.

He picked out a few shirts and shorts, and I did the same. He led me around me the place, holding my hand. When we had made our selections, we acted like we were entering separately, getting our changing room hanging tags from the dour attendant, and then we met in the same changing stall, where I stripped his naked his lithe body and then fucked the fuck out of his ass and boyed out inside him and then sucked his cute cock off as quietly and quickly as I

could possibly manage (he timed it with his phone: just over four minutes from the entry of my cock into his socket to the release of his nut-stream into my mouth).

And I did end up buying him the clothes that he picked out. He tried them all on and he seemed to puzzle over which one thing that he liked the most, as if he needed to pick just one, and he looked at me wide-eyed when I told him that he would be getting all the items if he liked all of them. "No, that's too much money," he said. I assured him that it certainly was not, that I have plenty of money (especially when dressing a cute young dude is a thing upon which to spend it), and that none of these items were very expensive anyway. We were in Target after all. "I'll take you to Nordstrom next time. I'll let you *really* burn some cash there. But you'll have to make me cum twice for it." He laughed at that, and he said this, and it delighted me: "This is like being a character in a billionaire-porn e-book. Do you know what I mean?"

Of course I knew about the billionaire trope common in e-book erotica (and have parodied it in the *Commander Jace* books by making Jace Dekka so stupefyingly rich that he can give huge trust funds to all his millions of offspring), but this comment by Braden made me wonder about it as an actual erotic hook rather than just a plot device, a McGuffin that makes the rest of story easier to tell without a lot of logic ruining all the fun. I don't usually get into, or even think about, buying things for guys with whom I am having sex, but I really do like buying clothing for a dude like Braden. It's because it's very intimate in the sense that

he will put these items on his body, and he will sweat in them. His new shorts will soon smell like the sweet rankness of his warm skin. He'll get random drips of his piss and preek and cum on them, and they'll smell like this hot boy's body.

As exciting as the Target excursion was, we needed, due to other obligations on both our parts, to take a break from our lust for each other's bodies on Saturday and Sunday.

But it occurred to me to invite Braden to my home this Monday. I wasn't sure if I actually wanted him to be a visitor to there, for him to actually know where I lived in case he somehow turned weird and started wanting more of a real "boyfriend" relationship rather than just a lustful fuck-relationship. But there wasn't a consistent schedule at his own home where it was safe for me to go to his house, and while I liked driving him into the park and sucking on his pretty penis in the car, it's just better and more practical to be in someone's house for sex, especially if one wants to ass-fuck, a thing almost too difficult to do in a car as to be worth it, and rather dangerous to do in public (though that has not stopped us thus far).

So I told him that if he was free all day this Monday, he could come over to my place as early as 7:00 am and stay as late as 5:00 pm if he wanted and we could see how many times we could manage to have sex in a single day. And shortly after issuing that invitation, I could amend the timeframe of it because Danny told me that he was going to be away for a couple days at a conference in Kansas City, one that he

was attending in lieu of another member of his team who could not attend for whatever reason.

I've said before that I would have liked to have seen if I could have had sex with Braden at least a hundred times before he turns twenty. But I wonder now what exactly constitutes a "time." It's straightforward if, for example, a Craigslist dude comes for a "blow-n-go," sucks me off and leaves. That's one time. There's a gang of dudes that I have had sex with one single time like that. If Danny were to fuck me tonight (yeah, right), blow a big load of cocksnot in my gut, roll over and go to sleep, that would be another time with him. But if Braden and I have an all-day fuck-a-thon for ten hours, is that also one time? What if I cum eight or ten or twelves times during that day, cum and cum again until I am totally out of semen and make the same happen to his body? I briefly decided to re-define a "time" with him as *me cumming*. When I get my rocks off with a dude, that's a "time." So, the times when I fucked him and came and then jacked off on his face and came again during the same session should count as two times. But I quickly saw the flaw in defining this solely and rather selfishly just by me getting off. What if I blow Braden, suck him all the way off, drink his jizz and then he leaves for some reason and I do not cum in any way by any means with him? That must also count as a "time" because I would have given him a blowjob, which is plainly having a sex act with him even if I don't also get blown and pop a load. After further meditation upon this, I remembered that I have in fact experienced a fair number of "times"

with guys where I did not cum. There was the time when I was senior in high school and I let a thirty-year-old teacher bone my ass in a storage closet—he came but I did not, because as soon as he was done, *we* were done (I had matured a fair amount in my attitude toward sex in the three years since getting on my knees for Jonny Petersen and had come to expect my partners to make me shoot a load, and so I denied that man a second hit at my hole since he was set on *not* getting my rocks off). There was also the time a few years ago when I fucked Danny for a long time but never got off because I was simply too drunk. I am sure I could find some more examples. I decided I'd tell him about my project of doing him a hundred times and we'd decide together which specific acts counted as a specific time.

I spent a few minutes trying to decide what, if anything, I would be wearing when Braden arrived. When I have a guy over for a one-time hookup, I always consider answering the door naked, but that seems kind of silly, and I always decide that it will be hotter if I am wearing at least a little something that I then need to strip off in front of him or make him remove from me.

I dug into the underwear drawer. I either wear underwear or pants but never both. I think it's just too much to have two layers of fabric covering my ass and my meat, and since I am kind of an exhibitionist I like being in public and letting my pole push out against the front of my pants knowing that if someone happens to look at my crotch they will know without any doubt that I am a horny male. I selected a black jockstrap-style brief, a good choice in that it made an awesome meat-pouch out of my junk and left my ass cheeks completely bare. I added a black tank top and purple rubber sandals.

Immediately after I dressed, Braden sexted me with a selfie, naked in bed, *(awake and ready!)* smiling, and another of his hand gripping his stiff prick. I texted back, told him that he is beautiful in the morning, that his penis is beautiful in the morning, and that he was welcome to show up whenever. *Do you want me to pick you up?*

He replied that he would like to walk, it's not far, he'd be on the way in a minute after he got ready. *"Don't shower or put on deodorant,"* I replied. *"I want you to smell like whatever it is that you smell like when you get out of bed in the morning. If I think your pussy needs washing before I eat the fuck outta it, I'll wash it here. If your dick is kind of cheesy this morning, I'll clean it up with my mouth."*

After a quick breakfast of oatmeal and blackberries, I stepped outside onto the upper back deck, smoked a cigarette, drank a cup of coffee and watered a few plants. It was already a very warm July morning. Braden would probably sweat a bit on his walk

and smell even sweeter. I traded the coffee for a huge mimosa and did a little more watering of plants. Arthur, the tenant who rented from us the downstairs level of the house, appeared in the yard with his own watering can, attending to his potted plants on the terrace below. He wore his typical summer garb, a bright aloha shirt, khaki shorts, flip-flops and one of those British jungle hats. He had been our only tenant the whole fifteen years we had owned this house, and he was a good, amicable neighbor. He said a cheery good morning. I always liked his voice, this strange patrician Mid-Atlantic accent that reminded me of William F. Buckley or Gore Vidal, and I always wondered when and where he'd picked that up since I think he is native to Saint Louis. Since I was facing forward, he probably couldn't quite see my bare ass, but it would have been no big deal if he could have seen it. He'd caught me fully naked down in the back yard more than once over the years. He had been retired for years from some kind of job with Boeing, and passed his days with various hobbies and a "lady friend" as he called her — her name is Gwynn — that he goes on dates with or has over to his place for dinner. He's a respectable home chef. I am not sure how old Arthur is other than old enough to be have been retired for a while. He is one of those people who could believably be any age from sixty to ninety depending on how the sun hits him. He wasn't at all gay, but he was very positively disposed toward "the young queers" of the neighborhood as he liked to call me and Danny and some of the other neighbors on our very fag-dense street. He even held a block party for the immediate

neighborhood when same-sex marriage was legalized. [15]

"Are you planning to be home all day?" I wondered.

"Actually, no. I have some rather full plans away from the house today," he said, and then gave me a long look as if to wonder why I'd asked.

"That's probably for the best," I said, "because if you were going to be here, you might notice rather more noise penetrating through the ceiling during the day than is normal for a Monday."

"So," he said, grinning. "You are planning something quite fun, I guess?"

"I'm having a very pretty young man over in just a few minutes. I intend to make strident love to him throughout the entire day. He may spend the night as well."

Arthur laughed long and loudly. "Even if I were home and overheard it, you know it wouldn't disturb me in the least. You boys used to party a lot more

_____

[15] If my understanding of Kyler Fey's chronology is correct, the legalization of same-sex marriage in our state (which did not happen until the Supreme Court mandated it for the entire country) had not happened yet and would not for another year (I think that *One Hundred Times* must be set in 2014). It is true that the city of Saint Louis and the adjacent county started issuing marriage license to queers earlier than the Supremes' order after a lower court ruling against the state's marriage ban, but I don't think even this move by the city had happened yet. It's not a big deal for the purpose of this story, but it jumps out at me because I have also noticed a lot of weird "retconning" in his *Jace* fiction in which previously-established history appears to no longer pertain. — Editor

loudly than you have in recent years." That statement was certainly true. Arthur had known us for a long time. He finished his watering and exhorted me to have a "brilliant" time with my "young visitor."

The night before, contemplating my day-long sex-date with Braden, I mulled over the topic of my own physical capacity for a day-long sex session. At thirty-eight years old, I did not kid myself that I could fully keep up with the capacious cum-capacity and superior erection durability of a man almost twenty years my junior, a nineteen-year-old boy who was probably at or near the apex of his physical prime. But I am still pretty cum-capable multiple times a day when sufficiently aroused, and I decided that I did not need to match Braden shot for shot, but just stay busy enough with him that he would be pleased all day and just let my own orgasms happen at the right times.

I had some things around that could help if I decided I needed them: a vial of poppers, some Viagra that I got after lying to my doctor that I had erectile dysfunction because I wanted to experiment with it as a recreational sex drug, a few old desiccated tabs of Erec-T. And there was something else that I doubted I would ever again touch: a couple little rocks of coke that have been sealed in a vac-bag in the bottom of my

underwear drawer for the last twelve years. I assume that shit expires at some point, but I don't really know, and I haven't been seriously tempted to find out since I stowed it there. But it sits there under my seldom-worn briefs and jockstraps like an erotic chemical talisman reminding me of some fucked-up nights in my twenties when I did believe that it was giving me crazy all-night fuck-stamina.

The buried coke plays a role in a recurring morning masturbation fantasy, one that I'd been having off and on over the last few years when waking up before dawn, kind of hungover and with that intense hangover horniness (do all dudes experience that? I know I always do.) that makes me want to lie in bed and fuck my fist and massage my nuts for an hour before attempting to rise even though I feel kinda like shit and need some coffee and fried eggs and sausage and hash browns and a screwdriver. In this fantasy, I snort the coke which has somehow become of a transformative vector of sexual augmentation and superiority. My body instantly undergoes some changes: my cock gets much longer and thicker, its fat shroom-head widens, and my cum-hole doubles in diameter. My nuts swell to twice their normal size, all the muscles of my body spontaneously harden and swell and tone, and for some reason, as I achieve this enhancement, I am in a vast gym locker room with a gang of twinky young men, twenty-one of them in various states of partial dress, and some of them are naked from having just gotten out of the shower or having just stripped off their swim trunks. They watch me with an affect of

dumb amazement as I pull on my pole, jacking off under the duress of a level of horniness that even I have never felt. Soon I cum but it's unlike any other climax that I have ever reached: from my huge veiny hose fires pulses and pulses of white ropey jizz that launch meters from my body and strikes the chests and faces of the young men watching me. They are shocked, but they cannot look away and some of them even come closer, some of them even kneel. One of them is brought to his knees when he slips on a slick of semen. And it continues: the cum-flow increases until it's like a garden hose spray of thick milky snot, and it splashes and splatters on all twenty-one of these dudes, soaking their hair, soaking whatever clothing they are still wearing. Those who are wearing trunks or shorts or jocks remove them, discard them on the cum-flooded tile, and they kneel closer as I continue to blast them with gallons of my hot ball-froth. These are all quite young men — some of them have never had sex before, some of them have never even seen another dude's cock while stiff. And then their own transformations begin: a skinny boy barely into post-adolescence and maybe four and a half feet tall suddenly grows a full two feet in a matter of seconds and new muscles bulge from his chest and belly and his cock grows until it's as big — even bigger — than mine. In quick succession, similar changes happen to all these boys. Most of them were actually straight before, but skin-contact with my supernatural homo-cum firehose has made every one of them a committed and incredibly horny fag. Some of them stroke their newly enormous pricks and squirt fountains of

cocksnot in a few seconds while some of them set upon each other in an orgy of cocksucking. Even after my impossible ejaculation, I don't need a break, and I take all twenty-one of them, one after the other in just a few minutes, and put a quart of seed in each of their assholes, fucking their young and buff and cum-sticky bodies, their hair still literally lathered in my spunk, on locker room benches. As each one gets his gut filled with my juice, the others cheer. This has yet another magical effect: like some kind of gay cum-vampire overlord, I find that I have enslaved all of them to me by breeding them, that I am now their master, that they will now be my faggot wild boy army that I will set loose upon the planet to conquer its every quarter and install themselves as invincible princes of unrestrained sodomy over the delighted and helpless masses.[16] Lately, when I have this fantasy, lying in bed, I do not—despite the enormous

---

[16] A psychiatrist that I saw briefly (mostly in dumb hope of getting a Klonopin prescription) suggested to me that this kind of blatantly narcissistic and megalomaniacal sex fantasy (there are many, many others like it) is probably rooted in the shame and persecution that I felt as a queer adolescent and that I have perhaps not resolved some old trauma. (Like, you think?) I asked if I should, then, somehow quit having these fantasies, and how would she suggest that I make a clean break from them given that they seem to be part and parcel of my own individual sexuality? Should I try to bury this part of me, by somehow denying myself these fantasies, under a surf of guilt and shame the same way that I tried to when I was a stressed adolescent? This query seemed to create an impasse in our conversation. And Klonopin was a shitty idea for me, too, so I quit seeing her after I tried that scrip. Vodka worked, and continues to work, much better. Though it's probably destroying my organs.

amounts of semen that I discharge in my imagination — let myself actually cum because I must continue with this regimen of staying horny enough to work on the *Jace* books at any available moment. I get horrendous blue-balls, but eventually it drains, an awesome and hot but not-quite-orgasmic ejac in my hand after I piss.

But I decided it was best to start by following my own normal regimen of staying very well-hydrated, not drinking too much booze the night before the date, and pacing my drinking during it. I have recently admitted to myself that I probably am a real alcoholic, but I comfort myself with how high-functioning I seem to be with this condition. But I still drink way too much, and knew that I would need to be aware of that fact during an all-day Braden-boning lest I become too drunk and go limp.

Braden arrived with a cute mop of bed-head hair rising awry over his brow. I kissed him on the front porch, deliberately in view of a couple people who were getting into cars parked on the street in front of my house, and then pressed my nose and mouth into both of his armpits. He was damp with sweat and smelled like a kind of candy made of caramelized young men. He wore loosely-belted olive shorts — one

of the items that I had bought for him at Target the other day — that seemed to barely stay on, hanging below the rise of his hip bones, revealing a bit of his pubic hair above the belt. It seemed that if it were not for surface tension provided by the pronounced bubble of his ass, they would not be able to remain aloft upon him as he walked up the stairs and into my home. He also wore a blue and white striped tank top that seemed a size or two too small for him and which left a strip of exposed midriff between the bottom of the shirt and the low-slung belt of his pants. His feet were clad in white Vans and no-show socks. He removed these foot items first as soon as he entered the living room. He sneezed hard several times and wiped his nose on a clump of his shirt. "Sorry," he said, "I think it's a bad allergy day, but I took my medicine. It should kick in."

He raised his arms and I stripped him of his snotty shirt. I undid his belt and his shorts fell from his hips. He kicked them aside. I pulled down his white button-fly trunks and his cute cock sprung upright. "Are you sure," he said, pulling his skin fully back from his shroom head, "that you actually like it *this* dirty? I haven't washed this fuckin' thing since last time you were down on it." He showed me how his cockhead was glazed with sticky curds of boy-cheese. I dropped to my knees, examined it up close and smelled its stench and tasted its tang. He murmured softly, and I cleaned his stiff dirty dong with my spit and my tongue.

8.

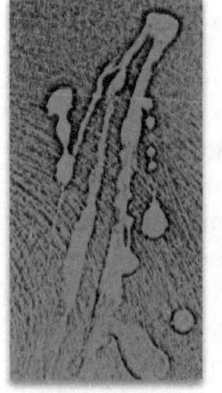

The young man shits, and the narrator indulges with his mouth in lust upon his lover's orifice; they experiment with a novel enema; some comments on the lad's body hair; a vigorous act of sodomy upon the narrator's living room floor; clearing the young lover's sinuses by a new means; more fluids injected into the lad's gut; the narrator exposes himself during an intimate bodily function; an experiment with make-up; they reverse positions and the boy sodomizes the narrator using an unusual lubricant.

Braden wanted to take a dump before he'd A-OK me eating out his cunt or sticking my prick in his hole. He wanted me to watch him do it, and he wanted me to wash his ass after he was done. I led him into the master bathroom, and he immediately squatted over the bowl. He didn't actually even sit on it, just lowered himself over it, bent low, grunted loudly and immediately ejected a couple logs of shit which splashed in the water, and a short spray of piss which landed mostly on the floor. "Sorry!" he said. I said nothing but indicated my approval of his piss by stepping in it with a bare foot and smearing it about on the tile. He was done with his shit in less than a minute. To

clean his ass, I didn't want to give him a full shower because I didn't want to destroy his perfect morning-sweat boy-stench, so I had him stand with his ass to the sink and I washed his crack and hole with water and little bit of soap the way I often do my own after I dump.

After I was finished, I had him turn around, face the sink, lean against it with his legs spread. I got to my knees, spread his ass-cheeks wide with my hands and inserted my tongue into his anus as deeply as I could. It felt like there was probably still a little bit of shit up inside there, which doesn't really bother me too much when I am eating out a dude's cunt, but it gave me an idea. I asked him if he'd ever had a club soda enema.

He was intrigued. "If you want to try it," I said, "I will squirt a liter of cold club soda into your gut. You'll see if you can hold it for a minute and then you'll blast it out onto the floor of the shower." He was game, so I went to the kitchen, grabbed a bottle from the refrigerator, retrieved my special "Apparatus" for this from my underwear drawer and returned to the bathroom. The Apparatus is a short tube, one of end of which pops over the opening of the bottle while the end slides into the dude's ass about four inches. it's hard to get all the liquid in there quickly sometimes because of pressure resistance inside the dude, but it usually works pretty well. "It's going to be cold," I advised, "and you might actually cramp a little bit, but it will pass quickly and it won't hurt you. I put a thick towel down on the floor of the shower stall to cushion his back and head, and had

him lie down face up and raise his knees to his elbows and open his pussy as if I were about to fuck him.

(A note on the shower: when Danny and I renovated the house, a structural issue precluded extending the kitchen and making it as big as I wanted to be — at least without spending a lot more money than he'd endorse — but as a compromise, he agreed to blow out the wall in between the master bathroom into what had been an extraneous third bedroom and make that an enormous luxury bathroom. We installed a giant shower area, curtainless and with enough space and spray heads for half a dozen dudes to be in it all at once as well as a soaking tub that one can comfortably bathe in with a partner. A perhaps somewhat weird feature of the shower chamber that always invites questions and comments from guests: it has an Asian-style squat toilet in one corner of it so that you can lower down and take a shit in the floor if you want to while showering. This was Danny's idea and he does this every morning, dumping his bowel with shower heads raining down in him; I do it sometimes, too, instead of using the sit-down toilet, but always when he is not in the room).

I lubed the ass-end of the tube and jammed some lube into his hole, and then quickly inserted the tube, upending the bottle. I squeezed and gave it a few shakes and he yelled a loud "oh fuck!" as it emptied quickly into his gut. I pulled the tube out and asked if he could hold any of it for any length of time at all. "I don't think so, kiddo!" he said. He rose into a squat, shoved the towel away and sprayed foamy soda on the shower floor along with another little glob of shit

which I picked up and tossed into the toilet. "Holy fuck! I guess," he said, "I'm pretty good and cleaned out now!"

Details of Braden's body hair seem worth noting, at least to me. He has a moderate and trimmed bush of pubes and just a hint of a trail up toward his navel, and some fuzz on his nuts. But he has no hair to speak of in his ass crack and none at all on his chest, not even a few shaved-off stray hairs around his nipples. I remember being his age and having no chest or abdomen hair even though I had full pubes by time I turned twelve. I still don't have much chest hair, and what I do have I tend to get rid of periodically, but Braden's torso looks like it's never even sprouted any. But he does have a thick thatch of sweaty black fur in his armpits with makes my mouth water. This was the first piece of him that I tasted that morning he finally arrived, sweating and clad in his minimal summer attire. He's exactly the kind of minimally hairy, lithe and barely legal boy that I sometimes think I want to put in a fuck-harness and bind with cuffs and straps and then fuck him alternately with a dildo and my dong and milk his balls dry until he cries and begs me stop atop and says he can't cum another time but I make him cum another time anyway. I might even

blindfold him but I wouldn't ball gag him because I'd want the neighbors to hear his cum-moans and cries for cock-mercy through the open windows. This is all if I were actually into bondage. But I don't know if I really am because I have had little opportunity to experiment in the genre. But t gets me stiff to write about it, so I might need to get some more real-life experience in it.

We fucked on the living room floor. First, I knelt and he took me from behind, on his knees, slamming his pole into my hole with great enthusiasm. "Louder, baby," I prodded. "I wanna hear how much you like fucking me! Make the fucking neighbors hear it!" He raised the volume on his moaning, his fuck-panting, high keening cries of pleasure. He told me how tight I am, how fucking good it feels to stab me with his prick, how I'm gonna make him bust his fucking nuts with my tight boy-cunt. And things of that nature. When he was ready to do just that, he pulled out and ordered me lie on my back. He stood over me, feet to each side of my thighs, aimed his rod downward and rained his batter upon me. A few drops landed in my open mouth, one in my eye, more of it on my chin and neck and chest. He lowered himself on top of me and kissed me and licked his jizz away from my face.

"Your turn now, baby. Use me just like that. My hole to make you cum!"

I rolled him off me and onto his back and told him to grab his knees and open his pussy wide for me. I licked and slobbered on his pucker for a few seconds, pulled it open with my fingers and hawked a thick streamer of spit into it and slimed my dick with some more drool. I aimed my shroom head into the hole, pushed it past his ring and he sobbed with glee. The spit was sufficient lube, and I slid in and out easily. As I drilled his body, I reached into his crotch with one hand and massaged his taint, pressing in just a bit harder than a normal caress and he moaned more loudly. I was sort of massaging his prostate from outside his body with my fingers and from inside with my dong. He thrilled me by being even noisier now than he had been fucking my ass. "Do that! Kyler! *That!*" he gasped. "Keep doing it!" Evidently I was hitting him just right: he gasped, grabbed his cock and instantly squirted another load onto his belly. And that pushed me over the edge: I withdrew, scooted forward, aimed at his face and fired. I enjoyed a crude manly delight that this spunk-load was quite copious, possibly the biggest one I could recall having shot lately. He lay there, grinning and spattered, and he cooperated as I carefully smeared my semen over pretty much every square inch of his face and neck.

"What else can we do like that?" Braden wondered. "Like the club soda enema. I wonder what else you can put inside me like that." I told him that if he would tolerate me inserting the neck of a bottle into

his rectum, it was theoretically possible for me to pour a bottle of beer or a glass of wine into his cocksocket and then for me to drink it from him as he shat it out. So we did this too. I put him on his back on the steel prep table in the kitchen, as if I were about to prep him like meat for dinner. I ended up drinking a good deal of two beers and some white wine from him like this. Since I was rather a mess anyway, I invited him to take a piss in my hair.

His nose was leaking again, a slow flood of clear loose ooze that he wiped away with his hand. I think I can help you with that runny nose, I said. I asked him if he would let me try to clear out his nasal cavity by sucking the snot out of his nose. He looked at me with some skepticism. I didn't know if it would even work, having never tried it nor having even been tempted to try such an outré thing before. "That is kinda super-weird, dude," he said. "But if you are into it, you are welcome to try." But how gross *is* it really anyway? Especially after some of what we had already done, just sucking out some runny snot from his pretty head? Was this fluid from his body any more repellent for any logical reason than his spit or his piss or his sweat or his semen, all of which I had drunk as delicacies?

I clamped my lips over his nose and sucked very gently. I tasted his hot snot immediately. He exhaled though his nose and I got a lot more of it. I sucked for another minute or so, and he blew out some more. This actually *was* kind of weird, and really (if I am honest about it) *not* at all as hot as having him fill my mouth with semen, but it stiffened my pole anyway, which he grabbed and stroked while I continued to drain goo from his head, so much of it that it felt as if my mouth would fill nearly to capacity in between each salt-syrupy swallow. When the nose-drool stopped and he seemed to be clear of it for the moment, I pulled away from his face and smiled at him. "Is that better, baby?" He said, in fact, that he felt much better. And how was it for you? he wondered. Everything you ever dreamed of? I laughed and confessed that it's not something I'd necessarily want to do every day nor with just anyone. "But if your pill wears off again and you need me do it again today, let me know and I will!"[17]

For all the openness that I have to any sort of sex behavior with men, and my general willingness to expose my body and its functions to others, I had never

---

[17] Interestingly enough, in the almost two years since these events with Braden happened, I have had sex with several other men, including another summer fling last year with another teenager, and I have yet to suck snot out of anyone else's nose, nor have I felt even slightly interested in doing so. I guess it was just something especially perfect about Braden as a perfect erotic object that made me ready not just to try anything with him that he was willing to do, but also to make up new things to do that neither of us had done with previous partners.

shat in front of another dude even once in my adult life, even though I'd been in the restroom plenty of times while other dudes were doing it front of me, and had just watched Braden do it a short while earlier. I don't even do it in front of Danny even though he casually does it in front of me in the squat toilet in the shower even when I am in the shower with him and sometimes I'll even take a morning piss *on* him while he does it. Because our master bedroom opens directly into that big bathroom with no provision for privacy, I always relieve myself either when Danny is not in the bedroom or I use the half-bath next to the kitchen in order to not be seen taking a dump. The last time I did it at all in front of someone — and I actually remember it vaguely — was when I was being potty-trained by my dad and being praised for taking a baby-dump in the "big" toilet.

So, Braden's insistence on being present for this, as I was when he did it earlier, was a challenge. But he had a good point: "Dude, you watched me shit and then you washed my ass. And then you gave me a club soda enema and basically forced me to take a huge wet fizzy dump in front of you, which made me shit on the shower floor, and you picked that up with your bare fingers, and I bet you thought about eating it *[he was perhaps correct]*, and then later you poured beer and wine into my ass from bottles that you stuck inside me and then you fucking *drank* that beer and wine out my ass! And you are now too shy to let me see you on the toilet! Really!"

But I felt some bodily urgency about it, and he had made it clear that he wasn't going to give me privacy,

so I sat on the bowl of the bowl of the conventional toilet, not the in-shower squatter, and did it, full eye contact with grinning Braden the whole time. He knelt in front of me and pulled my mouth to his and we kissed. My cock stiffened and stuck upward over the toilet seat. I pushed my way into the bowel action, and piss sprayed from my stiff stick and spattered Braden's torso. It dripped into his short pubes and onto his hard-on. He stood and put his prick in my mouth and let piss leak. I sucked on it, sucked my piss off his cock his piss out of his bladder and into my stomach, as I started to shit. He got back onto his knees and took my dick into his mouth. I squirted more piss into his throat and he swallowed it. The dump itself was a quick and mostly liquid affair. Evidently the blackberries, oatmeal and mimosas that I'd pounded for breakfast before his arrival had already worked their way through, and exited rather quickly and cleanly. I remained seated while flushing the toilet and let him clean me up as I did for him earlier. The event was remarkably hot, particularly when he asked me to stand, legs spread, leaning against the sink, and he, on his knees, pushed his face into my ass-crack and gave me a deep-tongue rim-job for what felt like a long time.

I asked him if he ever put on make-up. I told him that I thought he'd look like an astonishingly exotic andro-gyne (in the face at least—maybe not so much in the rest of his very *cis*-male body) if he had on some black eyeliner. He was willing to try it, so I applied it for him. We liked the look but he hated the process of it, worried that I'd accidentally poke his eye with the applicator, and he said that we'd not likely be doing this again. I also painted his fingernails purple, but we decided that we did not like that result at all, so we removed it right away. I suggested that his ballsack would be even cuter if it were perfectly smooth so he let me shave away its light fuzz (he'd complain a couple days later that it was itchy when it started to grow back).

In the refrigerator, he finds a wine bottle, slams a deep swallow of it, puts it back and pulls out a can of Reddi-Wip. "I wanna shoot this into your ass and cover my cock with it and fuck you with it. I wanna pretend that it's a spray can full of my cum that's somehow been aerosolized into a fuck-foam to use as a lube in faggots' asses." Put like this, the only plausible or possible response to this proposition is yes and *fuck yes*. We do it on the kitchen floor, me on my hands and knees. I figure that this floor will need a mopping eventually. Though I'd paper-toweled up a lot of the spilled Braden-ass beer and wine and his piss that my hair didn't soak up, there are still puddles of all of it by the prep island and his can of fuck-foam portends a further mess. He extends this whipped cream sod-omy for ten or fifteen minutes continually adding

more foam (which, by the way, is *very* cold when first dispensed!) to his cock and my cunt until the can is spent and then he is spent suddenly and with a loud and deep scream, leaving his real cream inside me.

Though I'd toweled it mostly dry, my hair actually smelled like Braden-piss to the point that it was kind of bothering me. I told him that I needed to rinse it. "Your hair's a big mess," he agreed. "I'll fix it for you." He took my hand and drew me along to the bathroom. "Face down, kiddo," he commanded. "Hands and knees, please." I dropped to the shower floor in the same position that that I'd been in during the kitchen fuck with Reddi-Wip. He turned on water and pulled a spray hose from the wall. He soaked my head with it, flushing filth from my hair. "I don't want to overdo cleaning us up, but this shit's sticky," he said, speaking now of the whipped cream. He gave my ass-crack a quick hosing and his crotch as well. "I'm not washing *your* junk though," he said. "I want your dick to keeping smelling and tasting like you've been fucking me." He took me to the vanity, towel-dried my hair and set to work on it with fingers full of pomade. He molded my hair into a spiky faux hawk and pronounced it to be "fucking cute." What was also *fucking cute* was this boy dominating me in this way, fucking my much older ass and then washing it for me, deciding how to restyle my hair.

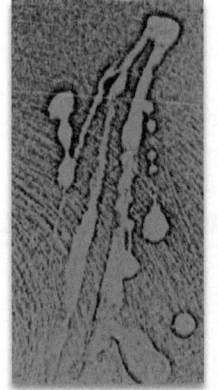

9.

Adding some artwork to his young lover's body; sharing cherries in an amorous fashion; a fantasy about an amazing new kind of sex organ; a messy and lavish lunch; an appreciation of kissing; Braden enjoys a remarkable snack

I used the post-fuck recovery time to add artwork to Braden's body. He'd shown me how he had set a pic of my cock that he'd taken earlier, when I was hovering over his face with it, as the background pic on his phone, and I was inspired to improve upon that. I got out the big jar of Sharpies — dozens of colors — that I kept on my desk in my office. I took his phone and opened the pic. He lay down on the area rug on the living room floor, and I set the open phone on his belly and, using the picture as a model, proceeded to draw a colorful and detailed picture of my cock on his inner thigh, the head of it crowning just inches below his nutsack. He laughed a lot during this because the action of my markers on his skin tickled him, but he held still well enough for me to do a very good (I feel) rendering of my meat on his skin, luridly colorful, complete with my big low-hanging ballsack and thick veiny shaft and wide mushroom head and the deep cleft of my cum-slit. I embellished it with a long and twisting fluorescent

streamer of semen arcing up his thigh through his short thick pubes and onto his abdomen and into his navel. I added to it this graffito in crooked, bold letters: *"Kyler's Cock: I Own This Shit!"* With his phone, I took some pics of my work, sent to myself a couple of them, and handed the phone back to him. Delighted, he immediately replaced the real pic of my dick with one of the drawing on his leg and its assertion that he owns my cock. "I *do* own this fucker, you know!" he said. In that moment, and throughout that day, I could not disagree.

Braden announced that he was hungry and started browsing through the kitchen to see what I might have on offer. I told him that soon my friend Zach from Taikonaut, the Chinese-Korean restaurant on the next block, was bringing over to us some stuff for lunch, but if he needed a snack right then, he could have freely at whatever was on hand. He looked over the fruit and vegetables on the side counter. "Do you like cherries?" I said. "They're really good!" He looked at the bowl of shiny, deep red orbs, considering it.

"I like the way they taste," he said, "but I hate trying to eat around the pits." He smiled at me. "Can you

take the pits out for me and feed them to me?" He laughed at himself for being so demanding.

"If you let me feed you like a bird feeding his baby bird, then I will do it." We looked at each, smiling, for a moment until he registered what I was proposing.

He nuzzled his forehead under my chin and whispered, "Feed me cherries like a baby bird, daddy!"

I took one into my mouth, chewed it carefully to dislodge the pit, removed the pit from my mouth, bit the flesh into smaller bits and drew Braden close, his mouth to mine. He opened wide and I dropped the mashed fruit and a lot of cherry juice spit onto his tongue. He chewed, savored for a few moments and swallowed. "That's the only way I am ever eating cherries again!"

"You want another one?"

"More, please! I want *six* more!"

Six more times, I fed him a cherry from my mouth to his, and each time it became more of a wet tongue kiss. By the time we finished the last one, both of our lips and chins were stained and glazed with juice.

I told Braden that sometimes when I rim a dude — or fantasize about rimming one while waxing my pole — I imagine having a cock-tongue that I can fuck him with. He was intrigued by this concept and I told him

to check out an erotic fiction website called Metabods in which the writers tell stories involving dudes with all kinds of fantastical bodily transformations such as impossibly huge cocks and balls, multiple cocks, multiple limbs, and any number of other variations. I told him that I read a story on this site in which two teenage friends are snooping around under one of the boy's older brother's bed and they find two little dildos designed to fit over one's tongue. They decide to put them on their own tongues which then transform by magic into cocks. Caught by the older brother, who alone can undo the magic spell, they are not released from this bizarre circumstance until first giving the older dude an ass-fucking by little bro's mouth-cock while big bro sucks off the other boy via his mouth-cock. This is so arousing to the boys with penises for tongues that they unload jizz both from their mouth-tools and their regular cocks. "If I could temporarily transform my tongue into a cock," I said to Braden, "I'd fuck your ass with it. If you could turn your tongue into a cock, I'd give you a blowjob by sucking off that thing and making you blow a nut right out your pretty mouth." Delighted with this premise, he asked me to draw another picture on his body, this, on his chest: a cartoonish rendering of Braden's head and neck, mouth agape, looking up at himself with huge manga eyes, his mouth wide open and, flopping out of it, a giant and lavish uncut dong leaking a fall of pre-jac. In tiny letters, on the shaft of the cock-tongue, I wrote: "Kyler! Suck this fucker now!"

Lunch would soon arrive, so I suggested to Braden that we have it outside on the deck. We covered our asses and cocks — his with the shorts he'd worn to my place that morning, mine with a pair of khaki carpenter shorts. I pulled on a white tank-top but Braden decided to eschew his shirt for the rest of the day. I'd asked Zach to bring the food through the back gate and upstairs to the deck, and as he arrived and made his way through the garden, Braden leaned over the table and whispered, "That dude's fuckin' cute!" I used to fuck him, I said. Delighted, Braden wondered, "Would he want to join us a for a little while?" No, I said. I'll explain later.

Zach scaled the stairs. "You weren't specific with your order," he said, setting a couple bags and a six-pack of Sapporo down on the table, "so I hope you both like what I picked out for you."

"I like everything!" Braden said, pulling open one bag and peering inside it.

"He's a very hungry boy," I said. Zach smiled, extended his hand toward Braden, they shook and introduced themselves. Zach remarked favorably upon the drawings that I'd inked onto Braden's body. And Braden briefly opened and hiked down his shorts to expose the entirety of the one on his inner thigh (and

his naked meat to Zach). "But I hope they're not permanent!" he said. Braden said, "No, but," and showed Zach his phone screen displaying the first pic.

"Can you stay for a bit?" I asked Zach, knowing what his answer would be. "Have some lunch and beer with us?"

"I'd love to," he said, (and I think he actually winked at Braden), "but I must get back to the shop. Somebody called off this morning, so I have to close the kitchen myself today." he told us to enjoy the food, said he'd hope to see us again soon, and left to walk back to Taikonaut.

As soon as he was out of earshot, I filled Braden in on my past with that handsome Asian dude: "Danny and I lent to him and his partner some of the money for them to open Taikonaut. Later I had a sexual affair with him where he would often come over here on Monday afternoons and we'd get drunk and snort narcowhirl and fuck each other's brains out. But that stopped a long time ago. He ended up marrying his partner and went wholly monogamous. Evidently, he no longer has sex with any man other than his husband of almost ten years."

"That's very sweet," Braden said, "if they love each other that much. But, still! I don't think I can imagine only ever having sex with one guy again in my whole life."

I wanted to point out the obvious: Braden is very young, he has probably never been in love and certainly not in the way that Zach and his spouse apparently were (nor the way Danny and I were, and certainly not the way we are now), his understanding of

"adult" relationships is probably rather shallow, and such other trite and glib sentiments as that. But fortunately, I realized before I'd opened my stupid mouth that this would all be very tedious to discuss and that I would probably sound utterly tiresome and patronizing to him and even to myself. So I just said, "I know, right? Me either!"

"You think he'll jerk off later? Thinking about me and how I showed him my cock?"

I had no doubt of it.

We opened the bags and all the containers inside, and we arrayed before us the food. I remarked that it was a lot of stuff but Braden felt quite confident that we'd eat every bit of it. These were the items: a bowl of slippery and glossy noodles in a spicy broth with shrimp and pulled pork and kimchi, dusted with crushed peanuts; a quartet of tiny slider-sized sandwiches formed of fried rice cakes which held between them braised beef short rib meat and pickled greens and Korean chili paste and pale strands of daikon sprout; nuggets of tempura-fried chicken in a glossy red sauce with dried chiles and wilted rapini, a fish filet roasted with sesame seeds and scallions and slathered with a fermented black bean sauce and slices of fried garlic; and, since we were in Saint Louis, a few obligatory eggs rolls and crab rangoon with packets of duck sauce.

Zach had brought us chop sticks and I had brought out a couple of forks and spoons as an alternative, but Braden ignored all utensils and reached into the fish with his fingers, broke away a big sticky chunk of it and put it in his mouth. He did the same

with a bite of the chicken and then lifted with his saucy digits one of the short rib rice cake sandwiches. "We will both definitely need to eat at least some of that one," I said. "It's garlicky as hell, so we both need to be inoculated. For later kissing, you know."

"We're both eating *all* the things!" He took a big sloppy bite from the little sandwich, fully half of it at once, and said with his mouth full of food, "Here. Open up wide." He reached across the table, I leaned in toward him, and he pushed the other half of the sandwich into my mouth.

We continued like this, eating with our hands, feeding each other bites of stuff with ever-stickier fingers, pounding down all the beers along the way. After a little while, Braden reclined back in his seat and conceded defeat: there was just too much food. "Okay, I need to stop," he said. "We got more fucking to do this afternoon and I can't be in a food coma for it."

We ended the lunch by putting away the leftovers and sucking each other's fingers semi-clean. Which was fun, but we soon agreed that we should wash our hands, as quotidian as that seemed in our food-ardent moment.

From the journal: I love it that Braden likes to kiss, and love it even more so that he likes to do it sloppily, with as much tongue and spit as possible. In this way, he reminds me a bit of a Mexican boy (who was also nineteen at the time) who accepted my Craigslist invitation one night about a year ago. That dude was very cute though a bit fat for my usual taste. He'd

wanted to get fucked in the ass, a task that I failed at somehow (save for with fingers) possibly due to a combination of me being a bit too drunk for it and his ass being a bit too fat and too tight, and too hard to enter for me keep firm enough a sadly condom-covered erection regardless which position we tried. He also never got hard himself at all — he told me "I don't usually get hard with guys," an odd quirk for a gay kid seeking hook-ups with random men. He had a nice fat dong, long and brown and limp and uncut. But he liked to kiss and he liked to get licked and bitten. I ate out his armpits and he acted that in itself was making him cum — though he stayed totally un-erect. I sucked on his nipples hard enough to make welts on his chubby boy-boobs and he cried out as if were shooting off. Eventually he gave me a thrilling blowjob, during which he paused a few times to say thank you when I told him that he was an awesome cocksucker. When I came — crying out loudly during it, blasting jizz all over his face and my stomach — he asked me if I was okay. I don't think I have been asked if I was okay by a boy, eyes wide with concern, after cumming my brains out under his skillful ministrations. It was very, very cute. We kissed for a couple minutes more before he put his shorts back on and went home.

But unlike that dude, Braden is a super-horny fucker, always hard, and kinky as fuck. For his rather young age, he is very sophisticated in his kinkiness, and very forthright in expressing it, with a comfort and honesty about what he likes and wants that most men don't attain *ever* much less before their twentieth

birthday. In this way, he reminds me (always back to the Delany references) of a real-life Denny (the sweet one from *Dhalgren*, not the insane one from *Hogg* — though his horniness may rival that of the latter). When he tells me exactly how he wants to cum, how he wants to make me cum, he seems like an old soul, much more experienced and wise than his years.

"I'm gonna eat one of these out of your ass," said Braden, lifting a banana from the bowl of assorted fruits and vegetables on the kitchen sideboard. "It can be done. I did it with another dude once." I was skeptical (and surprised that he was snacky again so soon after our huge lunch), and said that if he meant that he was going to first completely insert it inside me and then eat it out, that probably wouldn't work well because he'd need to peel the thing and then it would be way too soft to jam past my sphincter and up into my rectum. But if you mean, I said, that you're just going to mash some of it into my hole and then eat my ass, then I guess that will work fine.

"No," he said, "we're doing it more or less the first way you described. I'll show you." The banana, he said, was not over-ripe and therefore firm enough to use for this purpose. He took it to the butcher block and, with a paring knife, lopped off very ends of it,

leaving the skin just slightly open. He then made an incision down the length of the skin, carefully separated the skin in a single piece from the flesh of the fruit and the reassembled it. That's just going to fall apart, dude, I said, thinking I had some idea what he was planning. "No it won't," he said, "but we need to get you lubed up pretty good. Hopefully with something that tastes better than Stroke-Z since I'm gonna eat this thing straight from your socket."

We ended up concocting a slippery goo out of raspberry jam and extra virgin olive oil. He applied some of this to the flesh of the banana and then wrapped the skin back around it. Next, he injected some of the raspberry oil into my hole with the lube syringe from my Stroke-Z bottle. "I gotta loosen you up a little bit first," he said. "Bend over and spread, baby." I did so, against the prep table. He dipped his dick in the raspberry olive oil mixture and invited me to taste it. I slurped his cute rod clean of it. He re-applied and got behind me. A few moments later, he made his entry. I really liked his fuck-style, the sensation of that stiff spike of teenage boy-meat punching again and again through my hole. He gave it a couple/few dozen quick thrusts and I wondered if he was intending to go all the way and add a squirt of his cum to the oily, jammy froth that I suspected was forming inside my ass. But then, without any preamble, he withdrew his cock, inserted fingers and, while I could not see exactly what he was doing to me, I pictured him widening my fuck-opening with fingers as slender as calipers, and then there was the sense of something else larger going in, all at once, evidently

the banana. "Just hold still a second," he said, "in that position. I need to do one more thing."

At first I thought he was simply withdrawing the banana, but the pressure of something in my chute remained. "Check this out!" He placed on the table before me the skin of the banana, shimmering with our raspberry lube. He had evidently inserted the entire banana into my ass and then pulled out just the skin, leaving the flesh inside. "But that thing is fully inside your fuckin' cocksocket, kiddo. It's not even sticking out at all. So for me to be able to eat it, you need to literally *shit* it out. Into my mouth." I wondered if I was really going to be able to do this as easily as he imagined, but it seemed plausible that it would just kind of slide out like a raspberry-lubed log of sweet fruity shit. I remembered masturbating with a Vaseline-covered hot dog all the way inside in my ass when I was thirteen and then ejecting it easily after I'd gotten my rocks off. I just squatted on the floor and pushed it out.

We chose this position for it: Braden on the kitchen floor on his back, me squatting over his head, asshole against his mouth, basically sitting on his face. I felt him push his tongue into my hole. I pushed a little bit, feeling now as if I might take a huge dump on his head, and I wondered if any actual shit might end up following the banana out of my hole and into his mouth. But I wasn't too worried about this possibility due to my newly liberalized attitude toward shitting in the presence of a lover, and so comfortable with this new kink was I, and so intensely aroused by

my squatting position over his face that I could actually imagine dropping a log into his mouth and feeling totally great about that, and I didn't think Braden would be offended or surprised too much if I did. I almost hoped that this *would* happen, and I suspected that Braden might really go so far as to eat that as well, and I imagined encouraging him to do so.

I pushed a little harder and felt the banana start to slide out, and I felt it being kind of mashed by the crush of my ass-fuck-ring like a soft and squeeby squeeze of shit, and I heard Braden gulping it down, felt his lips and tongue in my raspberry-weeping ass-crack munching on this mushy mess. After a minute or so, I felt at least mostly emptied of the banana, and Braden, now laughing, seemed done with his snack, so I lifted off him and then back down, straddled his waist, lowered my mouth to his sticky face and kissed him for a while, licked his teeth and tongue, sucked on his nose. The flavor was, as one might expect, all of these things in small parts: banana, raspberry jam, the inside of my ass, olive oil, Braden's spit and snot, and his soft and sweet and salty skin.

10.

The boys indulge in a dark and transgressive fantasy; Braden undergoes a peculiar kind of sexual climax; a fantasy about another novel body feature.

Said Braden, "I'm gonna ask you something kind of fucked up, and you can be totally honest with me, because there is no possible answer that you can give that is going to bother me at all." He was sitting on my belly—not with all his weight, carrying some it on his knees and shins—his ass cheeks spread against my skin, and I could feel the wetness of his damp asshole against my navel. He'd told me a couple minutes before that he liked "how you are just a little bit chubby around there *[jabbing at my abdomen]*. Gives me a cushion!" I told him that I did not consider that to be a very good compliment, and he laughed. He smoked a cigarette, and I encouraged him to ash it on my chest *[note to self: add this detail to fictional Braden's behavior in the book]*. I was excited to know what he could possibly want to ask that he felt it necessary to preface it with such an insistence upon honesty. It stiffened my dick, wondering what he wanted to know, what he wanted me to confess. "Totally honest," he said. "Will you?" Of course, I said. "Remember," he emphasized, "there's *no wrong answer*. I am cool with anything you say, no matter how

fucked-up or weird or sick-ass, but be totally honest."
OK! I said. Ask! And he asked: "Have you ever, like,
forced a dude? Like, for *real*. Actually *made* him have
sex with you, or maybe did it to him when he was in-
capacitated and couldn't actually say yes if he would
have wanted to? And remember before you answer,"
he said, "I am A-OK with *any* answer to this!"

This kid was pretty freaky, so I couldn't always
tell when he is serious or maybe inviting me into some
role-playing or just trying to push a button. If he was
setting up a role-play, he might want a made-up, bizarre and extreme answer. I remembered a violent al-
pha/omega breeding scene that I'd read on an mpreg
site recently. I wondered if he'd be into it: *Braden in
lust, out of control with the need to breed, jumping on a
helpless heat-reeking omega, his cock knotting inside,
throbbing out a quart of jizz.* But not being sure what he
was after, I took him at his word that he wanted the
truth and said, "No, I haven't, though I have done
things kind of non-con with boyfriends a few times,"
and I related how I used to sometimes fuck Jay, my
freshman-in-college boyfriend, when he was wasted
on gin and Ambien. Jay didn't always remember
when this happened, and it was kind of hot to take his
ass when he was pretty much helpless. But that was a
"normal" feature of our relationship, a part of our
thing as a couple, he was very agreeable to it. It was
our "thing," and he never contended that he was being "forced" by me regardless of the superficial resemblance of the actual sex act to a date rape. It was

just a way that we fucked in our normal fuck-life together. "But no," I said, "I have never actually done
this to anyone in any way that you seem to mean."

"But have you ever *wanted* to?" he wondered.
"Like, even just in a fantasy?"

"I think," I said, "it's very normal for most guys to
fantasize about it sometimes, and jack off about it
sometimes while thinking about it or even looking at
porn about it, but I'm quite sure I'd not *really* do it."
But I did tell him that I have masturbated to porn vids
with premises such as *"step-dad punishes step-son"* by
brutally fucking him as a retaliation for some minor
transgression, or *"boarding school gang fuck."* I had just
watched such a one a few days earlier, a long scene in
which a trio of "half-way house" boys are sexually
brutalized by their older caretakers as the conse-
quence for having annoyed everyone by setting off an
alarm overnight.

And there are scenes in more serious literature,
such as in de Sade, where men and boys are subjected
to all sorts of sexual excesses including being tortured
and murdered for erotic purposes. "Dudes still read
that shit," I said, "and get hard-ons even though it's
totally grotesque and not about something most people would actually *do*. It's probably just in our prehis-
toric animal nature somehow." I told him that when I
read Delany's *Hogg*, a book that Braden knew and had
in his bedroom library, I got an involuntary hard-on
during the home invasion scene when the constantly
masturbating teenage character Denny fucks another
boy and then decides to give himself a cock-piercing
with a dirty nail. It's all totally awful and fucked up

and over the top, but it still makes me stiffen a little. "I agree," Braden said. "I freak out on that part, too. I have read it like a hundred times."

"But what if a dude," Braden persisted, "say some twinky, faggy bitch of a guy you found on Craigslist or Grindr, came over here for sex and you were really horny for him and then he decided that he didn't want to put out for you after all? Would you ever be tempted to just *make* him give you what you want?"

It has actually happened from time to time, I said, that I have arranged a hook-up and it hasn't worked out. Generally, I will at least attempt to complete the act even if the situation doesn't seem quite as hot when I actually see my one-off partner, but sometimes I don't appeal to the other guy enough and it just doesn't happen. But then—when I detect or am even told to my face—that I am not hot enough for the other dude to go ahead with sex with me, I tend to feel less aroused, and kind of embarrassed, and I just want to him to leave (which he does quickly), and it certainly does not ever occur to me to *force* the guy.

"I want *you*," Braden said, spitting on the nub of his spent cigarette and laying it in on my ashy chest, centering it between my nipples, "to do it to *me*."

Obviously he was asking for some role-play: we were so very, very far—at about hour eight—of our One Day of Sodom, from us requiring any further consent from each other for anything. We had fucked repeatedly, we had drunk each other's piss, we had spattered each other faces with boyjuice, I had given him a club soda enema and then later put a beer bottle in his ass (twice) and tipped its contents into his

cocksocket and literally drank foam from his beer-belching boypussy. I did the same with a wine bottle. I'd painted his fingernails, lined his eyes, drew a picture of my dick on his thigh, another one of his imaginary mouth-cock on his chest, took a shit in front of him and let him wash my ass and then rim me. We'd spit in each other's mouths and I'd sucked a quart of snot out of his nose and cleaned out his dirty ears with my tongue and sucked cheese off his cockhead. He had pissed in my hair and mashed a whole banana into my ass and then ate most of it right out of my hole. We had not yet delved into fisting, coprophagia, snuff-play or vampirism yet, but I couldn't think of much else that we had not already either explicitly or implicitly consented to with one another. And I'm really not any good at role-playing. I always break character. But I was willing to try since he seemed set upon it.

"Can you do some good fake-crying?" I asked. "Convincingly?" I imagined fucking his ass while he wailed and sobbed and this thought made my cock so hard it almost hurt. Immediately, his eyes widened as if in fear and a couple real tears welled over his brown eyes like a rising pond and then dripped. He added a little breathy sob to it and whispered *"please, no, please, no."* And, "You *like* that shit!" he said, breaking into a wide grin, jabbing me in the belly with his fingers, and wiping water from his eyes. "I *knew* it!"

"Okay, set the scene," I said.

He told me this: "I am your husband. We are married. You're even fuckin' *older* than you actually are, like forty-eight [*oh, thanks! I muttered*] and I am older

than I really am, too, but only like twenty-two. You cradle-robbed my cute boy-ass when I was eighteen and we got married. But we haven't been having sex at all lately, like not for weeks, because I'm never putting out for you lately, always making up excuses to keep your old dick off me, and you start digging through my computer and find a shit-ton of sex videos. I am in them. And so is my new lover. He's a hot and super-muscular freak-jock boy, like a superhuman creature from a sick-ass sex-manga, and he is way younger even than me. He'd only be like a fuckin' freshman if he even went to school but he doesn't, and he's like eight feet—almost eight-and-half feet—tall and he has a giant fucking eighteen-inch donkey-dong like a *hentai* stud, and it's like my whole fucking forearm and fist sticking out of his crotch, and he's got more pubes than I got hair on my head, and his giant hairy nuts are big as baseballs, and he shoots like a fucking quart of goo when he gets off, enough to make a dude die by drowning in dick-juice, and he has fucked almost every single faggot in the city already, but now he likes me the *best* because I will do a*nything* at all and I am like a slave to him and we make totally sick-ass fuck-videos together and put them on X-Tube. He has telepathic superpowers, too, like that dude in your book.[18] And you found this shit—me, your fucking *husband*—getting fucked half to death by this eight-foot-tall eighteen-inch-cocked teenage jock-ass stud who has fucked like a hundred

---

[18] A reference to his own namesake, the character of Braden in the *Jace* stories, a touch-telepath who can glean "stories" about people's true natures and intentions during sexual contact with them.

thousand other dudes already and has never once worn a fucking rubber on his big giant cheesy uncut prong, because they don't fit anyway because his dirty prick is too fucking huge, bro, you'd have to put a fucking trash bag on it! So you're totally blind enraged at what I have done. You are filled with hate for me over my betrayal of our marriage because I like getting fucked by this freak-monster-*kid* better than I like it from you!"

[I'll note here that I did not recreate Braden's monologue about this science fictional lover from memory. I actually recorded it on my phone, as I did with a lot of events of that day, thinking it would be some fun masturbation material in years hence long after this boy of summer is gone. And I'm glad I did so as a writer who usually skips over even trying to create extraneous "realistic" dialogue because I don't know how to make it interesting. To have something like this recording that I can just transcribe almost verbatim and find that it works in written form, unlike most normal human speech, is amazing. This kid is a kind of freaky fuck-poet.]

Nice scene, he laid out: playing upon my age by making me even older; describing a new lover two feet taller than me; suspecting that I am proud of my own big cock, and so giving his new lover a prick twice as big as mine; denying me the sex that I deserve from my husband, sex that this cheating little fucker *owes* me as his man. I imagined the headline on the porn vid: *"Cuckolded mature dude punishes cheating young twink husband."* It was a fun and funny thought for this fantasy scene since, in reality, I couldn't give a shit less about sexual monogamy and I'd never

dream of "punishing" a beautiful queer lad like Braden for fucking as many guys as he wants to, but I found myself nonetheless seriously aroused at the whole prospect of teaching a lesson to my faithless young lover, with my cock as the instrument of discipline to wreak upon his slutty hole. [19]

In my new persona as the betrayed spouse, I slapped him *(decently firmly)* and he opened the teargates. You fucking bitch, I whispered, and slapped him across the face again. I pulled him up from the bed, to his feet, and kneed him in the belly *(not too hard, don't worry)*. On your fucking knees! Now! And shoved him downward with a hand on top of his head. I picked his shorts up from the floor and removed the ropey belt from them and flung it over my shoulder. *"Kyler!"* he sobbed. "Please don't do this to me! I'm sorry! Please don't hurt me!" Shut up! I said and pulled his wet mouth open with my index fingers and pushed my cockhead inside, and pushed it all the way into the back of his throat. He gagged on it, blubbered, and streams of clear runny snot dripped from his nose and onto my dick as I made him bob his head on my pole. I pulled out, smeared his snot and spit over his cheeks with my fat pre-jac-drippy shroomhead. I stepped behind him, pulled his arms behind his back and he whimpered. Keep them there! I said. Just like that. "Please don't force me, Kyler! Please!"

---

[19] I do have recurring fantasies of being on the other end of this kind of scenario. I imagine Danny raping me as punishment for my constant hooking up with other dudes. Of course, he never has done this, and he won't role-play it with me either. I have asked him to do so a couple of times but it appalls him.

But I know you *like* this shit, I said, because I saw you do it with that dirty mutant freak. I saw the video, you fucking faggot! You, your arms tied, blindfolded, getting your hole stretched by that fucking baseball bat cock! I bound his forearms together behind his back with the belt from his shorts. I considered stuffing one of Danny's dirty jockstraps in his mouth, but refrained in deference to his stuffy nose and his probable need of an open mouth to breath. I pulled him up, back to his feet, fingers digging into his sweaty hairy armpits. He worked up some more tears as I shoved him forward out of the room and made him walk into the kitchen.

Face down, his smooth boy-belly on cool metal, I laid him on the stainless-steel prep island in the middle of the kitchen. He's so light, he was easy to pick up and put on the table — or maybe I had a lot of adrenaline going and he just felt that feathery-light. I'd not yet fucked Braden with him in the face-down position, but in this role-play scenario, it seemed that's how he should be, pinned face-down and helpless beneath me. Still blubbering and snotting out bubbles from his nose and begging for me to spare him, I pulled him into such a position that I could get at his ass while standing against the end of the table. I liked the look of the belt still binding his arms behind his back.

"I don't want you fucking that monster anymore!" I shouted. He cried out that it was all over, he'd never do it again. "I'm so sorry, Kyler! Please don't hurt me!" I don't believe you, you fuckin' monster-lover, I

said *(and somehow did not bust apart with laughter)*, prying open his damp red hole with two fingers, aiming my cockhead at it. He begged me to stop, promised again that he'd be all mine from now on, no more cheating! I didn't figure I needed to lube us up too much for this one. I just spat a couple times at his hole and on my cock and pushed forth.

He sobbed loudly throughout the entire fuck (and I was quite glad that Arthur was not home below us after all), perfectly in character, promising to love me and no other as I rammed him. When I say the "entire fuck," don't imagine that I am saying it lasted long. Since this was going to be my fifth orgasm of the day, I didn't expect much of it, but I was amazed that I put out a decently respectable load, and rather quickly. I considered leaving it fully inside him, but I pulled out instead and creamed his hole and asscheeks. I shoved a little bit of it inside him first with my cock and then with a finger. "That's better, baby," I said. "You're going to give me that ass whenever I tell you to from now on. And I am the *only* cock you're ever getting again!"

My ejaculation seemed to end the scene. I helped him off the steel table and was astounded at what he had left behind on it: a wet pool that shimmered in the afternoon light and spread over a couple square feet of the surface. "Did you cum? Or piss?" I wondered, touching it. I walked back into the bedroom, grabbed my phone and took a picture of it. It was almost as slimy as full-on cum but clear like drooly pre-jac, but there was a *lot* of it. I have seen so many interesting variations in how men's bodies behave during sex,

but this was a new one to me: a giant pool of a pre-jac-like fluid that I'd evidently fucked out of his dick during our pretend rape scene.

"I don't know!" he said. "But it felt fucking hot!" He told me that he needed to do something else immediately. "Kiddo," he said, clasping his hands to my face, "I don't know if I have to piss or cum! But I need to do something *now!*"

Do whichever happens, I said, dropping to my knees, grabbing his super-stiff prick, kissing it. He pushed it into my mouth, moaned a lot, and then started pissing despite his total erection. I gulped as he let out his stream, kind of slowly and even kind of fizzy because he was forcing it out through a full hard-on. It felt like two or three minutes that I kept my lips clamped around his stiff stalk, drinking his piss. "Keep going," he said, after the piss stream trickled to nothing, I sucked and pumped, and very quickly he filled my mouth with a cumload. I stood up, pulled him close and kissed him, fed him his spunk, sucked on his tongue and grew another full-blown hard-on.

We kissed a for a couple more minutes and I pressed my fat shroom-head into his deep pretty navel dent and told him about my recurring jack-off fantasy about how sweet it would be if certain boys' belly buttons actually opened into a deep, wet and fuckable orifice like a weird in-belly boy-vaj into which I could slide the full length of my dong, that I could fuck and

fill with my milk.[20] I imagined this navel-hole having something like a tiny cock-head or a clit hidden inside it that would get aroused by my in-and-out thrusting. I imagined this new kind of fuck-hole weeping a slick lube-juice that smelled like a sweaty boy's armpits and tasted like his spunk, and also an actual thick spunk that would flow uncontrollably from his belly and blast from his cock when my belly-fucking makes him cum. When I have this fantasy I usually imagine my cock being monstrously huge, like as big as my forearm, and a quart of belly-cum soaking my pube bush, soaking my nutsack, oozing into my crotch and running down my thighs. I'd want to take a fucking bath in it.

---

[20] Later, I made this a feature of Jace Dekka's body, and he periodically invites his lovers to fuck him in that special hole. His is an artificial body mod, but I also considered endowing the universe of that story with an entire race of homosexual boys who are born with natural belly-cunts that sexually mature at the same time as their nuts and cocks, but I haven't actually incorporated that detail yet. While the stories so far are set mostly on Earth, Venus and Mars, it is implied that there are human clades spread further out to Mercury and to the moons of Jupiter and Saturn, so perhaps in a place like that is where these specially-equipped dudes will be found.

11.

A visit from the boy's other young lover leads to sodomy and fellatio upon the narrator.

Out on the deck again Braden smoked and reacted to a blast of text messages. The sunset kissed his nearly black hair and reddened one side of it. "Ethan can come over here for like an hour," he said, "if you want him to. He's off from work but he has a date for dinner later." He stubbed out his cigarette and reached for another. "If you're up for it. I know you said you wanted to fuck him. He's game. He thinks you're hot. But we need to do it now if it's going to be today." I was reaching the point where I wondered if I might finally be shooting blanks for the rest of the day if I continued to have fuck, but the prospect of getting to do Ethan in front of Braden made me fully stiffen. He should come over now, then, I said.

Braden said, "But you need to know that he is not nearly as diverse a lover as I am. If you want fucking, in the literal gay sense of cock-in-ass penetration, you will have to be the bottom. He only tops. But if you don't want to do that with him, you can suck him off, and he will blow you as well. But that's about all he does. You can't piss in his mouth, he probably won't spit in your face, he won't rim you before he fucks you, he won't spit cherries into your mouth, and he

won't eat a banana out your ass. If you take a shit in front of him, he probably won't want to wash your crack."

"I wonder if he'd want me to suck snot out of his nose?" I said.

Braden laughed and said, "No, he'd think that's fuckin' gross, too. Like I did until you suggested it. And now I think it's totally hot, and I could probably use another sinus-clearing if you want to help me out again!" I sucked on his nose for a couple minutes, smoked a cig with him, and then we decided it would be appropriate to get dressed at least a bit for Ethan's arrival just so we'd have something to remove afterward. In the bathroom, he let me smear his hair with beach wax and style it into a messy mass of spikes and twists. I dressed him in one of my tanks and a pair of old and piss-dirty camo cargo shorts that I hadn't worn outside in a long time because there was big rip in the ass, but they had been worn around the house a lot of times and sweated in and pre-jac'd in a lot since their last wash. They were a bit big for him but the belt held them up over his ass cheeks, under his waist, just above the base of his prick with a slash of skin showing between the bottom edge of the shirt and the belt of the shorts, the scruff of his bush peeking above the belt. I love cladding a dude with my clothes, and made a mental note to make this a characteristic of Jace Dekka in the book, his love of dressing his scores of younger lovers. With the boy clothed and coiffed cutely, I selected for myself a pair of cut-off shorts that had originally been tight green denim

pants and a short-sleeved white button-down collar-less shirt that I left unbuttoned. He wondered if he should brush his teeth, concerned over cigarette smoke and residue of food from Taikonaut, but I tasted his teeth and tongue and assured him that there was no need, but we decided on a compromise: a swish and swallow of Rumple Minze, and another that we passed a few times between our mouths until we both had our own foamy shot of booze and spit to swallow.

Excerpted from *Kyler Fey's The Fuck Record*[21]:

---

[21] That Kyler Fey titled his private sex journal in such a formal way says a lot of about the meticulous way in which he documents his erotic life. *Kyler Fey's The Fuck Record* itself is a series of large documents, in several electronic volumes, comprising an exhaustive catalog of his sexual history and his sexual thoughts. Thousands of incidents of masturbation are documented (he claims to journal about it every time he does it), including many pages of scans from pages from handwritten journals that he kept as far back as his puberty. As the years pass, the entries become more detailed and occasionally include many pages of commentary and theory about his sexuality, along with many hundreds of notations of his sexual encounters all the way back to his first such. Entries from more recent years include hundreds of naked pics of the author and his genitals as well as pics of many of his sex partners. Also in it is an archive of other media: sex videos done with partners, solo masturbation videos, audio recordings

"Ethan" is the Name of Record of officially-counted partner number two hundred twelve, following partner number two hundred eleven, "Braden." Acts committed that constitute partner designation: anal sodomy performed by him upon me; fellatio performed by me upon him and by him upon me, in the presence of Braden who watched these acts, masturbated and took some pics during them. Ejaculations: one by Ethan upon my face; one by me inside Ethan's mouth.

Ethan is both a weirder and more conventional character than I had imagined. Braden was correct in his forewarning that Ethan is rather more "vanilla" in his in-bed behavior than either Braden or I. But that's fine in itself. Most people are less weird than me or even Braden. But the contrast after most of a day with ever-kinkier horseplay with Braden was striking. It's true, as Braden said, that Ethan's interest in anal fucking is limited to him being the one doing the fucking, and he does it in a very efficient lube-up/get-it-in kind of way without a lot of foreplay. He is a decently good cocksucker, but then again most dudes who like to suck other dudes' cocks are decently good at it. He is also a decent if not spectacular kisser.

But unlike Braden, who is a healthy gay youth with great sexual self-esteem, Ethan—a boy of the same age—seems to have already settled on an awkward semi-closeted lifestyle that seems like a throwback to an earlier era especially for urban American boys of his generation. He asserts that he is bisexual

---

of the author having sex or masturbating and a lot of erotic drawings. Fey estimates that the complete record to date may contain about a million words. — Editor

(but prefers gay sex when he can get it) and he has been in a long-time relationship with a significantly older woman (twenty-seven, I think) who's been riding his pole for a couple years already, since Ethan was seventeen and still in high school. His hope — his actual insane *hope* — for this relationship is that he ends up getting her pregnant because he expects that she will then want to marry him. This will please his parents, who he believes would disown or murder him if they knew that he liked having sex with other men, which he intends to continue having behind his wife's back while every year or two seeding another kid inside her until they have three or four. This way, he will wear the facade of a "normal" family man while still having the pleasure of putting his dick in other guys' assholes. It all seemed very sad to me.

Braden put it this way: "Ethan is a sweetheart and I really like him, but he is dumb as a hammer. Not only does he think this stupid closet-case future will be a good idea, he's super-worried that his sperm doesn't work because she's never gotten knocked up after all the times he's boyed out inside her. I have told him like eight hundred times that she is probably using some kind of birth control instead of making him put a rubber on his cock. And how do you not *know* that! Like, you never even talk about this topic with the woman that you're bare-cock fucking? And then he's like, oh yeah, I think she gets some kind of shot or implant. Then a while later her period starts again and he wants to go to the doctor and get his sperm count checked, and I remind him again that she is getting something done to stop him from knocking

her up. And he's like, oh yeah. It's so fucking dumb. It's hard to even like him at all when you remember how fucking dumb he is."

I agreed but, at the same time, I could imagine a dude like that, one who truly wanted to knock up his girlfriend, wanting to eventually get a solid confirmation of his sperm's viability. During the short period in my teen years when I was having occasional straight sex, I pregged a girl. Fortunately, she was not an anti-abortion zealot and we dealt with the situation together and quietly without anyone else finding out about it. While the whole stupid affair could have been avoided if I'd worn a rubber, it was in retrospect kind of hot in a kinky masculine way to know without any doubt that all that white sloppy boy-snot that shoots out of my stick all the time *can* actually cause a kid to start growing, even if I never want that to happen for real. Several years later I got a second confirmation that the stuff works when I donated sperm to a close friend, a woman who is a several years older than me, who wanted to have a kid but who was never going to do it the conventional way.[22]

Ethan was with us for about forty-five minutes, about half that time spent having sex with him. I took

---

[22] This kid, who is already fifteen years old (a fact that makes me feel quite aged sometimes), is aware of me and interacts with me on social media fairly often, though he regards me more as a family friend than his literal biological father. The coincidence that he turned out to be a boy and gay (he came out as such when he was only thirteen) inspired the part of Jace Dekka's backstory in the *Unsuitable Boys* books about how his far-flung sperm resulted in millions of offspring, every single one of them a gay male.

him and Braden into the bedroom. Braden asked if I wanted privacy with Ethan or if he could watch us. "Obviously I want you to watch!" I took off my clothes and knelt in front of Ethan, undid his belt, open the fly and zipper of his jeans, pulled his pants down to his knees, and did the same with his white briefs. The trend away from American parents always circumcising their sons' penises upon their birth has been going on long enough that I have started to notice it when I have sex with guys in their late teens and early twenties. If I do an American male closer to my own age, he is pretty much always going to be cut like I am (though my cut is less complete than some — I have some it left and can actually stretch skin fully over my head when I am less than fully erect). But when I do a dude in the eighteen to twenty-five range, there seems to be a fifty-fifty or better chance that these younger lovers will have their complete foreskins.

While Braden's skin was short, not quite fully covering his cockhead even when he's flaccid, almost as if he had been just partially cut, Ethan had a full sleeve of skin that completely shrouded and extended over and past the end of his head even when fully erect, as he was already when I exposed his meat. I skinned him back and took his slippery cock-crown in my mouth, slathered it with spit and sucked. Unlike Braden's cock this morning, Ethan's was immaculate, cheese-free, probably freshly washed right before he got here. I tasted his pre-jac drool immediately, licked his cum-slit, and he moaned. He placed his hands on the back of my head and thrusted a little bit into my

mouth, so I let him mouth-fuck me like that for a minute, and he seemed so into I wondered if he was satisfied with getting his rocks off by this method or if he wanted to fuck my ass. So I removed my mouth from his rod and asked him.

He was enthusiastic about this idea. I told him to take off his clothes the rest of the way, get fully naked, let me see his pretty bare body. He's got the typical male body that I like, not too super-muscular but firm and fairly toned. He's quite a bit hairier than Braden with black curls of it around his nipples, a fuzzy dark trail from his belly to his cock, a furry untrimmed bush and a lot of black hair on his inner thighs. I handed him the lube tube and got on my back on the bed and invited him to get on top.

He asked if he needed to put on a condom. I told him he didn't have to unless he wanted to and if he was clean and truthful about being so. He did not want to wear the rubber, assuming that I was also clean. After mutual assurances to that effect, he happily eschewed the latex, but "don't shoot that thing inside me," I said. "I want to see your batter. Pull out and squirt it on me when you're ready. You can shoot it on my face if you like doing that to a dude."

His dick is quite thick — maybe even bigger around than mine though not nearly as long — and he stretched me rather a lot more than Braden does when he pushed it inside. The fuck didn't last very long, he did it in rapid and deep thrusts, and he obeyed my cum-order by finishing himself off with a few pumps of his fist, dropping his juice on my face and into my

mouth, and it tasted sweet and salty and a little bleachy.

Braden, who had been standing near the bed and jerking on his cock the whole time, snapped a pic of it, my face spattered and glazed with Ethan-goo. Ethan offered me a blowjob. I told him to go ahead. He said it was okay for me to cum in his mouth, that he liked swallowing it. I told him he might be disappointed at my output because Braden had been milking my pump all day and I'd already had five wet orgasms with him. But he did it with good mouth-and-hand technique and I was surprised at how quickly I was ready to cum again. Maybe the prostate-massaging his stick had just given me somehow speeded up the refilling my reservoir. I did manage to give him some juice, and he opened his mouth to show me his tongue glossed with it before he swallowed. At the same time, Braden spurted a load onto the bed next to us.

Then Ethan got up from the bed, went into the bathroom, washed his junk with soap and water at the sink, toweled off with my bath towel and put his clothes back on. He hung out for a few more minutes, drank a shot of absinthe with us, smoked a cigarette, told us about his upcoming date with that older woman — it's her birthday tomorrow, he explained, but she has to work all day and I have a night shift tomorrow. He revealed that to make the time to come over and fuck me, he'd lied to her about when he'd be done with work that day. This really didn't seem like a good long-term strategy for a strong relationship, but I couldn't judge him for it given my own hook-up

behavior over the years. But I also decided that I did not really like him that much either, at least not in the sense of him being someone I'd enjoy spending any time with beyond the sex act itself, beyond using his body for a few minutes to get off. I could not picture spending a whole day with him the way I had been doing with Braden. He seemed, in contrast to Braden, intellectually rather barren and boring and I did not feel as badly for him as I did at first when Braden had told me of his great ambition to get his girlfriend pregnant and marry her and live a life of being on the down-low.

12.

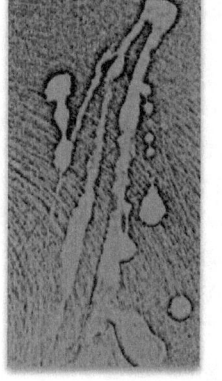

An invitation to share a bed; a dinner made from an exotic recipe; lithe Braden proposes another strange and thrilling fantasy play.

"When this day started," I said to Braden, sitting with him outside on the balcony just past sunset, strings of solar lights in many colors lighting the rails and the plants, "I wasn't sure if I'd make this next offer. But I will. And feel free to decline. My feelings will *not* be hurt."

He leaned forward, wide-eyed, a bemused smile forming on his lips.

I said, "I am still home alone here for a couple days—Danny is gone until Thursday and I arranged things so as not to need to go to work tomorrow at all. I would be happy to keep you here overnight if you want to literally *sleep* with me and then wake up with me in the morning."

He beamed brightly in the pretty lights. "Of course I would! But a couple questions."

"Ask."

"I assume we can probably fuck again at some point between now and when we fall asleep?"

I liked that question. "It seems like I keep being able to fuck today no matter how many times I do it probably because you're a perfect erotic object, so yes, I assume we will."

He said, "I wonder if at some time during the night, one of us will wake up and want to fuck again and then sleep some more."

"I suspect," I said, "that this, too, is quite likely."

"And I wonder," he said, "if you will be as fucking horny when you wake up in the morning as I always am and will want to fuck at that time as well?"

"You can be assured of it."

Braden laughed and lit another cigarette and sat back and smoked and looked very satisfied for a minute or two. Then he said, "So, I don't know if you have been keeping good track of the number of 'times' that you have had sex with me today — or even if we are counting the same things[23] — but it sounds like we just scheduled at least three more times."

---

[23] Later, when we compared notes, he declared that he counted it as a "time" with me when he jacked himself off while watching me fuck and suck with Ethan. I might not have counted this as a "time" with "him" myself, but his logic was pretty good: "You kept looking at me when Ethan was drilling you. And I think you watched me the entire time he was blowing you. I think you were actually having sex with *me* but using Ethan's cock and mouth in place of mine. And I came right after you did." So, yes, this counted as a time. I guess it was really a three-way with Braden and Ethan. Or, to be honest, a one-on-one between Braden and me, the two of us on a level above, using dumb Ethan as a kind of meat-based boy-shaped sex toy to get us off. The poor kid was just a walking talking version of the banana that Braden had jammed in my ass earlier in the day.

"This is fucking hot, dude." Braden said, still perusing the print-out of the formatted *The Intersex Boys of Venus*. "These guys, just two of them, fucking and knocking up like two hundred of these mpreg boys." He continued to read for a few moments, rubbing his stiff prick through his shorts as he did so, which I liked to see since the intent of the book is at least in part to cause erections in gay men and since it was evidently doing so to Braden, it made me feel as if I was at least somewhat successful in crafting some queer pornography. He laughed and said, "Yeah, I like this word: *cocksnot*. I don't think I have heard it called that before. I'm going to start saying that."

I pointed out that it's nice to have a lot of fun words like that at one's disposal for that stuff when writing a book featuring almost continual references to semen, both to the substance itself and to the male sex-act of ejaculating it. "I like that one, too. *Cocksnot*. It's kind of gay-sexy but also fairly gross and crude in a way that only men talking about their sexual functions and the slime of their horny bodies can be."

"I agree," he said. "It's dirty. Fucking dirty. Disgusting. I *like* it!"

He entertained me and himself for a few minutes suggesting more such terms, some that I'd heard and used before (like "nut-yogurt" and "boyfuck" which the character Trace uses in *Royal Rent Boy of Kasei* and

which reminds one of how the Marquis de Sade often called the substance simply "fuck" and how it invokes in a pithy way two of my favorite things: males and cumming) and some that were new to me (such as "boychata" — which I liked the sound of but didn't really "get" until a few days later when I saw a bottle of RumChata in the liquor room at work). He wanted more words for pre-jac. His own ability to leak that substance copiously probably made him especially interested in it. He liked that the characters in the *Unsuitable Boys* stories often call it "preek." I told him that I sometimes call it "dick-drool." He suggested these: pole-wax, fuck-primer, cock-leak, dickpetizer, ready-now juice, and ¡only-lube-you'll-need-faggot! spelled with the dual exclamation point.

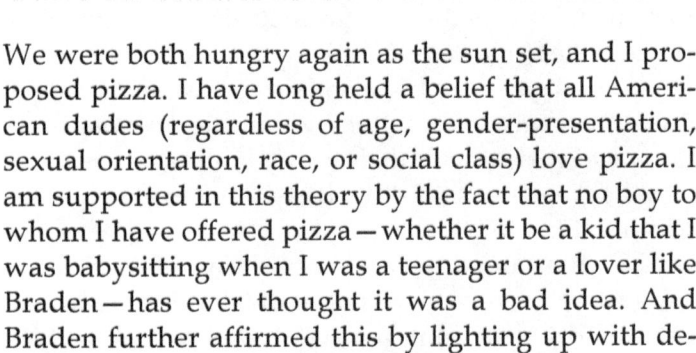

We were both hungry again as the sun set, and I proposed pizza. I have long held a belief that all American dudes (regardless of age, gender-presentation, sexual orientation, race, or social class) love pizza. I am supported in this theory by the fact that no boy to whom I have offered pizza — whether it be a kid that I was babysitting when I was a teenager or a lover like Braden — has ever thought it was a bad idea. And Braden further affirmed this by lighting up with delight when I suggested it. I led him into the kitchen

and his delight turned somewhat toward confusion or perhaps concern when I started getting out supplies from my baking center: flour, yeast, olive oil.

"Wait," he said. "Do you mean that you are going to actually *make* the pizza?"

"No. *We* are." I smiled at him and pulled him close for a kiss. "Worry not. It won't take as long as you might think, and it will be far better than delivery. And you are going to help!"

I dropped some yeast into the steel bowl of my stand mixer along with a pinch of sugar. "Do you think," I asked Braden, "that you could give me some cum again right now if I needed you to?"

He told me that he could probably be persuaded by my mouth. So I dropped to my knees in front of him, pulled his shorts down to his ankles and sucked his prick into my mouth, where it stiffened immediately. I blew him for three or four minutes, and when I could sense that he was going to spunk out, I pulled away, placed the mixing bowl in front of his crotch. "Finish it off, baby. Right in the bowl." He grabbed his pole, stroked it a few times and lobbed out a spatter of kid-goo on top of the yeast. I added a little splash of warm water, a pinch of sugar, a drizzle of olive oil, a glob of my own spit and his and stirred it all together with my finger.

Braden watched, rapt, as the slurry of yeast and sugar and spit and his own spunk started foaming and growing into a living sponge. He wanted to finish the project, hands-on, so I guided him through putting the bowl back onto the mixer, adding flour, adding more oil, a bit of salt and mixing it into a glossy

dough ball. We turned the dough out onto the table and I took his hands underneath mine and we kneaded it together until it was supple and elastic.

I put the dough back into the steel bowl and covered it with a film of plastic wrap. I advised him that it would rise faster outside since it was so much warmer out there than in my air-conditioned kitchen. I opened a bottle of prosecco and poured us each a large glass of it and took him and our dough back outside. There we drank and smoked for a little while, and talked about Samuel Delany books, and he watched with great interest the progress of the dough as it gradually swelled.

"You're its biological father," I told him, and he laughed and he actually blushed, and that was almost intolerably cute and I leaned across the table and kissed his forehead.

"Do you think," he said, peering into the dough bowl, "that my sperm cells are still alive in there?"

I offered that I thought it was possible. "It's a warm and moist environment. Maybe they are even reproducing by the millions." Of course we both knew that this is not how sperm works — it doesn't reproduce itself like the yeast that we'd activated with it. It was just a fun thought to share, and he liked the premise.

We talked about *Dhalgren*, which Braden had just read last year in bed while recovering from a tonsillectomy, and he admitted to a very incomplete understanding of it. *Nobody* really fully understands it, I assured him, other than perhaps the author. But it can be read as a story like any other novel without worrying too much over whether one is somehow Delany-smart enough to "get" it in its entirety. We agreed that we loved the young Denny character, and that we'd both had the same sense of worry and incompleteness about what may have happened to him toward the end of the book as that character kind of faded away into the background of the ending — that wraps back around to the beginning. But Braden was sure that I would have some kind of great insight into that book that he could glean from me, and he adhered to the fact that I had read it for the first time before he "was even born," and pointed this out several times, and that at my advanced age I must have accrued some revelations, accreted upon my old skin like a leathery patina of deep knowledge, not available to such a fresh youth as he. We traded observations about favorite scenes and concepts, which he enjoyed, but we reached an impasse when I could not explain the title of the book. This, surely, because I had read it before he "was even born" — making me practically a contemporary in his mind with the septuagenarian Delany — just had to be a thing that I could explain finally to his young and absorbent brain. "That word 'Dhalgren' shows up just once in the entire book," he said, "and it's just some dude's last name within a

whole list of names. *Dhalgren*. What the fuck does that shit mean?" and his mouth rounded into a great 'o' of anticipation and I feared that he would lose all interest in me, all respect for me, and that he would just leave in disgust and disappointment and that we would never fuck again after I had to admit that I had no godsdamned idea as to the answer to his question. But he laughed, and spit on his fingertips and reached across the table to my mouth to kiss me with that thick foam from *his* sweet and dripping mouth.

The dough rose quickly in the twilight heat, and we worked it over again together on the kitchen prep table, my hands guiding his, and soon we had a flat oblong shell that I docked with his fingertips and smeared with more virgin olive oil again using his hands as the utensils. I let him select its toppings, and he chose a fat purple heirloom tomato that he hand-crushed with garlic, basil from the garden, a tin of anchovy filets, fontina that he grated into large shards with a box shredder, some prosciutto that he rendered into julienne. I complimented him on his tasteful choices and his skill with preparing them. He revealed that he likes to cook, is better at it than his mom, and does it at home all the time. The temptation to simply tell him that I love him — to impulsively lie

to him because I am *crushing hard on* him — was never more pronounced during this day than at that moment. "But I never made a pizza from scratch before," he said, snapping me away from this impulse to tell him about my crush-love for him. "And was never the bio-father of one." We both laughed at this and kissed for a minute and slid his creation onto the stone tile inside the raging hot oven where it quickly puffed and crisped and bubbled.

We agreed — I think with neither of us lying — that it was the most delicious pizza we'd ever eaten.[24]

We sat on the deck for a while, post-pizza. I asked Braden if his brother is as cute as Braden himself is. "Even cuter!" he said, and laughed. "No, seriously, dude, I can't even tell you. He's fucking *adorable*, especially the last year or two since he kind of finished growing up. He had a big spurt last year. He's gotten muscly and really tall. The dumbass is like six inches taller than me! You'd totally pitch a big long tentpole in your pants if you saw him." Then it occurred to him that he could, in fact, show me. He opened the camera

---

[24] The day after this event, I added a scene into the rough draft of *The Lust Drug of Ephebos* in which Jace and Ethan make a cum-infused pizza.

roll on his phone and showed me a few recent pics of Eric:

one a grinning joint selfie with Braden, both boys with globs of frozen custard in their open mouths

another of Eric lying in bed with covers pulled to his chin, one bare arm reaching out to give his brother the finger

another of him standing in Braden's bedroom (cum-stiff Bieber poster on the wall behind him) shirtless, pelvis clad in cargo shorts, for some reason holding up a Pokemon toy

and another of him again in Braden's room, seated at Braden's desk, gulping from a Miller Lite can, a cricket cap tilted askew on his head

I certainly did not, based just on those pics, rate him as *more* handsome and hot than Braden, but he was very cute nonetheless. He looked more or less like a copy of his brother, but with somewhat lighter hair and I noticed in a couple of the pictures that his ears seemed to have a little backward bend that reminded me of those Scottish fold cats with those funny loppy ears, but in reverse. I remarked upon this and Braden said, "Exactly. That's *exactly* what I said! I used to make fun of him for that and tell him he had ears like one of those cats or like a lop-eared rabbit. But actually, it's kind of cute. It really is. Girls like his dumb ears, too. They gush and cry over them. Or so he says."[25]

---

[25] Fey made these quirky ears a feature of the fictional Braden in the Commander Jace books. In *The Intersex Boys of Venus* (published back-to-back with this book as the other half of the print

"I'm going to give you a scenario," I said. "And you tell me if it's hot or disgusting. Here: Eric naked on your bed, his bare back lying against your dirty cum-stained sheets, you on top of him hammering his ass with your cock."

He laughed loudly. "*Kyler!* Jesus Christ!" He laughed some more and said, "It's not *disgusting*, but it's pretty fuckin' sick. But I will admit that I would probably think it's pretty hot anyway if he were gay. And it would be wild just to do it once, just to be able to add that the list of things I've done. Not everyone gets to say they fucked their hot brother. But he's not gay, so it's hard to picture it. And I don't dig messing around with straight gay-curious dudes because they tend to chicken out and not get the job done."

"Would you consider Eric to be gay-curious?"

Braden said that his brother has said—and I recalled him saying this during one of our previous encounters—that he would consider trying gay sex sometime if the circumstances for it aligned correctly. "But I think his idea of gay sex," Braden add, "is a boy giving him a blowjob. He'd be horny, a gay boy would offer, he'd let the dude suck him off. And that's it. I don't think he'd recip at all. I think he'd get his rocks off, zip his pants back up, thank the fag for his fag-service and go home."

"But if he were gay," I adhered, "and he was willing to experiment with *you*, would you do it with him?"

---

edition double), the character Patrick refers to "another black-eyed, lop-eared rug-rat," a result that he speculates would come about if Braden could be impregnated and bear children. —Editor

Braden grinned and said, "If the dude was actually gay, I'd bone his fucking dumb brains right out his pretty head. I'd fuck him so long and hard my cocksnot would fill his skull and drain out his ears." He beamed widely, evidently pleased with his first deployment of "cocksnot" in conversation. "I'd gag him on my cock, jizz in his throat and piss straight into his stomach. And then I'd have *him* do all that shit to *me*, except a lot harder." He leaned across the table, dragged on his smoke, reached across to pinch my left ear. "You *like* that shit, kiddo. I *know* you do!" he said. "I probably wouldn't *really* do all that with *him*, but it is kind of fucked-up/super-hot to think about, isn't it? Me fucking the living shit outta my cute little bro? You love it, don't you?"

I had no denial to offer. He could see me reaching for my hard-on, gripping it through my shorts, imagining that beautiful sibling pair locked together like naked queer Gemini twins, one impaled on the other's prick.

"Later on, or when we go to bed," Braden said, "let's do another role-play. I have an idea."

I asked him to pitch the scene.

He combined what he had been reading in *Intersex Boys* with our previous conversation. He suggested that he would be a "maph" from Venus, a gay dude with a female-style vagina in between his ballsack and his asshole, and with a womb and the ability to get pregnant. I would, in this scenario, be his father and I would be determined to protect him somehow from being violated and forced to bear the child of a lethal enemy of our family. The method that I would use to

so protect him from such a defilement would be to knock him up myself. So, in this way, he had created an mpreg/incest scenario. Ideally, I might have preferred—since we were fantasizing about incest anyway—to have been his older brother in this scene rather than his father, and I suggested to him such a small revision. But my "extreme age," as he put it, precluded any "possible or reasonable plausibility" of us being brothers, and it would just make the whole scene collapse under the weight of its laughable preposterousness (though, of course, he being a boy who could get pregnant was well within the realm of reason somehow!). But I suggested that there certainly do exist in the world real siblings with as much as a twenty-year age difference between them, but he just wasn't going for it.

"Besides, it's kinkier and more sick-ass this way," he said. "Brother-sex isn't really quite as weird. I went to high school with a kid who said that he used to blow his older bro all the time. I don't think it would ever happen with me and my brother, but I can kind of *imagine* doing it for real and it not being really all that creepy if we both decided we wanted to get into that sick-ass shit. Dad-on-son is pretty fucked up and sick though. It's *super*-sick! Especially when dad wants to get his boy *pregnant*, using the same sperm on him that made the son with in the first place."

I had to agree with his logic. *Super*-sick!

I am going to heavily fictionalize my depiction of how we went about this role-play episode, much more so than I did with the previous one, because we wove

165

into it so much science fiction/fantasy back-story and detail that we actually paused several times to discuss and debate the details of the "universe" in which it was happening. In fact, most of the actual duration of "real" scene was comprised of us just talking about the story and its details (with us then fucking at some point). The following scene, then, can be taken as a piece of fiction derived from a real sex game that Braden and I played and a piece of fiction that he should be considered to have co-authored...

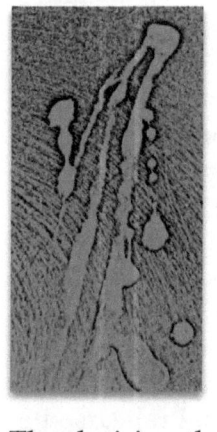

13.

"The Mpregnated Twinks of Phallos Vallis"
by Kyler Fey and Braden Vaieux

Characters: Lord Kyler of Phallos Vallis; his son, Prince Braden; Aaron, a servant-boy and Braden's lover
Tags: m/m, twink, mpreg, boy-vaj, incest

The decision that I made regarding Braden and Eric was not made lightly, and I may never have done it at all had it not been wholly necessary. In a few days, I would be sending my two eldest sons on a critical mission to Venus, and that world was still under the frightful effects of the Tong Tiphon's "spunk beam," that disastrous field of paranormal energy that had induced pregnancy in all the fertile maphs and females of that world, and with hideous results as the vampiric children started to be born.[26]

While Braden and Eric present themselves as young men, they are both maphs, and I could not risk the danger to them if they should conceive under the

---

[26]While this story, derived from Kyler Fey's sex-play with Braden, is replete with concepts borrowed from the universe of the Commander Jace books, its use of the "spunk beam" notion varies considerably from what is previewed in *The Intersex Boys of Venus* and later depicted in *The Spunk Beam*, and so cannot be taken as a "canon" entry in that universe. —Editor

effect of that beam while on Venus. No birth control method had proven effective for maphs under that energy. Both of these boys had been on a regimen of Null-Preg injections since their physical coming of age to prevent accidental impregnation by their many boyfriends or by the occasional breeding-capable pleasure slave (while most of these are, of course, Martian castrati with artificial sex equipment, we do occasionally have fully intact and spermy Earthmen employed about the compound), but this would not protect them on Venus, and it was now necessary that they be pregnant before their departure.

On my way to Braden's chambers, I rehearsed in my head how I would present my intentions to him, how I would rebut the various objections that I expected him to make, how I would comfort him when I revealed that he had been removed just yesterday by his doctor from the effects of the Null-Preg for me to accomplish my purpose with him. Because of my love for him, I genuinely wanted him to endorse my plan and believe in its logic, though it's true that I could, if necessary, compel him to cooperate with me by one means or another. Under the tradition of our clade, young men do not reach the age of majority until twenty-six,[27] and in our royal family, my sons are

---

[27] This idea of young men not reaching legal adulthood until such a late age as twenty-six recurs often in Fey's *Jace* writings (in the context of sexually conservative societies or ones with actual youth slavery such as the character Trace was subjected to) and is compatible with this attitude that he expressed in a journal entry:

technically my property until they reach that age. In effect, I own them as a kind of physical possession in the same way that I own the thousands of slaves that do the important work around our vast compound. But I did not want it to go that way. It would be so much better for us both if Braden assented to my plan.

When I arrived in Braden's chambers, I heard from the anteroom two young male voices talking and laughing — Braden's and someone else's. I entered Braden's study and found him on a couch with Aaron, one of the grounds boys.[28] Both lads were shirtless but wearing loose linen pants, obvious erections inside them, and appeared to be enjoying some wine and a snack. I saw Braden put a spoonful of red caviar in Aaron's mouth and then offer him a sip of white wine from his glass. They did not notice me until I said, "Gentlemen. So sorry to disturb you."

"It's hard to take seriously dudes in their late teens or early twenties as being fully 'men' even though the law considers them so for most purposes at eighteen. So many guys take so long to fully mature mentally and intellectually. Most of them, despite their physical maturity, seem like 'boys' well into their twenties, and often as late as thirty. But I am glad that ages of consent for sex with them in this country are (varying by which state you live in) sixteen and seventeen and eighteen because it would drive me batshit with unrelieved horniness if I had to wait until a hot dude is twenty-six before I could fuck him without perpetrating 'statutory rape' upon him, or if a video of two twenty-year-olds fucking each other was considered 'child porn'." — Editor

[28] A character named Aaron also appears in *The Hypnotic Lawn Boy*, episode #14 of the *Commander Jace* series. That one is depicted as a straight boy, though he does at one point fellate all the dudes in the Home. After his arrival, everyone becomes obsessed with a phone game that he shares with them.

Braden looked mildly annoyed but rose to greet me. "I was not expecting you, Kyler. You might have called first." But he smiled, stepped toward me, embraced me and kissed me on the cheek.

Poor Aaron looked quite embarrassed and uncomfortable with my intrusion. His white face and ears flushed deeply red, almost as red as his brilliant hair. This pretty youth had been one of my own favorite bed companions in recent months and perhaps he feared that he was breaking an arcane code of conduct by also making love to my son, but it didn't concern me in the least. Aaron was sterile. He could cum inside Braden's pussy all he wanted and never sire a child.

"Aaron, I am so sorry," I said, "but I have an important matter that I need to discuss with Braden privately. I hope you don't mind finding some other entertainment for the rest of this evening, or until Braden calls you back."

Aaron stood immediately, found his shirt on the floor next to the leather couch, put it back on quickly and said, "Of course, my master! I shall leave at once!" He was still blushing so I gave him a friendly wink and a gentle pat on the ass as he passed me and exited the room.

After he was gone, Braden slumped back into the couch. "Really! Is it *really* so important that we must meet right now?"

I went to his bar and poured myself a glass of wine and treated myself to a line of narcowhirl. "Did you have sex with him?" I wondered.

"I was *about* to!" Braden gulped from his glass, emptied it and went to the bar for a refill, his bone still tenting out the fly-front of his pants.

"I have had him a few times myself," I said, rather enjoying Braden's annoyance with my cock-blocking intrusion.

"Kyler! *Dad!*" he cried. "I *know* you have but you don't need to belabor the point, especially since I'd be 'having' him right now if you had not dropped by!"

"He's a very tight fuck," I persisted. "And if you bottom for him, he pounds like a jack-hammer. And he can deep-throat a cock like a champ."

Braden clapped his hands to his cheeks. "Jesus Christ, dude! I am getting the worst case of blue-balls! I am going to go into the bathroom and jack off real quick before we meet."

"I'd rather you didn't," I said. "Because your arousal may actually be useful to us and with what I need you to do."

"Oh god, Kyler," he sighed. "You know I love you," he said, and kissed me quickly on my mouth, "but I really do not want to fuck around with you tonight. We haven't done that lately anyway, and I am not nearly drunk enough for it!" He pounded down his new pour of wine in a single gulp. "If that's what this is about, maybe go see Eric. He is more into that scene than I am anyway." He poured another glass and took a small but determined sip from it.

"I saw Eric last night, but not quite for the reason that you are thinking," I said. "Doctor Arush confirmed for me this morning that Eric is now pregnant after my visit to his bed."

171

I thought Braden might actually spit wine out of his mouth in a spray as he absorbed that statement. "What the fuck! How did *that* shit happen? We're on Null-Preg shots!"

"Not anymore you're not. At the time of your booster shot the other day, the doctor gave you the antidote to it as well as a fertility stimulant. I wonder if you have noticed feeling extremely aroused lately? Even more so than is normal for your sex-hormone-soaked nineteen-year-old body? Even more desire than normal to have a cock inside your vaj?"

He looked down at his pants, still tented. He admitted that his hard-on had not flagged all day, to the point of it being an annoyance when he needed to piss. Braden frowned and said, "Eric's pregnancy, then, was not an accident."

"Nor will yours be. And it is necessary, as I will explain. You should also know that Eric fully consented to it as I think you will also."

Braden took a couple steps back. "Dad, Eric may have agreed to this crazy idea, but he's kind of dumb. We both know it. It's not a secret. Furthermore, I don't want to be pregnant right now! I do *not* want to have a kid, and I certainly don't think that *you* should be the man to put one inside me!" He paced around in a circle. "We are not that kind of family! We are not like the Martian jeddaks, all interbreeding with each other all the time! We are the princes of Phallos Vallis! We have standards! Sure, I will admit that I have fucked around with you, and with Eric as well, and enjoyed it, but *you* getting *me* pregnant is a whole other thing!"

I explained to him the simple fact that if he goes to Venus without already being pregnant, then he will become so there and by a method that will be very dangerous to him. "Even if we abort the Venusian pregnancy when you come home, your body will be permanently infected and damaged. I can't allow that to happen to you, sweetheart. You leave in two days and you *will* be pregnant by then. There is no other choice."

"But I do not want to have a kid now!" Braden cried. He gazed into my eyes, his own becoming wet and shiny. "I always imagined that someday I would have a son of my own, but I imagined doing that after I am married to a man that I love and want to share my whole life with!"

It was hard not to laugh at this act. He even managed to let a single fat and shiny tear fall from his left eye. My boy had practiced this doe-eyed rendition of heartfelt pleading all his life, and it warmed me inside just a little bit to see him try it again now. But I said, "Braden, that's fucking ridiculous! Bitch, please! You have *never* imagined wanting a son of your own and certainly not with a *husband,* for fuck's sake! You are quite possibly the most promiscuous and sex-addicted young faggot I have ever seen in my life! It's the rarest of days when you have sex with *just* one man! In fact, I know that you were involved in a sixty-way orgy in the garden baths just a few days ago! And if your fuck-blog is to be believed, you added another few dozen first-time partners during it."

"Ugh! Whatever!" Braden shouted. "I just hate the idea of being pregnant! It seems like such a fucking

inconvenience! Who's even going to *want* to fuck me when I am all fat and gross and can hardly walk because I have a fucking soccer ball in my gut!"

I had no doubt that I could easily find men who would love—would even *pay!* —to fuck him if he were in exactly that state, but "Calm down," I said, grinning at him in a way that I am certain he found intensely infuriating. "I am not going to make you actually carry the kid all the way to term *inside your body!* What, do you think I am some kind of sadist? Obviously, when you and Eric return safely from Venus, we will remove the fetuses to axolotl tanks and they can finish cooking there. Your pretty bodies will not be affected in the least. You might gain two pounds at most!"

"Okay, fine! I accept the logic that I ought to be pregnant before I get to Venus, but why does it have to be *you* who does it to me?" He poured yet another drink and hit the narcowhirl,[29] clear signs that despite

---

[29] "Narcowhirl" is a recreational drug in the *Jace* universe, constantly used by several of the main characters, often along with alcoholic beverages. The nature of its effect is never fully explained, but it appears to be compatible with sexual arousal and fuck-performance, and its method of ingestion would certainly remind anyone of powdered cocaine. It does not appear to be intended specifically as an aphrodisiac or performance-enhancing drug (unlike their other omnipresent drug Erec-T), but I wonder if it perhaps works to mitigate the effects of the staggering amount of alcohol that Jace Dekka and some of the other characters are depicted as consuming. A note in Fey's journal indicates that what he and Braden were really doing in their play-act of this scene was sniffing poppers, though elsewhere in this account Fey refers without explanation to both smoking and snorting narcowhirl as if it is a real-world drug. —Editor

his continued protests he was getting ready to accept what was going to happen to between us just as his brother had accepted it last night. "If you hadn't barged in here when you did, Aaron would probably be jamming his fag-pole in my cunt right now. Since I'm supposedly super-fertile now, *he* could have knocked me up."

No, he couldn't have, I had to let Braden know. "He is a totally sterile. He's got enough libido for three boys, but his nuts have never made a live swimmer in their lives."

"Well, there are still other breeder-capable males around this joint," he said, and swallowed some more wine. "I still don't get why we have to accomplish this in such an over-the-top incestuous way like we are some kind of rutting Martian brother-fuckers!"

I told him that we needed to sometime in the next generation reinforce our genetic line. I opened my phone and showed him some data that Arush had compiled. "Our son, and the one I have made with your brother will become super-breeders who will spread our DNA throughout the solar system." I pulled Braden close and he let me kiss his forehead. "We were going to need to do this eventually. And we might as well do it now since the urgency is here for you to be carrying before you to go to Venus." I released the embrace and lined up some more narco-whirl on the bar. "Braden, I think you understand now that you are going to carry my seed one way or another. We can accomplish this here through an act of love from me to you or we can go to the doctor's lab and get it done there with a syringe. Your choice."

"Fine," he said. He unbuttoned his pants and let them drop to the floor. He stepped out of them and stood naked, his prick upright. "Take me right here," he said. "On this couch. But let's not spend too much time on it!" He knelt on the couch, leaning over the back of it, ass raised. I stripped, and my cock drooled a long streamer of preek as I contemplated my boy's perfectly formed ass cheeks, the tight pucker of his socket. But, of course, this was not the hole that I needed to enter that night. My target was of course the other wet opening between his nuts and his anus. Though I had made love to my son a number of times before, I always prefer ass over vaj even when fucking a maph, and so I had actually only done this particular act with him once before, and that was a long time ago when I went to his bed to end his virginity and initiate him into the life of extreme sexual promiscuity that he now lives (not that it was my explicit intent that he become instantly a huge slut—it's just what developed with him as it has with Eric as well). That day—it was in the morning at about sunrise—he experienced ass-fucking for the first time both as the bottom and as the top, and I also broke the boy's hymen with my prick and flooded his baby-box with a big load of batter (he was already on Null-Preg at the time). But it was the tightness of his perfect ass that thrilled me the most that morning and the memory of tapping it for the first time still stiffens my stick every time I see him cavorting in the baths with his dozens of cute naked boyfriends.

I took Braden from behind, easily sliding into his wet cunt. As much as he initially protested this idea,

his arousal was extreme and he cried out loudly and had a vaj-orgasm within seconds of my entry. Maphs have an organ inside their slots resembling somewhat another cock-head, though smaller, and they can be brought to climax by the friction of a man's shaft thrusting past it. When this happens, they ejaculate a semen-like substance from it and sometimes also sometimes shoot a load from their cocks at the same time. Braden did both, spattering the leather couch beneath him and drenching my pole and nutsack with his vaj-spunk. His body, flooded with its desire for pregnancy, overrode any objections he'd had to this fucking. He pushed back against my pelvis, grinding his cunt over my stick. He screamed again and came a second time. As much as I would have loved to have drilled him for an hour like this, making his body quake with climax after climax from both his fuck-organs until he was reduced to a quivering and wholly fucked-out boy-mess, I couldn't trap in my own load any longer. I pushed in one more time, very hard and as deeply as I could, and released my nut-juice inside him. He cried some more, cumming a third time, and I held him by his hips, keeping my dong buried all the way inside for another full minute until my jizz-spasms finally stopped and I was satisfied that I had gotten as much sperm inside him and as *deeply* inside him as I could.

I pulled out, reached under him, lifted him and turned him onto his back. I lifted his legs, raised his knees and told him to lie there like that a bit, pussy elevated. "Let's not let too much leak out right away," I said.

He smiled and sobbed and laughed. "Jesus fuck, Kyler! Oh my god, *Dad*!" He wiped tears from his eyes and sweat from his forehead. "That was *stupid*-hot! I don't think it ever felt like that before!"

"Your body never wanted to be impregnated that badly before. You've been on Null-Preg since puberty all the way until yesterday. It's a natural response for boys like you when you are at the height of your fertility."

"You think it took?" he said. "Your baby-batter and my little egg?"

"Most likely." I kissed his forehead. "Your brother conceived on the first attempt. The doctor will come here to test you in the morning. If you have somehow not conceived, he will call me back to try again. But I suspect you are knocked up."

"I feel amazingly good," he said, smiling up at me. He raised his head and kissed me on the mouth. "But very tired for some reason! I think I need to lie in bed and read for a while." I agreed that this was a good idea, and I told him I'd send sweet Aaron back there later to sleep with him. He liked this idea, and I liked the image it conjured: my son and his friend, two pretty and sleepy twinks wrapped naked together in Braden's huge bed.

I lifted him from the couch and carried him to his bed. He told me that he had been reading A-R Kanayda's planetary romance queer porn serial *Lords of Ephebos*. He asked for its next two volumes, slim books which I pulled from one of his shelves (*The*

Twin Cocksuckers of Triton and *A Martian Youth Deflowered*).[30]

He picked up one of the books and curled up with it, head immersed in a pillow. I wandered back to his bar, poured another glass of wine and messaged Aaron that Braden would like him to spend the night. When I went back into the bed chamber to bid my son goodnight, he was already asleep.

---

[30] These were discarded possible titles of volumes of the *Jace* series, discarded simply because I do not yet have a story to hang upon them. But they could reappear again someday if I ever do a second serial.

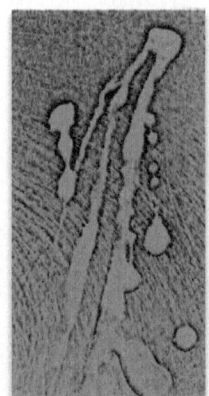

14.

A night and early morning of quiet sleep, quiet affection and masculine pleasure; the narrator tries but fails to deny his body's desire; Braden describes an outré wet dream; later, the boy needs to indulge further in his intense queer arousal, and the narrator obliges with great enthusiasm.

At Braden's request, I diminished the air conditioning in the bed room and opened the windows so that it would be a bit warmer in there, so that we could enjoy sleeping naked and completely uncovered. He told me that if sometime during the night I feel at all chilly to not reach for the sheet but rather just hold him close until our skin sweats together. I awakened at about two a.m. from an erotic dream about him in which his whole body shimmered with a glaze of cum. He lay on his back next to me, very soundly asleep, gently snoring, illuminated by the soft and multicolored glow of the solar lanterns hanging from the deck roof outside the bedroom. His cock was fully stiff, and I wondered if it was just a random nocturnal erection or if he was also having a sexy dream. I stroked my bone, gazing at him, and let myself almost reach climax two or three times. His pretty penis remained stiff and he remained asleep. I scooted down the mattress so I could reach his crotch with my mouth. I

licked his cum-slit and around the ring of his foreskin that just barely encircled the corona of his shroom-head when he was erect. He remained asleep, breathing gently. I took his dong fully into my mouth and drooled over it for a few moments and the started sucking on it, bobbing my head softly upon it.

I assumed that this cocksucking, even as gently as I was doing it, would wake him up. Guys have attempted to blow me in my sleep before and it always wakes me right up. But he did not stir. I continued the wet and slow suck, and he seemed to continue to sleep. He did not gasp or moan like he normally would during a blowjob. I could sense his respiration deepen and quicken, but that was the only change in his restful posture. Soon — faster than I'd expected — he released his nut-juice. It didn't really squirt the way it does when he is actively fucking or pumping his cock with his fist, rather it oozed out in a few slow pulses over my tongue, languidly, almost like the goo I'd sucked out of his nose earlier. I released his boy-stick from my mouth and slid back up to eye-level with him, expecting him to be fully awake now, but he still did not rouse. He shifted onto his side and then back onto his back, but he stayed asleep and continued his quiet snoring. I jacked off quickly — knowing I'd not be able to sleep again lying beside this gorgeous and naked young man without the relief of semen-release. I aimed at his navel and filled that hole and streaked his belly with it. A couple minutes later as I was starting to doze again, he reached an arm around my back and pressed his belly, still wet with my cocksnot, into mine. He pulled my mouth to his

and kissed me. "That was real, wasn't it?" he said, voice quiet and sleepy. He rolled onto his back and touched his stomach. "Is this yours or mine?" he smeared the remains of my jizz over his skin. "Mine," I said. "I swallowed yours."

He told me about his dream: "I already can't remember much of it, but I was really turned on because you had put a baby inside my cunt, but it wasn't like in our game earlier where we pretended that you were getting me pregnant by fucking me and shooting a wad inside me. Instead your cock was inside me and your cum-hole opened up really wide and somehow placed a little fetus inside me, and I somehow knew that what had happened was that I had gotten *you* pregnant somehow but now it was time to transfer our son into my body to finish growing. He was already growing inside your cock and you had to cum him out into my pussy almost like my cunt is a kangaroo pouch where the babies finish up after being born."

I was impressed with his dream imagination and this variation on the mpreg theme that I had never heard of before (though I wouldn't be surprised if someone has written about this before), and I was delighted that he evidently experienced this dream while I was, in fact, attempting to suck him off without waking him up. "I want to hug you and sleep some more," he said, pulling my head into his furry and rank armpit. In a few moments, he'd drifted away again and I followed him quickly.

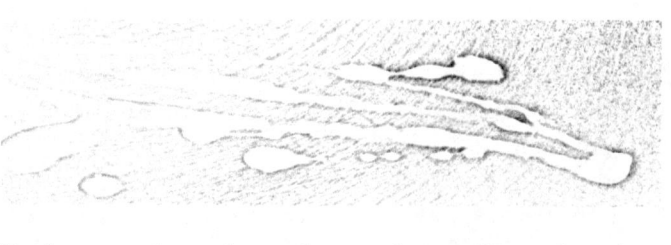

Perhaps an hour later, he awoke again and woke me by complaining of a hangover. "I have that weird hangover horniness going on," he said. "I want to fuck again but I need to sleep a little more first and my head hurts and I am thirsty." I went to the kitchen and fetched a bottle of water and a couple ibuprofen. I helped him sit up enough to drink and he gulped down the whole bottle. "A little better already," he said. "Water is good. But I already had to piss really bad and I need to make myself get up and do that. Then more sleep."

"Just lie right there and do it," I said. "I won't spill a drop."

"For real?"

"For real," I said.

"You're the fucking best!" He lay back and I clamped my lips over his dick and in a minute he started to empty his bladder, which is evidently capacious because it seemed that I was swallowing his piss for a full two minutes before he was done. He thanked me and cuddled up beside me again. Of course doing this made *me* need to piss in short order, but I let him fall back asleep first before getting up and going to the bathroom. But before he nodded off again I asked him if it really was okay with him that I sucked his cock and jacked off on him while he was sleeping and not

able to agree to it, that this wasn't too rapey. He said, "You fuckin' kidding, bro? I want to get sucked off in my sleep *every* night now!" He related another fact about himself that I had in common with him: "Remember when you're growing up and they tell you in school that boys have wet dreams when they start making cum, as if that's the first and only way that any young boy ever rocks off?" I certainly remembered this teaching from sex ed class. He continued: "I have never *once* in my life—until tonight!—had a wet dream. Because I was jacking off already way before I could even shoot a load and the first time I made some sperm I was wide awake for it! And I kept doing it every single day."

A note on pissing and the queer male:

While I was, until my encounter with Braden, shy about shitting, I have always been a piss exhibitionist in that I like to be seen doing it by lovers as well as by strangers in public restrooms. There is something about men pissing in the same room as each other that is inherently sexual in its character. Because the organ that we use to piss is obviously the same one that we use to fuck and shoot cum, it's always a kind of sex act when a dude enters a restroom, opens his fly, exposes his meat and takes a piss. He touches his cock,

holds it and aims it and often does this while standing at a urinal next to some other dude doing the same thing. In a situation such as the one above in which I invited Braden to piss in my mouth and I swallowed all of it, it was plainly a homosexual act in the obvious way that we were two male lovers in bed together and I took his cock into my mouth to achieve the act, but also in the sense that man's piss becomes in that context not just piss but an actual sex fluid as much as his semen is because I am enjoying receiving it as part of a gay sex act (even a gay *love* act) and he is enjoying giving it to me as part of our sex-play with each other.

Ostensibly straight men who engage in piss-play as an act of hazing or degradation to other males need to think about what they are really doing and what it might say about their innate sexuality. One time, when I was a senior in high school, I was in the park one evening cruising for sex and I interrupted and stopped what I believed to be an act of gay bashing. A trio of boys close to my age had corralled on his knees a younger boy who appeared to have been stripped of his shirt, and he was being pissed upon by one of his assailants. It occurred to me that what I was seeing could possibly be a consensual sex act, but it didn't feel quite like that and the boy on the ground had the look of being forced. My intervention was not some kind of dramatic thing where I physically attacked the assailants and rescued their victim. All I needed to do was appear, yell out "hey, what are you doing!" and they dashed away at a full run and disappeared into the woods like the kind of cowards who gang up three-to-one on a weaker kid. The boy

who had been pissed on was clearly shaken but he put on a brave face and tried to act like he wasn't "scared of those assholes." I offered to take him back to his home, but he stated that he couldn't go there in this state with his hair and clothes soaked in piss. So I took him first to my home so he could take a shower and I gave him some of my clothes to wear home. He admitted that he, like me, had been in the park looking for a sexual opportunity when these bullies set upon him. I advised him that this can be a dangerous activity, but if he's going to do it anyway then to do like me and carry some pepper spray, advising him that aside from the danger of thugs like ones he encountered there could be much worse things out there. While there were usually enough like-minded sex-seeking men in that area of the park in those days that it was relatively safe, there was still the slim chance of getting taken by a serial killer of teenage boys or a pimp seducing them into drug-addicted prostitution.[31]

I just wished that I would have had the opportunity to horrify the boy's attackers (dudes who prob-

---

[31] I wonder if this sort of park-cruising really exists anymore. A couple years ago I did go to see what I could find, inspired by all the fantastic cruising described in Delany's *Through the Valley of the Nest of Spiders* (set in a upornotopian world built for the practice), but I didn't turn up any kind of action. The incident that I mention here happened before the age of Craigslist and all the gay hook-up apps when it wasn't as easy as it is now to find a sex-date from home on one's computer or smart phone. I suspect that this technology has made a lot of the old spots for finding anonymous sex obsolete.

ably all imagine themselves to be straight and enemies of "fags") by presenting them with this incontrovertible fact: they were committing an act of male-on-male sexual assault. They were using their exposed penises to put fluid from their bodies onto another male's body and in, so doing, expressing in a very unhealthy and psychically fucked-up way their own homosexual desire for him. Ironically, if they'd been willing to admit to themselves and each other this desire, they probably could have had it satisfied in a much better way: that kid was in the park that evening because he wanted to suck some cocks and he probably would have willingly given all three of them blowjobs if they'd asked nicely instead of deciding to attack him in a homophobic (but still homosexual) fashion. And they could even have continued to lie to each other that they that were still "real" alpha-dudes just using a fag for what a fag's for. But everyone would have gotten what they'd really wanted out of the encounter.

Around six o'clock, Braden awakened again and rolled on top of me, lying on me chest-to-chest, his stiff cock pressed into my pelvis. He kissed me and said, "Can I fuck you, kiddo? I really need to stick this

thing in something. I'm still kind of hung over but I can't wait."

I agreed but told him that I needed to take a dump first. Because there is no door or other partition between the sleep area and the bath area, one can see the toilet from the bed, and with my new willingness to shit in front of Braden, I didn't mind him watching me. I gave my ass a quick wash at the sink. "You can wash your ass-crack if you want," said Braden. "But leave your dick and nuts alone. I want them just the way they are. I'm gonna teabag that sweaty ballsack in a little while!"

I got back into bed, on my back, knees raised, legs spread. He squeezed a glob of Stroke-Z onto his cock-head, slicked it over his shaft and got on his knees in between my legs. In a few moments, he was in, stabbing my chute with that cute prick. With one hand, he alternately squeezed my balls and stroked my pole. I don't always maintain a full hard-on while getting my ass drilled by most guys, but I always did so when Braden fucked me. He let spit drool from his lips and it landed on my chest. "Give me some more of that, baby," I said, and opened my mouth wide. With excellent aim, he landed a big glob of it on my tongue. After a couple more minutes, he cried out loudly and said "I'm gonna nut, kiddo. I'm gonna fuckin nut off now! Can I do it inside you?"

Do it, I said. *Right now, baby-face.*

Moaning, almost sobbing, he launched it. He spasmed a few times and stayed inside my ass for a minute or so after his climax subsided. He pulled out and rolled over onto his back and told me get on his

188

face: "I told you I'm gonna suck on those giant fuckin' nuts, dude. Get them in my mouth!"

My balls *are* actually pretty big. I always compare this trait to other men when I have sex with them. About fifty percent of every guy that I have ever done has had what I'd call considerably smaller nuts than mine and I'd only rate maybe ten percent as having ones close to my size or even larger. Interestingly, Braden's were on the larger side of the spectrum as well, an unexpected and nice trait for a boy who wasn't overall that big a guy. I doubted he could get both in his mouth at once, but he was welcome to try. And try he did, and with some effort, he soon had stuffed his mouth entirely full of my ballsack. But his stuffy nose, I assume, precluded blocking his mouth off completely for very long, so he pushed them back out and spent a couple more minutes licking and gently biting them on one at a time while pulling on my pole. "You're going to make bust it, dude," I said, gasping out the words through intense pleasure over his mouth-and-hand action on my junk. He told me to do it: "Right in my face, Kyler!" I hit him with it on his nose and in both his open eyes and in his open mouth. He wiped jizz off his eyes with fingers and licked his fingers. He laughed and said, "I fucking love that! How I can't see for a second because there is cum on my eyeballs." He told me that, when jacking off, he deliberately tries to do this to himself by hitting himself in the face with his own wad.

We have breakfast. I give him a mimosa, which he gulps hungrily and has another, but insists that he can't drink anymore because he has an afternoon shift at the grocery store. For breakfast I make us hash browns and sausage patties and glistening runny sunny eggs. We feed each other like we did with the Taikonaut food yesterday, with fingers, giving each other our own portions by hand. After we eat, we smoke a narcowhirl-laced cigarette in the bathroom and he takes a shit and I clean his ass with my tongue and I take him back to bed and we fuck again, him inside me and me inside him and we both cum on each other's bellies. He wants to go home and nap for a little while before he needs to go to work, and as much as I want to keep him for another day, I have work to do as well, and I agree that it's time for our long date to end. But he likes my bathroom better than his and asks me if he can take a shower in there before he leaves. He insists that he needs to smell not as much like twenty-four hours of sodomy as he does now before he goes to work, and I reluctantly agree as long as he agrees that I will wash him myself, and I get under the shower spray with him and rinse his hair and clean his ears with my tongue and grudgingly apply some soap to the crack and hole of his ass and low-hanging ball sack and I get under his foreskin

190

with it and he laughs when I scrub his smelly armpits and sadly most of the ink of the cock-art vanishes (and some had rubbed off in bed, too — *note to self: get new sheets before Danny comes home*). I dry him off and take him to the sink and shave his face scruff and dress him in my underwear, his shorts, my tank top, his shoes. I offer to drive him home, to his own bed, to his pre-work nap, but he says he wants to walk back. Though he doesn't want to drink anymore he accepts a shot of vodka when I offer to spit it into his mouth from my mouth and I walk him downstairs to the street and we kiss on the sidewalk and a couple neighbors see us as they get in and out of cars like some of them did yesterday morning. "I love you, you cute fucker," I say even though I said to myself that I'd not say that, *not* say that I love him, but I think I said it with a tone that suggested I was not too serious, just horny.

He says, "You are stupid-amazing. I know I bag on you for being old and shit, but you have taught me so much about fucking, about what to get out of sex." I tell him that he taught me some things as well.

He laughs and asks like what. I say, "That I can cum as many times in day as I want to—-even at my extraordinarily advanced age— if I am with a hot enough boy; that a peeled banana can, if fact, be inserted into my rectum; that if a cute fuck-boy is hot enough then even his snotty nose is also hot; that I can totally get into shitting in front of a dude while he is staring at me; that it's hot when a pretty guy eats with his hands and feeds me sloppy food with his filthy fingers; that cute and uncut gay teenagers should be

banned by law from ever washing their penises because their cock-cheese is delicious."

And "That's fuckin' gross, dude," he says and grins at me and says "Even *I* get grossed about how filthy my own cock gets. It smells like hell!" We kiss again and he says text you later, kiddo, and love you, baby, and he jaunts down the street.

15.

A postscript, and a reflection on a boy of summer.

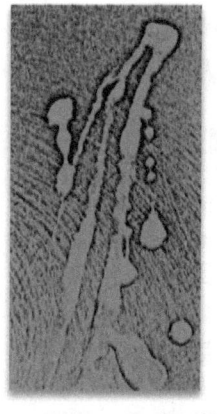

Braden was, of course, despite all our thrilling fuck-time together, just a boy of summer for me just as much as I was for him. He got accepted with a big scholarship to a college in New York where he intended to major in English and then do an MFA creative writing, and he left Saint Louis in mid-August. Evidently this had been his plan all along, but he didn't tell me about it during the first few weeks we knew each other because he was afraid his money wouldn't come through and he wouldn't really be able to go. He said it would have embarrassed him too much to have stated such a grand plan and then not actually carried through with it. I understood that feeling very well, and I was very, very happy for him that it had all worked out.

We did not quite make it to one hundred times before he left. We compared notes and arrived at a consensus tally of seventy-one times encompassing about that many orgasms for him and a dozen or so fewer for me. After our epic One Day of Sodom, we kept hooking up over the following weeks. I even spent a night of sweat and spunk in his boyish bedroom, under the cum-glazed static gaze of the Bieber poster, and a few days later we even had another day-long

fuck-session during which we "wrote" another science fiction fuck-tale and performed another non-con-fantasy play this time with me in the role of Braden's "victim."

I did end up taking him, as promised, to Nordstrom where I poled him in the changing room and bought him over a thousand dollars-worth of clothes. Later, I booked a honeymoon suite at the Chase and we pretended to be a newly married couple and we fucked in the spa tub in our room and drank four or five bottles of champagne and snorted a couple bags of narcowhirl and sniffed a lot of poppers and pissed down each other's throats. But, as fun as all these sequel-fucks were, I think we somehow got the best of each other's imaginations and bodies during the day described in above chapters, and after that we were just acting upon routine horniness and enjoying some carnal company until we needed inevitably to part ways forever.

I gave him a list of three hundred books that I wanted him to read. Some of them he had already read but most of them he hadn't. I told him that I would love it if he would send me a "book report" on each one as he got to them, just stating why he liked or didn't like them: as short as tweet, as long as a whole tract of criticism, just any reaction at all would be fine.

A couple weeks after school started, Braden texted me a long surf of pics and vids, each one of them featuring him and another dark-haired skinny-dicked twinky kid engaged in a series of queer fuck-acts. "Miss you so much, Kyler!" he said. "School is so

great! I thought you might like to jack off to me and my new dumb-but-cute fuck, so here's a bunch of pics! XOXOXO!" That same day, he also sent me his book report on Burroughs' *The Wild Boys*, and it was in the form of a piece of fan fiction based upon it, starring himself and me as characters inserted into that world, and he made us winged cat boys cock-bulging big in shiny green jock straps with cyanide claws raising hell in a spunk-spattered jungle.

He continues to send me his book reports.

—Saint Louis, 2014-2016